REIGN

REIGN

BILLIE LUSTIG

NRA Publishing

AUTHOR'S NOTE

Since you probably picked this book up because you're a mafia romance lover, I'm assuming you won't bat an eye when I tell you my characters curse like sailors, fuck like bunnies, and don't give a damn about a drop of blood.

Or a bucket.

But this book leveled up a bit, and I'm not talking automatic guns and torture sessions. I'm talking about the characters being confronted with child abuse, sexual abuse, suicide, and prostitution. If you have any question's about it, you can email me through my website, or slide into my DM's. Don't worry though, they still get their happy ending.

Sienna

"I'll see you in the morning, Mom!" I pull the door closed behind me, my black nine-inch boots tapping loudly as I pace down the brick steps of the front door. My hands reach for the buttons of my woolen coat to keep me warm in the brisk fall air, when my gaze catches a familiar set of green eyes. My heart stills, and instantly I halt, sucking in a deep breath.

His eyes may not belong to the one who once had my heart, but they are similar enough to make goosebumps peak along my skin as he keeps his piercing gaze trained on me without moving. He has that ability. They all do. But his comes with a sense of authority you can't deny. He's older now, and with his age, his stance has become intimidating. He went from a boy on the streets to a up in the air as I avert my eyes. The thought of being around the Prince Charming of the Wolfe's every day sounds like hell.

"It's not just Reign's bar," he argues, making me snap my gaze back to him with wide eyes. "It's Killian's too. And Connor's. *Mine*. It belongs to all of us. Reign and Killian are just the ones running it. It's supposed to be the start of our legal empire. But it's not working."

"Because you don't let two manwhores run a bar! They'll probably be busier pulling some biddy every night to entertain their dicks rather than selling some drinks." My tone gets more frustrated with every word, feeling my buried emotions bubbling up like air in a water tank.

They run as deep as the fucking ocean, and I know it will be an endless source of annoyance if I tap into it.

"I haven't seen Reign with a girl in at least six months."

"Doesn't mean he ain't sleeping with anyone, Franky," I counter, a little pissed he wants to argue with me on this. He knows what happened between Reign and me. I know it's his brother, but he does not get to defend him against me. Not after the stunt Reign pulled.

He tears a breath from his lungs, shutting me up with his stern expression.

"You're still pissed. I get it. I'm pissed at my brother ninety percent of the time, and if you want to give those little shitheads a hard time, go for it. I'm giving you free rein. I'll even buy you a damn whip if you want me to. God knows they deserve a good whipping every now and then," he mutters before he continues. "But you're the best event manager in the city. You're the only one who can turn this bar into profit. I'll pay you. *Good*."

I keep staring at him, my teeth pressed together as he plays into the one thing that actually would make a difference.

"I know you've been saving to buy your own bar," he remarks with a smug grin tugging at his lips, making me realize I should have known no secret ever stays a secret when it comes to Franklin Wolfe.

"You asked Reign to check my bank account?" I quirk up a brow, unimpressed.

"I know you won't accept me to pay for it all, so I'll pay you enough for the deposit and the remodeling," he informs, ignoring my question.

Right now, I earn decent money with my job as an event manager in one of the hottest clubs in town, but with the bills all dropping on my shoulders, I've barely made it halfway in the last two years. At this rate, I'll be able to buy my own bar in a few years, but I'll have no money left to really start fresh.

My thoughts are interrupted when my phone beeps, and I pull it out, reading the message on my screen.

LUCAS: Hey, beautiful. Do you wanna grab dinner tomorrow night?

"Boyfriend?" Franklin's voice makes my head twist back up.

"That's none of your business," I reply drily with a glare.

"I don't care who you date, Sienna." He pauses. "Will you do it?"

My eyes roam over his face, trying to detect the bullshit. But I'm not surprised when I find none. Franklin isn't the brother to serve you a load of crap, and I know he's not the type to play matchmaker either, ruling out he's doing this for Reign.

12 YEARS OLD

My teeth sink into the chocolate donut, welcoming the sweet taste as I bounce in my seat, listening to the radio. With my eyes locked on the screen, I wipe my fingers off on my jeans, then start tapping the keyboard again.

Let's see, Hyde Park High School.

Doing what I do best, it takes me no more than two minutes before I hack into the system and look for the student I need.

"What are you doing?" I glance over my shoulder to Killian standing with his arms crossed in front of his body, leaning against the doorpost. A big crest is on his head, and with his leather jacket, he looks like he walked straight out of a scene from *Grease*. He could be Danny Zuko's little brother.

"Oh, you know. Eating some Dunks. Upgrading some grades." I twist my head back, then hear him shuffle closer behind me.

"Hyde Park High? Tell me those chuckleheads didn't give you that black eye to force you to hack into the system."

"What? You mean this?" I look up, pointing my finger at the eye in question. "Nah, I got into a fight with Barry."

"What did that little fucker say now?"

"Nothing." I avert my gaze, feeling how my brother's eyes are trying to burn a hole in my shaggy brown hair.

"Reign." His hand lands on my shoulder with a firm grip. He's only two years older, but he's grown a head above me in the last year, giving me the feeling I'm the kid brother. Okay, I am the kid brother, but up until last year, Killian and I were the kid brothers *together*. We were the same height, same build, and we may be two years apart, but we looked the same age. Now, I'm the shortest, and it's wicked annoying.

"What?" I keep my gaze trained in front of me.

"What. Did. He. Say?" he growls, that brotherly loyalty clear in his voice. He's going to give Barry a wicked shiner to match mine.

"Nothing, Kill."

"Don't make me ask Barry."

"Kill, you're going to give me detention if you do that!" I snap my head up, shrugging his hand off my shoulder.

"Then tell me what he said?" A frown forms on his face as he scowls at me. "I won't get you into trouble. I promise. I got your back."

I sigh, leaning back into the chair, my arm resting on the desk while I look at my brother's stern face.

"He said I look like Dad. That we're criminals and he'd be visiting me in jail. Said it was only a matter of time before the last Wolfe was locked up."

"Whatever," Killian huffs. "Since when do you care about the people in this neighborhood talking about us?"

"I don't," I disclose before continuing with a quieter voice, "but then he said Franklin was a murderer."

Killian's brows move up, his stern look softening.

"And then you snapped." There is understanding in his voice, because he knows how loyal I am to my brothers. Especially Franklin. With a deadbeat dad like ours, Franklin has always been my role model, stepping up whenever Sean Wolfe was too drunk or awol. Which was always. My father once took me to the candy shop when I was five and made me pick out a big bag of whatever I wanted for my birthday. It was the only day I experienced him relaxed and smiling. It's the only good memory I have from my father. A memory that's now permanently overshadowed by his abusive fists and love for alcohol. He never hit me, not like he did Franklin and Connor, but not for lack of trying. I was just always covered by one of my brothers taking his wrath instead of me.

Franklin, however, has been to every school function, making a lame ass excuse for my parents even before Sean Wolfe beat my mother to death in one of his drunken episodes. My father is the murderer. Not Franklin. My father is the one who abandoned his sons to run off with his new girlfriend the minute his wife was cold and under the ground. Not Franklin. Franklin has always put us first. He gives me the feeling I matter, and I'll be damned before I let anyone talk shit about my big brother.

"And then I snapped," I concede.

Killian nods, leaning his back against the desk. "Did you give him a shiner like yours?"

"I did."

"Good." He pauses, glancing at the screen. "You're not changing grades for nothing, right? Franklin is gonna lose his shit if he finds out you're hacking into school systems."

I reach down into my drawer and pull out a brown paper bag before throwing it at his chest. He catches it, pressed against his body, then peeks inside.

"I ain't doing shit for nothing, Kill. Got a wicked big bag that will be worth those two minutes I can get caught. Besides, I'm almost done, and no one will ever know I was here." I bring my gaze back to the screen and start typing.

"How much is this?"

"Five hundred."

"For changing *one* tool's grades?" he asks incredulously.

I lift two fingers in the air, never averting my eye. "Two."

"You charge two hundred and fifty dollars to change grades?"

"Not bad, huh?" I smirk.

"Reign, we should do something with this. Make it a business. We can make some serious money. I know a shit ton of kids who would pay for this."

"Well, I can't just go and upgrade everyone's grades. That would be suspicious."

"Yeah, true." I can hear his thoughts trail off, probably thinking about a way to make money with this without being a risk.

Killian is business minded, just like Franklin. Always looking for opportunities to make money, starting from a young age.

"Kill! Reign!" Connor's voice booms through the house, his footsteps drumming on the stairs like he's a damn elephant. "Where the fuck are you guys?" There is panic lacing his tone, and we exchange a look of confusion before he appears in the doorway.

"What, bro?" Killian questions.

"It's Franklin." Connor's skin is as white as snow, bringing out the yellowness of his blonde hair, his eyes wide and raging. "He's been arrested."

"What?! Why?" Killian yelps.

"For what?!" I shriek.

Connor lets out a troubled sigh, rubbing a hand over his face.

"Second-degree murder."

"Are you okay?" Connor asks. The tone of his voice is insecure and shaky, raising my worry about this fucked up situation. When we got to the police station, we weren't allowed to see Franklin, with us being minors and all. After we threw a fit, Connor finally got to see him for two minutes. No more. They are charging him with the murder of Declan Murphy.

I don't know him. But I know of him.

He's an eighteen-year-old druggie foot soldier from one of the many gangs this city holds, living next door to my best friend, Emma Walsh. We've seen him around in the neighborhood, but he's nobody important and he certainly has no connections with Franklin. Though only eighteen, it's no secret that Franky has been moved up the criminal ladder quicker than expected. It was one of the things my father hated about him. He never even got a glimpse of the

One day, he was here and mine, and the next, he abandoned me for New York.

"Sienna Brennan, are you lost?" Killian turns his body toward me and a smile spreads to his cheeks. Seeing his familiar face, I can't help but return his smile with a genuine one of my own.

His black leather jacket hugs his lean torso, and with his button-down peeking from underneath, and chocolate brown hair sitting on his head in a slick cut, he looks like the ultimate bad boy.

Killian is the perfect mix of his three brothers. He's charming, like Reign. He can be merciless, like Connor. But most of all, he's as cunning as his oldest brother, seeing right through your bullshit within a heartbeat and having no pity when you play them. Equally polite as ruthless, even though Killian will snap quicker than Franklin. He lacks the patience his oldest brother has mastered over the years.

"I wish I was," I scoff, one foot moving past the other as I close the distance.

Franklin is standing behind the bar, his coat molding to his broad arms as he crosses them in front of his chest with a friendly yet amused expression taking over.

"Sienna." He greets me, and I reply with a slight nod, then I take the stool next to Killian. "Do you want something to drink?"

"How about an Old Fashioned?" I sigh a little, relieved that the tension is leaving my body now that I know Reign isn't here to mess with my head. The corner of my mouth lifts in a small smile, but he returns it with a blank expression, as if I just placed my order in a different language.

"I'm guessing you're not the man to ask for a cocktail?"

Franklin tilts his head, shooting me a mocking look before he takes matters into his own hands and reaches for the bottle of Scotch beside him. He grabs a tumbler from the wall, throws some ice cubes in it, and splashes two fingers in the glass.

There is a look in his eyes that says *dare me* when he places the drink in front of me, and I roll my eyes, mumbling a 'thanks' as I bring it to my lips.

"Glad you're here," Franklin tells me.

My eye catches Killian twisting his head from me to his brother and back.

"So, how have you been?" Killian turns his body toward mine.

Franklin nods at me in encouragement, and I take another sip to calm my leftover nerves. When Franklin stood there in front of my house, an aching feeling crept inside of me, and I realized how much I've missed these men. They were a big part of my life many years ago. We all continued our lives in different directions, but after all these years, their presence gives me a settled feeling I shouldn't be experiencing. They bring back memories that are buried in the past, making me forget about all the evil things they did to get where they are now. The only reason I was able to stay away for so long was by convincing myself that there is no safety in running with the Wolfes, but now I wonder if I've been lying to myself for way too long.

You're here for the money, Sienna.

I relax my shoulders away from my ears, cracking my neck from side to side, when the door to the stockroom flies open, and I lock eyes with Reign's compelling greens. They are just as I remembered, completely drawing me in. He freezes, his shoulders tense as he stares at me, gaping.

Even though he's at least four yards away, his irises cut like lasers through me, making my heart pound like a jackhammer. Every inch of my skin seems to burn up when his eyes move over my body, as if he's trying to figure out if I'm really here or if I'm just a mirage. I've done my best to avoid him in the last few years, making sure I never set foot in Wolfe territory, and for the first time, I see how much he's changed.

His face has matured since I last saw him. Whatever baby fat was still on his face, completely gone and replaced by a scruffed jaw. But it's not his face that has my heart having a hard time keeping up. It's his energy. His entire stance. He's more intimidating and brooding like his brothers now. Gone is the boy I once knew. He's always been the easiest Wolfe. Whispers on the streets call him Prince Charming, but if you know him, truly know him, you know he can be just as vile and dangerous as his brothers. He rarely shows it, and I never thought he was cruel, but it's there. My gut tells me he shows it a lot more nowadays.

"Sienna," he grunts, running a hand through his brown hair. A hint of hope flashes over his face. "What are you doing here?"

Realizing what he's asking, I squint my eyes, rearing my head back to Franklin.

"You didn't tell them?" I clip.

Franklin drills his gaze into mine, unimpressed by my sneering tone, as he just shrugs without any explanation.

Asshole.

"Tell us what?" Reign takes a step forward while I hear Killian chuckle next to me.

"Wicked." The tone of Killian's voice tells me he's enjoying the show, and I lower my head, pinching the bridge of my nose while I wait for it to land with Reign.

"Sienna is here to kick some life into your bar," Franklin explains, pointing his glass at me.

Killian snorts beside me, at the same time Reign blurts out a *"what the fuck."*

I keep my gaze trained on the bar, avoiding eye contact to pull myself together. I have no clue how they are going to respond to my sudden appearance, and I'm not prepared to stir up a fight between these brothers. Killian and I have always been friendly, even after Reign and I broke up, but that could change if he knows I'm here to boss him around. Reign, however, is always looking for a reason to be pissed at Franklin, and I have a feeling he just gave him the perfect opening.

When I look up, Reign's giving his brother a dirty glare, grinding his teeth like a maniac, nostrils flaring. "Thanks for the heads up, *bro."*

I can only blink, completely dazed, when not one muscle in Franklin's face responds. There're no fucks given that his brother is upset. My shock only lingers a moment, though, as I feel Reign's attention move back to me. Driving my head back, my eyes tangle with his before a tight smile forms on his handsome face. It's friendly, but laced with unspoken words and resentment.

A jittery feeling bounces through my stomach while a heatwave flushes the skin on my neck. He moves in front of his brother, bending his body over the bar so that now his ass is directed at Franklin. I glance over his shoulder, just in time to catch Franklin rolling his eyes before I'm being impaled by Reign's gaze head on. His face is only a foot from mine, completely entering my aura even though the bar separates the rest of our bodies.

Brown hair falls in front of his forehead, and my fingers itch to feel the softness of the silky strand and run my hand through it, my pulse pounding harder and harder at the unwelcome temptation. It's a freaking pain to keep up my unbothered stance, making me hate the effect he has on me.

Why the fuck does he have to be so hot?

"How have you been, *baby*?" His voice is soft and sweet for anyone else to hear, making a shiver travel down my spine. But I know it's a silent sneer my way, a taunt to piss me off. I used to love it when he called me that. Reign always called the female species darling or sweetheart, and when he first called me *baby*, it made me feel special. As if he kept that hidden just for me until now. Or at least that's what I told myself. History tells us that's bullshit, though.

"I'm not your baby," I snarl, hiding my nostalgia. "And I'm fine. Which is more than I can say about your bar." I glance around the room, trying to put his focus somewhere else, but when I move it back, I freeze when his head never moved. He's staring at me like I'm this magnificent creature, his eyes daring me to bite his head off, and I can't help but shift in my seat.

"Can you stop that? Please?" A scowl is aimed his way, and he raises his brows in question, never dropping the mischievous smirk stretching his cheeks.

"Stop what?"

"This. You." I wave my hand in front of his face. "Stop staring at me!"

His head shakes marginally, and I can hear Killian snicker beside me.

"I can't," he states, simply. "I haven't seen your face in ages. It will take me a while before I can stop staring at it."

"Charming." I roll my eyes.

"You sound surprised," Killian drawls.

"Shut up, Kill," I bark, keeping my eyes locked with Reign, frowning at him with annoyance. I'm doing my best to let my frustration with him surpass the zoo of activity he seems to ignite in my lower body.

He holds my gaze for what feels like forever before he finally opens his mouth again.

"What's wrong with our bar, *Sienna*?" My name comes out just as softly as when he called me baby a minute ago, but this time it also sounds impatient. For some reason, a disappointed pang moves through my chest.

"What isn't?" I bring my glass to my mouth, throwing back the contents in one go before sliding off the stool to walk around the area. Anything to create some distance between us. "Inside it looks great, classy even. Love the old 1800s photos of the city and your bar is a real eye-catcher." I look at the middle of the bar that's stacked with bottles of liquor with a big blackboard above it, listing a number of numerous cocktails in a classy font. There are two arches on both sides acting like a little nook that displays all the special bottles of whiskey. Then on both far ends of the bar is a wooden arch that houses the lighting over the shelves, holding all the glasses with a register on each side. "But it doesn't match the rest of your interior, not even mentioning the outside."

"How come?" Killian gives me an interested look.

"Those old wooden chairs make it feel just that. *Old.* [] I move my gaze between Reign and Killian. "This doesn't scream *speakeasy*. It just screams ancient."

"What makes you think we were going for speakeasy?" Reign frowns as he straightens his body, then folds his arms in front of his chest.

"Oh, please. I know all four of you. The epitome of sophisticatedly bad. A speakeasy screams Wolfe. But please, enlighten me to what look you were going for if I'm wrong?"

I bring my hands to my sides, my boots tapping on the hardwood floor as I prance back to the bar.

When all three of them just look at me with entertained smirks on their faces, I hold still.

"Right. You did an okay job, but you left out the comfort of the twenty-first century."

"What are you suggesting?" Franklin asks, his voice deep.

"Booths along the wall. Then only a few smaller tables in the middle here," I say, bringing my hand up to show them what I mean. "And a small podium at the back where you can have live music once a week. I'm thinking cream-colored furniture and some dark blue accessories around the entire bar. Maybe mixed with gold."

"Gold?" Reign huffs. "Can we keep it a bit manly? I don't need this place filled with just women every night."

"As if you have any issues looking at the female species every single night." I snort.

"Oh, you're jealous, baby? You know I only have eyes for you," he mocks quicker than I expect. His words are working to tear down the wall around my heart, yet I refuse to let him woo me over with his charm, while the taunting tone only raises my anger.

"You didn't when you left me for another girl." The snarl is filled with venom, and I see Killian press his lips together in amusement.

Reign rubs a hand over his face, groaning. "I didn't leave you for another girl." Malice is dripping from his tone, but he can fuck right off with his frustration. He has no right to be angry when he's the one who is responsible for our break-up in the first place.

"What about outside?" Killian muses.

A grateful glint takes over my gaze as I look to him, thankful for the interruption.

"It looks like a sports bar. If you want, we can keep the black paint, but right now it feels dull and cheap. I'd go for a lacquer black combined with gold arches and definitely put back a sign with a Celtic font."

I keep my focus on Killian, avoiding Reign's broodiness at all costs. I'm not here for him, and I'm not here to work out all the issues that have grown over the years. He can give me all the pretty words he's got, and God knows he has a lot, but I'm not as forgiving as he might hope me to be. I don't know if he wants my forgiveness, but either way, I'm not ready for it. I'm helping them because Franklin asked me to, and he's giving me the cash I need. Enough for me to finally get my own place and start building my own future. It just means I have to run with the Wolfes one last time.

"Sounds good," Killian agrees. "When do you want to start remodeling?"

Strutting back toward the bar, I grab my bag. "As soon as possible. The sooner that's done, the sooner you can re-open, make some money, and I can be on my way."

"I'll set it up and let you know when it will be done," Killian confirms.

I give Killian and Franklin a tight smile, still avoiding the roving gaze Reign has pointed at me, hoping no one notices the pebbles forming on my skin.

"Have a good day, boys." I twist on my heels, then carry myself back to the entrance to leave.

"Sienna, stop. Can we talk?" Reign's voice feels like a sledgehammer being thrown at my back, almost making me stumble on my feet. My mind tells me to keep going, to ignore him, but my heart can't help looking over my shoulder, though with grinding teeth. I really need to work on my ability to ignore him.

"Please?" The balanced mix of hope and rage is noticeable in his eyes, reminding me of the sixteen-year-old boy I fell in love with. Filled with trouble, yet still consumed by love even after the hell he's been through. A love that was once reserved for me.

Until it wasn't.

My shoulders square, my mind reminding me why I'm here.

"No," I grate, as I continue my way out of the door. I can feel the wall around my heart wobble, but I ignore the sensation, pushing it away as soon as my skin is touched by the cold air.

Reign Wolfe had more than enough of my time, and he took it for granted.

Too late, Prince Charming.

4

REIGN

I watch how she walks out of the door without glancing back, my heart cracking before I snap my head to my oldest brother with a clenched jaw.

"What the fuck, Franklin?" He's still leaning on the back of the bar, relaxed and indifferent, and it's pissing me off. "Did you know?" My eyes land on Killian, whose brows instantly shoot up in innocence, holding his glass still in front of his face.

"I didn't."

My eyes lower to slits, trying to detect the bullshit.

"I didn't," he screeches. "I swear. This was all him." He points his glass at Franklin.

"I figured you'd be happy to see her," Franklin offers with a straight face.

"Fucking hell, you just gave me a heart attack. At least if you would've given me a heads up, I'd have put on something nice. Maybe show some more skin or something," I respond with a bucket load of sarcasm, shooting him a smile that doesn't match my eyes.

"I hate to break it to you, brother, but showing your lack of abs isn't going to do the trick," Killian chimes in.

"What lack of abs?" I bring up my shirt. "Don't be mad because you have none."

The door opens and my eyes fall to my fourth brother joining the party.

"Was that Sienna?" He points his thumb over his shoulders while his big strides make a loud thud with each step as he crosses toward us. I glance at Connor's bulky physique with a cynical smile.

"It was. One of Franklin's gifts of the day."

"You seem pleased." He takes the stool next to Killian, reaching over the bar to pick up the bottle of Scotch Franklin left on the workstation. Like the asshole that he is, he grabs Killian's now empty glass, splashing in two fingers for himself.

"I wasn't done with that." Killian scowls.

"I don't care," Connor counters, then turns his attention back to me. "Is she finally ready to talk to you?"

"What?" I jeer, getting aggravated with these assholes I share the same DNA with. "No. For fuck's sake. I wish," I mumble, barely audible. My hand moves up, running it through my hair. "Franklin apparently hired her to help us with the bar."

A frown creases on Connor's head. "Like a bartender?"

"Nope," Killian answers, popping his *P*.

"I hired Sienna to re-design the bar. Take over the place until it's profitable."

"No-suh!" Connor flashes his teeth, looking between Killian and me, then breaks out in laughter. "This is some wicked shit. Sienna is going to be bossing you two chuckleheads around all day?"

"Err, no," Killian mutters, confused, before I chime in.

"No. She's just giving us pointers. Doing the remodeling. Helping us out." I pause, suddenly not so sure of my words. My head turns to Franklin. "She is, right? She's here to *help*? Please tell me you didn't give my ex-girlfriend free rein to take over our bar and boss us around like fucking kids?" The tone in my voice gets grittier with every word, knowing exactly where this is going. Franklin is the one running our business, being the drive behind the fact that we have more money stashed around the city than we can spend. I don't care that he calls the shots most of the time, but this is my bar. Killian's bar. *Our* bar. As much as I'd love to see Sienna more, playing her little bartender is not how I imagined that scenario.

"You gave Sienna a carte blanche? Because if that's the case, I'd rather be dealing with other shit until she's done with everything. Pick up more rounds or something, but I'm not going to watch those two piss each other off all day. *No offense*," Killian offers when Franklin keeps his mouth shut.

"Offense taken, *asshole*. You're going to let me deal with my ex by myself?" I bite back.

"You dug the grave. Doesn't mean I need to lie down next to you."

"You're supposed to be the brother who has my back." I huff, then nudge my chin to Franklin. "Not put a knife in my back like him."

Franklin's eyes shoot daggers at me while I grant him another fake smile.

"Sienna will stay until this bar is profitable and you two know exactly how to copy it for the next one. We need to legitimize our businesses. This is the first step, and she's the best event manager in the city. She knows her shit."

"You really are the biggest asshole there is, Franklin," I grunt.

"You loved the girl once, Reign. Hell, pretty sure you still do. I'm sure you can get over your tantrum and work with her for a few weeks."

"It's not the fact that you hired her." I take a step forward, pointing my finger at his bored gaze. "It's the fact that you didn't share your plan. You gave *us* this bar, yet here you are calling the shots again! Like always. You could've been less of an asshole and expressed your worry with us, *discussed* it. Not hire my ex-girlfriend behind my back to fix it all."

Franklin holds my stare, blank-faced as always, not uttering another word.

After a brief moment and no words coming from his mouth, I grab my jacket from the end of the bar, rounding it, then give him one last glare as I put it on.

I'm not surprised by his silence, but it's still annoying me. After he met his girlfriend, Kendall, I thought he and I were getting along better, feeling a certain mutual respect forming between us. When he bought this bar, I was skeptical at first, but in the last few months, we've exchanged more words than we have in the last eight years. Even though I know we have a long way to go, I assumed we were establishing more trust between us. Or that's how it felt.

Guess I was wrong.

"But why should I be surprised? You never share anything," I finally say as my last jab, strutting out of the bar while feeling all my brothers' gazes at my back as I disappear from sight.

5

Sienna

I walk through the front door, soaking wet, then slam it behind me.

"It's a wicked shitstorm out there!" I rant, shrugging out of my wet coat and taking off my black boots.

"You forgot your umbrella?" Ma yells from the kitchen. The smell of fried goods enters my nose, and I breathe it in greedily, closing my eyes to enjoy the warmth and comfort the house instantly gives me.

"Yeah, I wasn't expecting the rain."

"I told you to check the forecast. It's fall."

I smile as I walk in just my socks over the hardwood floor of the parlor to the kitchen. My mother is stirring something in the frying pan, an apron protecting her clothes. Ambling over to her, I press a kiss to her gray hair.

"Hey, Ma. How was your day?" I grab a towel out of the lower cabinet and start to somewhat dry my black hair.

"Fine. Took the T to get you some munchkins at Dunks."

"Ma," I blurt, holding still.

"It was your last day working for the Abbey. You deserve a treat."

"That's really sweet, Ma. But you shouldn't do that. You gotta rest your leg." I give her a slight scowl, even though she doesn't bother to turn around to face me.

"I know, but being cooped inside all day is making me wicked mad." The sound of her voice is etched with desperation, and I feel for my poor mother.

She's been working at the factory for as long as I can remember, enjoying her job and coworkers as much as someone can while working for a big manufacturer. My mother never needed much in life other than the reassurance she could take care of the two of us after my father bailed when I was four. I don't remember much of him, but word goes around that he was a real tool, though Ma has never uttered a bad word about him.

"If you don't take the doctor's advice, it's gonna take even longer for you to really get back on your feet." I wrap my arms around her, pressing my chest into her back as I rest my cheek against her warm shoulder.

"I'm on my feet now!" she exclaims like the stubborn woman that she is.

"You know what I mean. We're eating fish and chips for supper?" I peek into the pan, noticing the battered cod that makes my stomach roar and my inner child clap with excitement. When I was younger, this was my favorite dish. Since I grew up and realized how bad this shit is for you, I don't eat it quite as often, but it still makes my mouth water every time it's on the menu.

"I told you. You deserve a treat."

"You're the sweetest, Ma," I say, kissing her silky cheek.

Letting go of her, I walk across the room to the sideboard to start setting the table.

"What's this?" I pick up the Providence postcard after I've put two plates on the wooden surface, then flip it around.

To Sienna with love. It says, though no name is listed.

"Oh, yeah, that was in the mail. I figured it was from one of your college friends or something?

"I don't have any friends from Providence."

"You don't? Well, maybe they moved there." She puts the food on a plate, then sets it down on the table.

Shrugging, I take out the cutlery, then take a seat at the table while Ma does the same. "Yeah, maybe."

Eagerly, I fill up my plate and take a bite of the hot fish. The greasy juices coat my tongue, and I close my eyes to enjoy the taste before I swallow and pop a fry into my mouth.

"Is the Abbey ready to do it without you?" Ma brings a bite to her mouth.

"Yeah." I nod. "They're ready. They seemed confident and excited for it all. Though they asked me if they could call me if they needed anything else."

"That's good, honey. So," she drawls, a suspicious look in her now Bambi-looking eyes. "When do you start working for Reign?"

"I'm not going to work for *Reign*," I scold.

"It's Reign's bar, right? You told me that."

"It's Reign and Killian's bar. But Franklin hired me."

Her head tilts, boring her gaze into mine. "But you'll be seeing Reign every day, right?"

"I guess," I mutter, putting another piece of fish in my mouth.

"Good. It's about time the two of you worked this out."

Baffled, I drop my fork. "We are not *working* anything out, Ma. I'm helping the Wolfes with their bar. Like I've been doing for a handful of bars the last two years. They are just another client. This has nothing to do with the personal shit Reign and I have created in the last decade," I spit out.

"There is that Italian temperament." She offers me a smile. "I'm not saying you have to get back together. But this could be the perfect opportunity to clear the air. Become civil. Maybe even friends."

My eyes turn to slits as I stare at her. "What is it with this boy, Ma?"

I know what she's doing. She never made it a secret that she loved Reign. She's thrown hints at me since before we got together. She was over the moon when we were a couple, and she has been throwing comments here and there since the day we broke up. She has a weakness for the boy, and though I can't blame her because I would be lying if I denied I feel the same, I'm not ever going to admit that. Not to Reign. Not to my mother.

"What do you mean?" she counters sweetly.

I lean back against the chair, crossing my arms in front of my chest.

"You're always pushing me to work things out with him. Even when we were still together, you'd pick his side on almost everything."

"That's some wicked bullshit," she sputters, avoiding my gaze.

"No-suh!"

She pushes out a long breath, then brings her eyes up. There is a sad, compassionate gleam in her eyes. "I know he hurt you. But I don't think he intended to in the first place."

I roll my eyes. "Don't even go there."

"He's been through hell with all those years in foster care."

"You don't even know that because he refuses to talk about it."

"Oh, I *know*," she disagrees. "I saw the look in that boy's eyes when he came for supper the first time. The bright twelve-year-old he was before all that shit went down was nowhere to be found. Instead, there was a man who was hurt, troubled, and dealing with all the ugly shit in this world." She pauses. "But over the months, you brought that spark back into his eyes. You're the–"

"Don't you dare say love of his life." I point my finger at my mother with a glare. "If I was the love of his life, he wouldn't have left me for a *year* when he was supposed to go for a month. He wouldn't have left me for another *girl*."

She presses her lips together to a firm line, then brings her arms up. "Fine. I'll shut up."

We keep our eyes locked, and I grind my teeth in annoyance.

"Look," I add, "I get what you're saying. But Reign and me? That's in the past. I agreed to this because Franklin is offering me a wicked amount of money that will be the first step to my own bar. I'm making enough so you don't even have to go back to the factory."

"I don't mind going back to the factory."

"I know. But wouldn't you rather help me out around the bar during the day? *Our* bar?" I emphasize. I know she can't disagree with that because she always wanted me to have a better life than her. She encouraged me to do the things I love and pursue the college major I wanted. When I chose Communications, there were a lot of people who frowned, wondering if that was a bit too broad. Don't even get me started about the responses when I told them I wanted to be an event manager. Half the neighborhood had been spewing about how I wanted to be a glorified bartender, having no clue what an event manager really did. But my mother always supported me. She motivated me even on the days she was exhausted as fuck from working at the factory and I was being a lazy teenager. She knows this is my dream, and she wants to be a part of it.

"Course," she agrees.

"Well, this job is going to make that happen. I'll be working for the Wolfes for a few weeks, getting their bar out of the slump it's in, and after that, I'll have enough money to open my own bar. They are the key to a brighter future, but I have no desire to rattle up the past."

"Okay." My mother shifts in her seat, and I can see she's not done talking.

Slightly shaking my head, I roll my eyes. "What now, Ma?"

"Just try to be nice to the boy." Her tone is calm, yet firm, tolerating no contradiction. "You'll be running around like that wicked storm outside for the next few weeks if you don't at least manage to act professional." One of her brows quirks up in a reprimanding way, knowing me well enough that I wasn't planning on making life easy for Reign Wolfe for the foreseeable future. She does have a point, though. Reign is the one person who can affect my mood within seconds, and that hasn't been a good one for the last couple of years. Reign might deserve my wrath, but Franklin and the rest of his brothers don't. They are paying me for my expertise, and I'm expected to act professional. Even if I can't stand the person I'm working with.

"Reign Wolfe will get the polite woman you raised," I jeer, "but that's it."

She grabs my hand, a soft glance washing her face. "That's all I ask, honey."

6

12 YEARS OLD

I t looks like a haunted house. Like one of those houses you ride past a little quicker than all the other houses, just to make sure no one snatches you in and you turn into an urban legend. I imagine this house being a real pretty sight at its prime. But there is an ominous feeling forming inside of me that weighs on my stomach like a ton of bricks. The chipped paint on each wood panel combined with the rusty gates on the porch tells me those times have long gone.

"They will take good care of you." The social worker's hand lands on my shoulder, and I shrug it off while I look at the dead plants along the borders.

"My brother was taking good care of me," I scoff. "

"Your brother is a criminal." I look up at her with a glare, wanting to scratch her eyes out. Her brown eyes peer at me from under the glasses that sit on her nose, her brown hair up in a tight bun. For most people, public workers are an example of trust. The people they can confide in when they are in trouble or help through hard times with aid or support.

But I'm a Wolfe.

Life has been different for me since the day I was born. I was taught to be cautious of cruisers, to distrust the people working for the government. To me, *they* are the criminals. The ones who hide under a uniform and a permanent mask, pretending to honor the law. But they did nothing when they found out my father was beating up my mother every single day. They did nothing when one of Franklin's classmates got raped in broad daylight when she was walking home from school. They didn't do shit when Connor got bullied by one of the richer kids in middle school. Public workers are not there for everyone. They don't give a shit if you're born on the wrong side of town. They didn't give a shit then and they don't give a shit now. The look in her eyes tells me exactly that.

I'm nothing more than an inconvenience that she's about to dump somewhere in Providence, Rhode Island.

"Go on. Let's go." She gives me a push and I shuffle forward, feeling like there is lead hanging on my feet. I suck in a deep breath, thinking about Franklin and how he'd want me to act before I straighten my shoulders. Closing my eyes, I push the nervous feeling to the side, doing my best to replace it with fake confidence before I open them again. She's moving up the small steps to the front door and I watch her with her stately attitude and hideous heels as she rings the doorbell.

Bitch.

"Get over here!" she hisses over her shoulder.

With a grim look on my face, I slog her way, then hold my breath with my eyes trained on the worn-out wooden door until it swings open.

Right away, the smell of cigarette smoke hits my nose, accompanied by the drenching odor of liquor. It reminds me of my father, but I already have a feeling there won't be anyone here who will protect me from getting beaten up if I so much as breathe funny.

In front of us stands a big guy, a beer belly pointing at us with his shirt barely covering his stomach. A cigarette is dangling from his thin lips. His dark eyes are almost as brown as his scruffy beard, impaling me with a devious grin tugging on his cheeks.

He looks like an obese bulldog. And not the cute kind. More like a villain in a very bad movie. Like a wicked sleaze ball.

"You must be Reign." He smirks with a smile that creeps the shit out of me.

When I keep my mouth shut, the devil's helper gives me a slight kick to my ankle, keeping her fake smile focused on the fat motherfucker in front of us.

"Yes," I reply, reluctantly.

"Well, come on in, boy. We've been waiting for you." A shiver runs down my spine when I look at his insidious expression. Without waiting for my reply, he forcefully grabs my shoulder and pulls me over the threshold.

"We will be checking in—"

"He's not the first. I know the drill," he interrupts. I glance over my shoulder one more time before he slams the door shut in the social worker's face. I keep my head up, doing my best to ignore the bad feeling in my stomach, then turn around to scan the living room.

It smells like garbage and mildew, and when I look around, I'm not surprised. The living room is cluttered, with empty beer cans scattered around the floor.

"You look like a little prince." I twist my head to the girl's voice coming from the kitchen.

A girl is leaning against the counter, her curly brown hair messy and dirty, like she hasn't washed it in ages. Or brushed it, for that matter. She looks like she's a few years older than I am, though the little girl next to her can't be older than eight, maybe nine.

"Aubrey, you show the boy his room and tell him what is expected," the bulldog barks as he moves past me before flopping his disgusting body onto the couch. "And once you're done, go to the store. Your mother will be home soon."

"Yes, Daddy." She rolls her eyes, then bounces off the counter, offering me her hand. "I'm Aubrey. This is Nova, my sister."

I eye her dirty hand, and when I wait too long, it falls back down.

"Who are they?" I nudge my head to the two girls sitting on the couch with vacant looks in their eyes.

"Foster kids. Not important." Her lips twist. "Like *you*. Don't worry about them. They'll be gone and replaced by a fresh set of girls every few months. But we actually live here." She points at her little sister.

"I'm Reign Wolfe," I reply with a glare, tugging my bag tighter on my shoulder.

"Nice to meet you, *Reign Wolfe*." A smile that doesn't match her eyes travels across her face. "Welcome to hell."

7

Sienna

Taking a deep breath, I give myself one last glance in the window of the bar next to the Pack. I straighten my black leather skirt with long strokes, then tug on my cream sweater. Bringing my hands up, I adjust a few strands of my black hair while exhaling loudly before I plaster a smile on my face. When I look at my reflection, I see a strong, confident woman, but really on the inside, I'm screaming from anxiety that's making it nearly impossible to keep my professional attitude in check.

"You're in charge, Sienna. You tell them what to do. He's just a client," I whisper in a mantra at myself.

Deciding there is no better time than now, I take the final stride to the entrance of the Pack and push the heavy door open. I expected all of the brothers to be here, since we're discussing the plan for the next few weeks, but instead it's just Reign who's sitting at the bar with his nose in his phone. He's wearing a white shirt and an open denim button-down with his sleeves rolled up. Sunglasses sit on his hair even though it's a cloudy day, and I can't keep my lips from parting. He's tapping the screen with his thumbs, showing the tense muscles of his tattooed hand, and uncontrollably, a vision jolts into my head. A memory of his tattooed fingers wrapped around my neck as he moved his other hand over my body makes my cheeks grow flush as I just gawk at him.

After what feels like an eternity, his head twists my way and my mouth snaps shut, feeling completely busted. A smile tugs on the corner of his mouth, an amused spark clear in his gemstone green eyes. Can't he just look like a troll or something? It would make this so much easier.

"Sienna," he beams, turning his body on the barstool before dropping his phone on the bar.

"Reign," I reply stiffly.

I roll my shoulders, trying to pull my confidence back from wherever it just went and approach him while his piercing gaze never leaves my body.

"Where are the rest?" I ask.

"They'll be here shortly. Have a seat." He motions to the stool next to him.

Feeling extremely uncomfortable, I sit down at the same time he slides off. His chest brushes against my arm and the hairs on the back of my neck stand up, making me briefly close my eyes.

"You want coffee?" His tone is gentle, warming my insides. It's going to be fucking hell to keep up this unaffected stance I was going for if he's going to bring out all his charm every single day. I need dickish Reign.

"Please."

"Coming right up." He rounds the bar with a big stride, his grin never disappearing. I expect him to fill the void with his usual smartass comments, but instead the silence creates a thick curtain between us. He easily whips up a latte macchiato without asking what I'd like, finishing it off with one spoon of sugar before he places it in front of me with a sweet smile.

I hold his gaze, muttering a 'thanks' and completely ignoring the fact that he remembers how I like my coffee and how that makes me feel. Silently, I fold my hands around the warm glass before I bring it up to take a sip.

"Look, baby," he coos, running a hand through his honey brown hair.

And just like that, my anger ignites, burning like a damn bonfire.

"Don't call me *baby*," I snarl, my coffee now hanging midair in front of my face.

"Fine," he replies with an eye roll, placating. "Sorry. *Sienna*. I know you're mad at me. And I understand why—"

"Oh, thank fuck," I interrupt sarcastically.

"But, [] he continues, unfazed, "I hope we can start over."

"Start over?" My rage rises when I listen to his choice of words. Call me a resentful bitch, but I have a hard time starting over when the love of my life ditched me for someone else.

"Well, no. Yes. Maybe. No," he stammers, rubbing a hand over his face. A little amused at flustering him, I keep my mouth in a straight line, urging away the smile that's tugging at my lip. I've never seen this man speechless in my life, like, ever. He's the one who always has something to say, always ready with a taunting remark about anything. He's quick and witty, hence his notable charm.

"Somebody please call the Boston Globe. Reign Wolfe has lost his tongue." Our heads snap to Killian, who's standing in the doorway with a teasing look. He's sporting his leather jacket as always and his hair sits messy on his head as if he just rolled out of bed.

"Shut up, asshole." Reign sneers while I crack my body a bit as Killian saunters toward us.

"Rough night?" I ask, glancing up at his hair.

He rakes his hand through the messy mop on his head, then shoots me a lopsided grin that tells me he got laid last night. Or this morning. Maybe even both.

Who knows with Killian.

"Something like that."

"*Anyway.*[] Reign's voice sounds gritty, and I meet his pinched expression. "I hope we can be civil. Professional. I appreciate you helping us out."

"I'm not helping."

"What do you mean?"

"Franklin offered me a big bag of money. Don't flatter yourself, Reign. I'm not here to *help* you out. I'm here because the amount of money your brother is offering me gives me the chance to buy my own bar. I'm not here for you. I'm here for *me.*"

Killian snickers next to me and I can feel his eyes focused on the stare-off that Reign and I are starting. A slight frown forms on Reign's face, his lips pursing with annoyance at my harsh words.

It's true, though. I'm not here for him. If Franklin had tried to hire me for my regular fee, I would've declined. The only reason I'm here is because he offered me enough to secure a better future. Dangled it in front of my face like a piece of candy and I'm happily taking it with both hands. But like I already told my mother, I'm not here to fix anything with Reign. I'm not here as a favor.

"Can you please just make me a coffee so I can move to a corner table, and you can continue this weird display of affection without me until Franky and Connor get here?" Killian questions.

We both twist our heads at him, silently telling him to shut up with united glares, and his mouth snaps shut.

"You're not even gonna sugarcoat it, are you?" Reign's gaze has hardened when I rear back.

"Why would I? I work best with clients if I'm upfront about the things they can expect. You're my *client*. Well, technically, your brother is."

He brings his elbows to the bar, leaning closer.

"Customer is king, right?" He dares me with a smirk that doesn't match his eyes. One that says he's going to ruffle my feathers every chance he gets, like I was planning for him to.

Shit.

I swallow, grinding my teeth. That son of a bitch has me right where he wants me, and he knows it. If he's going to play this game with me, it's going to be a wicked pain to keep my calm and stay professional all the time.

"There are limits," I say, sticking my nose in the air, "but yes."

"Good," he clips, moving his body back up. "Happy to have you, *Sienna*." He shoots me a wink, like the bastard he is, then walks toward the stockroom. "I got some inventory to do. Just let me know when Connor and Franklin get here."

My heart falls down to the floor when he moves out of sight. My confidence is taking a beating because I just know he's going to push my buttons as much as he can, and as much as I don't want to admit it, he's better at it than I am.

"You'll be fine." I turn to see Killian offering me a coy smile. "You know what he's like. He's going to poke until he gets a response. Just don't give him any room to be anything but professional and you'll be fine." The words leave his lips as if he's making a pastrami sandwich. As if it's the easiest thing to do. But the glint in his eyes shows he's mocking me.

"Can you *not* do that?"

"What?" he yelps.

"Use that bullshit reverse psychology on me. We both know Reign isn't even capable of having a normal conversation with the female species, let alone being professional to *me*, of all people. He's going to push me as much as he can to get his way, and I'm not here to work shit out with my ex-boyfriend."

Killian holds my gaze, softly tapping his finger on the bar. "What?"

"You know he has a weakness for you." He pauses. "And I know you have one for him."

I close my eyes for a second. "I don't. Not anymore. I'm here to do my job. And if you or Reign are going to make that hard for me to do because you're pissing me off all the time, then I won't hesitate to call Franklin and tell him I'm only taking this job if the two of you are out of the picture. I expect you to keep Reign off my back, Kill." I point my finger at his face with a scowl.

"You know I don't control my brother, but fine. I'll keep my mouth shut." He rolls his eyes at the same time Franklin and Connor walk through the door before he moves his face close to my ear, whispering, "Just be prepared to hear *I told you so.*"

8

12 YEARS OLD

I grew up with the knowledge that my father was the biggest piece of shit alive. He was more drunk than sober, regularly abusing my mom and even us kids. None of us were left unscathed. Being the youngest meant my brothers did as much as they could to protect me, making sure my father couldn't reach me. But I saw how he treated my brothers. How Franklin would fight him every single day to make sure his attention was anywhere but pointed at the rest of us. Unless I was home alone with my dad, I was somewhat safe in our house. But there was no denying he was the devil himself.

After a week in my new foster home, I'm not so sure, though.

The food in this house is scarce, showers are something you almost have to fight for, and comfort is not something they're familiar with. After Aubrey showed me my room, which is more like a broom closet, she introduced me to the two other girls who live here. I didn't listen to their names, and I could barely get a wave hello, but Aubrey told me not to bother because they wouldn't be staying for long anyway. I have no clue why, or what that means, but to be honest, I was too angry to ask. I went to sleep and thank fuck they let me.

The next morning, Aubrey rode the bus to school with me, which was a nice escape from that hellhole, explaining the dynamics of the family. Apparently, I'm the first boy they've ever taken in. Her dad wasn't happy with it, because he preferred girls, but the agency told him he didn't get to pick them anymore. They had to take me or they wouldn't get anymore girls, period. It was a revelation that brought a pit to my stomach even though I didn't know why, but I chose to ignore it. My life right now gives me one big stomachache anyway.

"Are you a foster kid too?" I asked, while sitting next to her on the bus.

"No," she explained. She and Nova were the only biological kids of Jefferson and Rita Brady. They've been taking in foster kids for as long as she can remember, referring to themselves as the Brady Bunch. She chuckled while telling me that, but I couldn't squeeze out more than a frown, having a feeling they weren't anything like the happy family you see on TV.

"What about the other girls? Why aren't they coming to school with us?" I continued to pry.

She gave me a tight smile, then explained in a whisper how they are being homeschooled. How they were *special*.

It was on the tip of my tongue to blurt out who the fuck was homeschooling them since her parents seemed like they were not the brightest, but I bit my tongue and settled with that answer. When we arrived at the school, we split up, with her being a grade above me, and I had my first day at school as awkwardly as you can imagine.

I hated it there. But I didn't hate it as much as I hated being at the hell house that was now my home, so every morning I waited for that bus with relief.

"Did you do the dishes?" Aubrey is standing in the doorway, looking down at me while I'm doing my homework on the floor of my closet. Or room. Whatever the fuck you wanna call it.

"Did you check the sink?" I glare before dropping my eyes back to my homework.

"Look, don't be smart with me. It's an important night. The house needs to look clean, and it's your turn to do the dishes."

"The house is never clean," I scoff.

Aubrey squats down, gripping my hair and tilting my head back to force me to look at her.

"Get the fuck off me, you tool." I slap her hand away, glaring.

"If we don't make sure the house is looking decent tonight, he's going to freak out and not spare any of us. Do you get me?"

'He' is her deadbeat dad, I assume.

Part of me wants to spit in her face and tell her to go fuck herself, but there is a fearful glint in her eyes that grips my heart and doesn't let go.

"Yeah, Aubrey," I say, annoyed. "I did the dishes."

Her face softens with relief, and she gets back up, bringing my attention to her clothes.

"What are you wearing?" I frown.

Her skinny legs are barely covered by a denim miniskirt, her belly peeking out from under a crop top while there are knee-high boots covering her feet. It's completely different from the dirty jeans and hoodies she normally wears.

"Nothing." She huffs, then gives me a reluctant look. "I told you. It's a special night."

I hold her gaze with suspicion when the doorbell rings, and she glances over her shoulder. "Are you sure you did the dishes?"

"Yeah."

"Okay, just do yourself a favor. Stay here. Don't come out of your room."

"Okay," I drawl, not sure why she's acting all sketchy.

"I mean it, Reign." She snaps her head my way, her face now in a slight scowl. "You have to stay here. All night, okay? Don't come out before I'm back."

"Where are you going?"

"Just do as I say, okay?" she barks impatiently.

"Fine!" I bellow back before she mumbles something, then jolts off to the living room.

A little confused, I roll my eyes, moving them back to my textbook until I take note of the unfamiliar male voice in the house.

"Yeah, she looks good."

"Aubrey, spin around," I hear Jefferson order.

Even though I told Aubrey I'd stay here, my curiosity gets the best of me, and I stand up. Carefully, I slog toward the living room, trying to stay as quiet as possible.

I shift my eyes around the room before they land on the odd man out.

He's big. Huge even. With eyes that are a deep brown that make them appear black. Almost as black as the slick hair on his head. He's wearing a leather jacket, and he pulls out a roll of bills before throwing it at Aubrey's dad.

"She will do," he rumbles, raking his ominous eyes over Aubrey's body with hunger.

My attention moves to Aubrey, holding her chin in the air to hide the fear that is dripping from her face. The look in her eyes is vacant, but she manages to give the man a coy smile that makes me want to hurl up my dinner.

"You get two hours," Jefferson tells him.

The man takes two big steps toward Aubrey before he grabs her arms, tucking her body flush with his. She's bigger than me, older than me, but next to this big guy, it's perfectly clear she's just a little girl. A kid. Nothing more.

My chest starts to move up and down rapidly with rage, suddenly connecting the dots.

"Two hours is more than enough." He drags a finger along her jaw, and she snaps her head to the side, her gaze locking with mine. Panic quickly replaces the absent look in her eyes, and she gives me the tiniest head waggle, pleading with me to go back to my room.

"No!" I growl as much as a twelve-year-old can. My fists are balled beside my body, my teeth pressed together so hard it hurts.

The man holding her arms turns his head my way with an amused grin splitting his face, then glances at Jefferson. "Who's this?"

"No one," he thunders, then quickly gets his fat ass up from the couch.

"Reign, *please*, go to your room," Aubrey begs.

"Fucking let her go!" I charge forward, ready to pull her from his grasp, but before I can reach her, Jefferson knocks me to the ground.

A ringing in my ears keeps me there while I hear the muffled sound of Aubrey shouting through the room.

"No! Don't hurt him! I'll go. I'm going. Please!"

A black boot connects with my stomach, making me hunch forward in agony.

"Just get to the basement. I'll take care of this shithead," Jefferson booms.

Aubrey gives me a sad glance as she's dragged away before Jefferson's foot slams against my back. I cry out, instinctively gripping my head to protect myself.

"What do you think you're doing, little shithead?" Kick.

"You think you can barge in here messing with my business?" Slam.

"You gonna earn the money around here?" Kick.

He pulls me up by my shirt and I look up at him with narrow eyes. He smells like beer and cigarettes, a mix that will forever be engraved in my brain as vile and wrong.

"Well?" Before I can say anything, his fist connects with my head, a splitting pain pounding through it before he throws me back on the floor, then gives me another kick in the ribs. I yelp in anguish, trying to crawl into the hallway while he keeps kicking me wherever he can.

"You pull that shit again and I'll make sure you won't be able to crawl back to your room, boy." I wait for more pain, but when I glance over my shoulder, he's still standing in the living room with a furious look. He pulls an empty beer can from the floor, throwing it at my head, and I duck, still crawling away as tears stream down my face.

"Go to your fucking room. And stay there." Not having to be told twice, I scramble up, running to my room as fast as I can before slamming the door behind me. I press my back against the wooden surface, my knees tucked in front of my body as I stare into nothing with wide eyes. My heart is slamming against my chest in fear, my breath jerking, making it impossible for me to calm down. After a week in hell and keeping up a strong appearance, I break down, letting my emotions take over.

My vision is going blurry, making me feel dizzy, and I drop my head between my knees, welcoming the darkness that blocks out the light as I just sob uncontrollably.

Killian was right. When Franklin got arrested, that wasn't just everything going to shit. It was our lives going up in smoke. The day they split us up, Franklin promised me he would get me out. I believe him. I do. My brother will always do anything in his power to save me.

I just hope I'm still alive by the time he does.

9

Sienna

Working for the Wolfes hasn't been as awful as I expected it to be. Although, to be fair, I was expecting it to be awful with Reign. Not with the rest of the brothers. If anything, I've felt more myself being around them than I have in a long time. Even with Reign, I'm growing more comfortable. At first, everything was awkward, and I kept glaring at him with every word he said. But the last few days, he's been okay. I still feel my body go rigid every time he enters a room, and I still overthink everything I say, but at least I don't have a stomachache before I get here. More like a flutter I desperately try to ignore. A flutter that he seems to ignite just by staring at me like he's doing now. I'm sitting at the bar, while Reign polishes the glasses for tonight.

"I'm really proud of you, you know?" Reign brings his eyes up to me, then lowers them again as if he's trying to not make me uncomfortable. "You really nailed your goal. You're the best event manager in the city."

"Thank you. It took me a while, but I'm proud of the reputation I have." It's something I've worked hard for. At one point, it was fueled by showing the world I was more than Reign's ex-girlfriend, although sometimes I wonder if it's more myself who I'm trying to convince.

"You should be. Though, there was never any other outcome. You've always gone after what you wanted."

"Like what?" I ask, quirking up a brow.

"Like me." The arrogant boyish grin on his face makes me snort, but the corners of my lips pull up without my permission.

"What? I'm pretty sure you asked me to be your girlfriend."

"True. But you're the one who chased me." He smirks, leaning his elbows onto the bar to move his face closer to mine.

"I did not!" I scoff.

"Yeah, you did. My sixteenth birthday party. You were there. You made it no secret you wanted to hang out with me."

I get up in an attempt to hide my flushed cheeks. I did chase him at first. When he came home a few weeks before his sixteenth birthday, Emma pushed me to be brave and at least show Reign I still had that childhood crush on him. A crush that now seems like it's everlasting.

I walk around the bar with an approving expression, taking in all the parts they've renovated. It's a lame attempt to change the subject, but it's all I can think of this fast.

"It's looking good." They took everything I said to heart, and I'm pleased to say it's a big improvement. It shows class. The kind of class that feels like a *night out* instead of *getting a beer at the corner pub*.

"I know." Reign's voice vibrates close to my ear, making my heart drop before I spin around. My eyes snap up, looking into his piercing retinas that are focused on one thing and one thing only; me.

I've seen the moments he's stared at me a little too long over the last few days, and even his slight touches when he walks past me haven't gone unnoticed. They've slowly been sparking my body alive, reigniting a longing that I haven't felt in forever. As much as I want to keep my distance, I can't seem to shake the feeling he's giving me. In my heart, I can't deny my crush is still very much alive, burning like the Olympic flame, but I'm not going to show him all my cards just yet.

"I'm talking about the bar." A scowl is on my face, but the crack in my voice shows how nervous he makes me.

"I'm not." He smirks. The tension forms when he takes another step, now close enough for me to feel the warmth of his body radiating against mine. My head is telling me to not go there, to keep my distance, but in the last few days, my heart has been giving my mind a big *fuck you* every chance she's gotten. I can feel my pulse throbbing in my neck, and without thinking, my lips part from my desire. Within a split second, his eyes lower, and he reaches his hand up to touch my face. I shouldn't allow him to touch me, to cross the boundaries I've been trying to set, but I do nothing. I want to feel strong enough to slap his hand away, but instead, I lean into it. For a brief second, his touch warms my skin just how I remember, his knuckles caressing my cheekbone and trailing into my hair as he stares down at me. I wait in anticipation for his lips to touch mine until a set of heavy boots is audible behind us, and he quickly drops his hand.

"Am I interrupting anything?" Killian asks while Reign scowls over the top of my head.

I hold still, sucking in a deep breath, then twist my head, giving him a coy smile.

"We were just discussing how well the renovation turned out."

"Right," Reign chimes in, though with a voice that tells me I'm full of shit.

Killian looks at both of us, a smile haunting his face before it goes back to the uninterested one he's known for. "Yeah, whatever."

He rounds the bar, pulling out three tumblers.

"Let's sit down, and Sienna can tell us exactly what we should do now."

"I thought this was a brainstorming session?" Reign questions as we both take a stool in front of the bar.

Killian splashes two fingers in each glass. "We both know we don't have a clue what we're doing, so why don't we save ourselves the time and energy and let her fix it."

"Good point. So, what's the plan?" Reign's eyes fall on me again, and I roll my eyes as they both stare at me with expectation.

"You two tools are not even going to try and come up with any ideas?"

They both shake their handsome heads with matching cocky grins.

"Nope."

"You know you'll have to do it yourselves in a few weeks, right?"

They both just continue staring at me, not even attempting to appease me.

"Fine," I grumble. "I want to start with an opening for no more than forty guests."

"Forty? There is room for at least a hundred." Reign looks at me like I'm crazy, making it that much easier to scowl at him.

"Your guest capacity never changed. But what you're selling should. You've tried the let's-wing-it-approach, and it didn't work. We need to show the city you're not a typical bar. You're open for everyone, but we want to give them a reason to wanna be there. We need to create exclusivity. If we invite no more than forty people, others will want to come for the simple reason they can't."

They look at me in awe. "What?

"You're quite the little vixen, aren't you?" Reign says with a craving look that makes me shift on my stool.

"Keep it up, and I'll scratch your eyes out," I sneer.

"You wouldn't, but you can scratch something else." His gaze impales me once again, his smirk nowhere to be found, and all I can picture are my nails dragging down his back as he makes me scream his name. Just great. Up until now, his flirtatious comments were nothing more than playful, like he is. But today, he seems different. *Determined.* Like he woke up this morning, deciding he wasn't going to give me any slack anymore. Going straight for the kill.

The worst part is that my damp panties tell me it's working.

"Ay!" Killian snaps his fingers between our faces, then moves his finger back and forth. "Can you two do this when I leave?" He gives us both a glare, though the amusement flicks through his eyes. "So who do you wanna invite?"

I clear my throat, going back to the plan.

"A mix of high society and Southie. I want to make sure we represent the entire city. This bar doesn't care if you're from Beacon hill, Roxbury, or Southie. We have to show people that this is a bar for everyone. Not just one group of people."

"Yeah, that makes sense," Killian concedes, knocking his knuckles on the bar. "So, what do you need me to do?"

"Be here and mingle next Friday."

"That's it?"

"That's it," I confirm with a tilt of my head.

"Wicked." He throws the contents of his glass down his throat, then puts his sunglasses on his nose. "If that's all, I'm out." With big strides, his feet move from behind the bar.

"Where are you going?" Reign calls as we watch him get to the door.

"Leaving you two to do... well, whatever the fuck you two wanna do." He chortles with his green eyes glittering devilishly.

Before I can open my mouth and tell him we won't be doing shit together, the door opens, and a delivery guy steps over the threshold. In his hand sits a long white box with a perfect red bow around it, and naturally, a frown brings my eyebrows together.

"Reign Wolfe?" the guy calls out, moving his gaze from Killian to Reign.

Killian brings up his hand, pointing at his brother, and curiosity washes his entertained features. "That one."

Killian follows the delivery guy when he places the box in front of Reign on the bar, apparently not ready to leave just yet, then the guy gives Reign a clipboard to sign for the package. I do my best to keep a straight face, though a little green monster seems to settle on my shoulders while I wonder if he's been dating without me knowing.

"What the fuck?" Reign mutters when the delivery guy makes his way out again.

"You got a secret admirer, bro." Killian rests his elbows on the bar, his chin in his hands, as he glances at the box with a big grin stretching his face.

"I don't," Reign argues before quickly giving me a pleading look. "I really don't."

I shrug nonchalantly, pressing my lips together, trying like hell to feign not caring.

"I really don't, Sienna." He rolls his eyes while he pulls the ribbon with his tattooed hand.

"You don't owe me any explanations, Reign."

As much as I hate the thought of him with a girl, I'm not stupid. Not only is he very capable of picking up a new piece of ass every single night, but I also know he hasn't been a saint for the last few years. I don't expect him to get romantic gestures, but it also doesn't completely surprise me.

"No," he says, his gaze locked on mine, "but I also don't want you to get the wrong idea." He lifts the top of the box, and my eyes grow wide before I abruptly shove my stool backwards.

"What the hell?" Killian jumps up with disgust.

Shock is written onto Reign's face as he takes a step back, peering into the box. On a piece of blue silk lay three red roses, the thorns still on them. But it's not the flowers that have us staring at it like we see water burning. It's the dozens of worms crawling over them, accompanied by a note that's handwritten with the words; *I miss you.*

It takes me a few seconds before the corner of my mouth curls up, and I give him a mocking look.

"Who did you piss off, *Prince Charming*?" I taunt.

"Funny." He glares.

"No-suh, that is some fucked up shit, Reign. Who hates you?" Killian bellows.

"Nobody hates me!"

I snicker. *"Somebody* hates you."

The three of us stare at the crawling worms, holding still until I give Reign a questioning look with a chuckle coming from my lips. "Pulled a biddy and never called her back, Reign?"

With a cramped expression, he shakes his head, then he rubs a hand over his face, looking at his brother.

"I have a bad feeling, Kill."

"What do you mean?" Killian asks while I watch both of them with an incredulous look.

"Remember those paper swans we used to get?"

"She's dead, Reign." He gives his brother a sympathetic look.

Who's dead?

"I know!" he retorts. "But what if it's one of the other girls? What if they want to get back at me for something?"

What girls?

They keep quiet, a silent conversation being had between the two of them. The tiniest flexing of the muscles on their faces has me watching raptly, and I cock my head to try to decipher what's going on.

"What about Bella?" Killian offers.

"Who's Bella?" I ask.

Reign rubs his hand over his scruff. "She was Cary's girlfriend, the one who took Emerson's crew over after we killed him for messing with Kendall and Franklin's horses. She kidnapped Colin a few months ago."

"What?" Shock overtakes me. I've never met Colin, but I heard about him being Connor's little boy.

"We handled it. He didn't get hurt," Reign reassures me. "But Bella got away."

"I don't know, man," Killian chimes in. "Bella was sleeping with the leader of a rival gang that wants all of us dead. This seems personal, though."

"True," Reign agrees.

"We gotta look into it." Killian snaps a picture of the box. "I'll call Franklin."

I huff. "It's probably just some girl who's pissed at you for either dumping her or not calling her back after sneaking out. Are you really going to bother your brother with this shit?"

Killian blinks at me. "You know we have a lot of enemies, right?" he deadpans.

"You think this is one of your enemies? You're pretty well known in this city," I mock. "I doubt your *enemy* would be sending you roses and worms."

"Maybe she's right." Reign offers a tentative look, but the tension in his jaw shows his worry. "Maybe we're overreacting."

Killian shrugs, bringing his phone to his ear. "Could be. But let's see what Franky says. I'm gonna go."

"You gonna kill some people?" Reign calls out to his brother's back.

"Probably." With a mock salute, he disappears through the door, and I turn my head back to Reign.

"He's joking, right?"

He snorts. "I doubt it."

When both of us stay quiet, I realize I'm alone with Reign again.

Shit.

"You should throw that out." I point at the box with crawling insects, my lips pursed in repulsion.

"Right." He picks up the note, placing it on the bar, then puts the top back on, picking it up to bring it to the containers out back.

"Okay, I'm gonna go too," I tell him right before he goes through the backdoor.

"Hold up!" Instantly, he turns back around, putting the box back on the end of the bar before he closes the distance between us with determined steps.

Putting my jacket back on, I wait until he's in front of me, then look up.

Please don't give me any of your charm.

"Have dinner with me."

Goddammit.

I take in his handsome features while an indecisive feeling builds inside of me. The hairs on my back jolt up, one by one, at a slow pace, and I let out a deep, reluctant sigh.

"Reign."

"Please." The word is a plea, but it's laced with demand, nothing more than a courtesy, telling me he won't stop until I give him what he wants. "I know you don't want to fight me forever. I can see it in your beautiful eyes." Boldly, he brings his hand up, cupping my face. His touch causes my neck to grow flush, and my heart rate speeds up. "I know I hurt you. I'm not going to apologize. Not now, because I know you won't believe me. But give me the chance to show you that I do regret it. Just have dinner with me."

My mind seems to turn into mush because all I want to do is say yes. I don't trust him. But I want to. I want to give him that chance to gain my trust once more, to get access to my heart, even though I know he's the only one who can break it into a thousand pieces all over again.

My feet shuffle on the hardwood floor, my eyes never leaving his. I shake my head, wondering what the fuck happened to my defensive stance, and I watch his face fall for a brief second.

"I can't believe I'm doing this," I whisper, shocked by my own decision.

He runs a hand through his brown hair, a strand falling in front of his face in the most seductive way.

"Fine." I give in. "But you're buying."

10

13 YEARS OLD

"I didn't see you in school today." I drop my body onto
Aubrey's bed, keeping the door wide open. "You were
smoking pot with that Gino guy again?"

She glances over her shoulders, her brown curls bouncing
around her head before she turns her gaze to the now open
door. She pulls down the headphones covering her ears,
giving me a glare as she gets up and slams the door shut.

"You know I don't like it when the door is open on a
Saturday night."

For anyone else, it's just Saturday night. The night you go
out to the movies. Have fun with friends. Spend time with
family. But for us, Saturday night is money night. I need to
make sure the house is clean and one of the girls brings in
the money. The first few weeks, I couldn't control myself,

desperately wanting to save each one of them from the ugly fate that was waiting in the basement. But I learned quickly. I soon found out that if I wanted to stay alive, I needed to keep my mouth shut and do as I was told. That was the only way I'd be able to go back home to my brothers... whenever that may be.

I roll my eyes at her. "As if not hearing anything will make it any easier."

"You've been here for over a year. This is life, Reign. Just accept it." Her headphones circle around her neck as she goes back to the paper in front of her.

"What are you doing?" I move my body up, looking at her desk. The surface is poorly lit by a small light, giving the view of three swans folded from paper. "You made those?"

She nods. "It's origami."

"What's that?"

"Japanese. I saw it on TV once."

"Can you make more?"

"No. Just swans."

"So you just fold swans all night?"

"Hmm."

I bring my legs onto the bed, cross-legged. "Why?"

"It keeps me busy." She shrugs.

"And the headphones?"

"To block out the noise." She gives me a look that says *duh*, as if that's all it takes for her to just block the ugly that's going on in this house.

"Right." I drop my head onto her pillow, peering up at the ceiling with a melancholic feeling. "You ever wonder if your life could've been different?"

"No." Her answer is firm, surprising me.

"No?" I parrot, incredulously. "Why not?"

"Because this is it. Look around." She spreads her arms. "At least we're not out on the streets, begging for money. We are lucky, Reign," she tells me with a smile.

"No, instead you need to spread your legs," I counter, my tone unintentionally vicious.

Anger flares in her eyes, and I offer her a remorseful look. "Sorry."

She pushes the air from her lungs. "No one is going to save us."

I quirk back up, my voice low. "But what if we can save ourselves?"

"How?" she scoffs. "We got no money, and nowhere to go. Besides, social services would pick us up in a heartbeat and throw us right back in. Or worse, in a different foster home. At least here I know what to expect." She's serious. The defeated look on her face tells me she never even considered to just pack her bags and go, and it baffles me. Everything inside of me tells me to run. Hide. Live on the street. Anything and anywhere but here. The only reason I haven't left yet is because my heart can't leave Aubrey and Nova behind.

"You'll be sixteen next year. We can run. We'd stand a chance."

"And leave Nova behind? Never." Her fire reignites when she mentions her sister.

"No. We'd take her with us. Just think about it, Aubrey. We can start over. Just the three of us. We can get a job and get a place. At sixteen, you can get emancipated. We might even be able to get custody over Nova if we tell social services about what's happening here. My brothers can help us."

"Don't you dare tell your brothers." Her finger snaps my way, a reprimanding tone in her voice. "Don't you get it?

You think no one ever tried to out them? Social services is in on it. They can't help us. No one can."

"Fine, but *we* can. We can run." I pause, watching her carefully as she takes in my words. "Just think about it."

When she doesn't reply, I cock my head a little, forcing her to look at me.

"Just promise you'll think about it."

"Fine." She gives in with an eye roll. "I'll think about it."

A coy smile tugs on the corners of my mouth before I lie back down. "Thank you."

I stay there for a few minutes, staring at the ceiling. Anything to not be alone.

It's weird how you can be happy while being in an unhappy situation.

In these brief moments I spend with Aubrey and Nova, being together in this room that represents a little bit of safety, I feel happy. But I guess my standard has changed. When I was younger, I was happy on Christmas morning. Unwrapping gifts. Then happiness was when my father didn't beat my mom up that day. Nowadays, happiness means being fed, being able to dodge any fists coming my way, and enjoying the quiet of our own rooms. It shows me the house I grew up in wasn't as bad as I thought it was. My father wasn't as bad as I thought he was. And my brothers mean more to me than I ever showed them.

Franklin says he's trying to get custody over me. To get me out of this hellhole. The first few weeks, I believed him. Thought that any day now, he'd ring that doorbell and take me out of here. But as the months passed, I knew that wasn't going to happen. Not because he wasn't trying. But because there was no way a judge was going to let me live with a criminal.

The irony, right?

Here I am living with the biggest piece of scum you'll ever meet, running a whorehouse with his children from his living room, while my innocent brother is trying to get me out. I learned at a young age that the world isn't fair. But I could've never prepared myself for the moment when I would find out just how true that was. How fucked up the world was.

"Do you hate them?"

I watch how she turns her head from the corner of my eye while I keep my focus up.

"Who?"

"Jefferson. Your dad. Your mom?"

"Why would I hate them? They love me."

A frown knits my brows as I slowly turn my head to look at her. "You can't be serious."

She gives me a puzzled look, as if I'm crazy. "What do you mean?"

"You get raped every single weekend because they whore you out."

Her eyes grow cold, and I watch her as she squares her shoulders, her chin up high. She fiddles with her fingers and the weird look on her face makes the hairs on my arms prick up.

"We all have to do our part in this family, Reign. Food isn't free. Neither is rent." The words roll off her tongue, rehearsed, like she's acting.

My eyes grow big, wondering if I heard her correctly.

"Don't look at me like that," she continues. "It's not that bad."

"Being raped is *not that bad*?" I ask, incredulous.

"It's not rape when you enjoy it." She gives me a daring look and I sit still, even though I feel like I'm being punched in the stomach.

"You enjoy it?"

She twists her mouth, giving me a look that reminds me of a stuck-up librarian or something.

"Not at first," she discloses, "but I learned to enjoy it. I do it with Gino all the time."

My mind can't process what she's saying, and I'm seriously wondering if she's losing her mind. Is this what happens when you're in hell too long? When you're surrounded by psychopaths all day, do you become one? Do you go crazy? Panic grips me and I press my hand against my chest, trying to ease the sharp sting that's seeping through. My skin burns up while I have a hard time breathing.

Trying to pull myself together, I suck in a deep breath, then exhale as slowly as possible.

"It's just sex, Reign. You wouldn't understand." She sighs.

"I understand it's wrong!" I snarl. "Does Gino know you're a prostitute? That your dad is your pimp? Student during the week, whore on the weekend." My words are meant to hurt her, cut through her, anything to get a reaction from her that makes sense.

A reaction of anger, despair, tears, anything that tells me she's still a normal girl underneath. But instead, she glares at me, smirking, running her tongue along her teeth.

"I'm not a whore, *Reign*," she sneers. "And you better watch it, because I can make your life a living hell around here."

"You mean this isn't hell already?" I scoff.

"Ha!" she jeers. "You have no clue if you think this is the worst you can do. Just be lucky that the only thing you have to worry about is doing your chores and ducking some fists. Maybe if you're lucky, you'll even graduate in a few years.

You got it easy, Reign. Like I said before, this is just life. *My life.*"

"Don't you want more?"

"There is no *more*," she barks, getting annoyed with me. Our eyes stay tangled, an invisible cord holding us together while we stare at each other in anger. Both are frustrated about life. Refusing to believe that, I vow to not back down, determined to make her see differently. My nostrils flare with every exhale as my chest slowly moves up and down, the tension rising with every passing second. I watch as her jaw ticks and a hateful spark laces her dark eyes.

Our connection breaks when I hear a girl scream, and I strain my neck to listen to the piercing sound entering my ears. My shoulders tighten, and I snap my head back to Aubrey. Her gloomy expression has disappeared and a vacant one takes its place.

"Where is Nova?" I ask, holding my breath.

Aubrey shakes her head, her eyes closed, as if she wishes my question away.

"Aubrey!" I jump up, things clicking in my head when I realize the reason why Nova isn't in the room with us. My mind goes dizzy, rage taking over as I dart to the door, ready to do... I don't know. *Anything.*

Aubrey jumps in front of me, blocking me from getting out of the door, and I slam the wall beside her face. "Let me out!" I roar.

Her head frantically moves from side to side, a panicked look in her eyes. "No, Reign. You can't. You know what's going to happen if you do that."

"I don't care!" I shout.

"You can't save her! We always knew it was going to be her turn one day!" she yells back with the same anger.

"That is your sister!"

"I know! But you won't get it! This is our life! You can't fix it! You can't save us!"

My knees weaken underneath me, and I slump to the floor, a tremor in my voice.

"She's nine, Aubrey." Every muscle in my body starts to hurt, a fog entering my mind that I can't seem to control when tears start to stream down my face. I wish to wake up from this nightmare. Everything about this is wrong. Everything inside me screams to go and help her. Help the little girl that is now ruined. Her innocence completely shattered under the pressure of a grown man's body. My stomach feels like it's somersaulting inside of me, and I try to swallow the nausea away.

"She's nine," I croak out, even though everything I do or say feels useless.

Aubrey drops to her knees, wrapping her arms around my chest.

Sobbing, I hug her back, rocking us back and forth while I try to think of a solution.

But there is none. I'm a thirteen-year-old in junior high. I can't do shit other than do my best to protect these girls as much as I can. That's all I can do. That's all I can offer.

"It's okay, Reign," she hums into my chest as we sit there on the floor for what feels like forever. But I shake my head. Nothing about this is okay. Nothing about this will ever be okay.

I grind my teeth together, the muscles in my face tensing. The blood is rushing through my ears while I bring up my chin before pressing it into her hair as I hold her tighter against me.

"One day, I'm going to get us out of here. I'm going to find a way to get out of this hellhole. All three of us. You, me, and

Nova. Do you hear me?" I push her back, forcing her to look at me, and I see the disbelief written on her features.

"I mean it, Aubrey," I groan, pained by her doubt. "I'm going to save us."

She presses her lips together in a coy smile, then brings her hands up to cup my cheek. Her thumb brushes away the tears before she gives me a sympathetic look.

"Okay, Reign." She gives in, though I don't believe her.

"I mean it!" I shout.

"I know you do." She nods. "I believe you."

She gets up, then reaches out her hand to me. When I grab it, she guides me back to the bed with a look filled with pity. She doesn't believe me, but I will show her. I will convince her. I will tell her every day until we finally escape.

I watch her as she walks to her closet, grabbing a big box. She grabs out another pair of headphones before she walks back and hands them over.

"What is this?" I wipe my nose with the back of my hoodie.

"It helps." She shrugs.

I give her a confused look.

"With the noise," she clarifies.

I accept them from her grasp, a little shocked as she walks back to her desk. She sits down, putting her own headphones back on, giving me another glance.

"Go on," she urges.

"You know it doesn't make it go away, right?" I tilt my head, perplexed about her approach to the problem.

"Suit yourself."

I'm not sure what I expect, but she just shrugs her shoulders, then turns her head and goes back to folding her swans. Letting her fingers work as if nothing is wrong, when in reality, there is nothing right.

11

Sienna

"Thank you for having dinner with me."

My eyes stop scanning the surroundings of the quaint little bistro he took me to, meeting his moss green eyes. They show a warmth no one else gives me, yet they also represent a hurt that I've been feeling since he left. I hate how they effortlessly lure me in, erasing all the awkwardness that should be between us, but I love it at the same time.

"Don't make me regret it." I grab my glass of red wine, bringing it to my lips. My eyes stay locked with his, looking over the rim while the red wine graces my tongue.

A smile stretches his face. It's one of those smiles that makes me feel like I'm in trouble. A boyish grin that makes my panties melt and my heart beat faster. It makes me wish we could forget about the past and move on in whatever way that might be.

"I won't."

My fingers are wrapped around the stem of my glass, and I stare at the red liquid as I softly swirl it around. We're sitting in a booth in the back of the restaurant, giving us the privacy I long for. We are both well known in this city, and I don't need the women at the bakery to start whispering about Reign and me by morning. That's not what I want. I don't even know what I want. In fact, I don't even know why I said yes to dinner, but here I am. Sitting in a back corner booth, with the man I've learned to stay angry at with a passion. I guess I don't really want to be angry at him anymore, though.

"You guys really climbed on top in the last few years."

He drapes his arm over the back of the booth, his fingers drifting to a lock of my black hair to play with. My instinct is to tell him to stop doing that, but I keep my mouth shut, loving his little display of affection.

"Franklin worked hard to get us where we are."

"Just Franklin?"

He shrugs, tilting his head with a smile haunting his lips. "You know I don't really do the heavy lifting. I just sit behind my computer whenever he asks."

"You say it like you are not part of the Wolfe empire."

"It feels like that."

"He bought you and Killian a bar."

"True," he concedes, "but *he* bought it."

I keep my eyes aligned with his. There was a time Franklin was his big example. A time when he would do anything to even remotely be like his big brother. But now all you see is disappointment and frustration whenever you bring Franklin up. I swore to stay out of it, but it kills me to see that hurt little boy still deep inside of him. They are wrapped up in a misunderstanding when their past should've brought them closer than they ever were.

"You still haven't worked things out with him?" I take a sip of my wine.

"What is there to work out? We are brothers. We just don't get along. Lots of siblings don't get along."

"It wasn't always like that."

"It is now." His tone is cold and sharp, pushing me to drop the subject.

But it kills me to watch this. Now that I've been spending most of my days with these brothers again, it's impossible to not care about them. To care about Reign when I see how his heart still bleeds like an open wound. He thinks he knows it all, but really, he's always been too stubborn to dig deeper.

Just like Franklin.

"You're going to hate him forever?" My tone is teasing, trying to get rid of the icy tension that just occurred.

"Maybe." He throws his whiskey down his throat before slamming it on the table with a loud thud. "Are you seeing anyone?"

Wasting no time, are you, Prince Charming?

Fire glitters from my eyes at the sudden change of subject, but also because I'm annoyed that he thinks I would be here if I were.

"You think that little of me?" I ask with a pinched mouth.

He breathes out, sliding his hand under my hair, resting it on the back of my neck. The heat of his palm instantly settles my annoyance while he gives me an apologetic expression.

"No. But I also realize that you're not here because you are willing to give me another shot. So it's a fair question, right?"

"I suppose." He holds my gaze, silently waiting for more than just those simple words. "I'm not seeing anyone exclusively. But I do date."

"Yeah?" He tries to keep the look on his face light and interested, but I can see his glare etching through his fake smile. He hates hearing this.

"Anyone pass the first date?"

"Just one." I keep my mouth in a straight line, not showing any emotions while Lucas flashes in front of my eyes. We've been to dinner a few times, and I'd really started to like him. But ever since I started working for the Wolfes, I've been holding him off. Hiding behind excuses like *"I'm too tired"* or *"I have an early morning tomorrow."*

"Why? Jealous?" I bring my glass to my lips.

He leans closer, our faces merely a foot apart. His voice is husky and low, stirring my lady parts alive.

"I don't have to be jealous. Because we both know there is no one who can make you feel the way I do." His grip on my neck tightens before his thumb starts to make scorching circles below my ear. His moves are filled with purpose, meant to remind me of the spark that's always been there between us. Our undeniable chemistry never faded, even when he moved to another city.

"Whoa, you're wasting no time, are you?" My tone is snappy, but I still don't remove his palm from my skin as it runs the length of my arm, landing on my thigh.

"I've wasted enough time, baby. You can date whoever you want, but I know you'll always wonder what could've been." He pauses, his flirty attitude changed by a serious one, and I decide to ignore the fact that he calls me *baby* again. "Like I do."

My lips part, taking a deep breath to ignore the swirling longing and desire in my body while my mind is trying to keep up the fight and not roll over too easily.

"You didn't wonder that when you stayed in New York."

His face darkens in a way that makes me hold my breath. In the last few days, I've noticed the maturity of his physique, the aging of his face, making him even more handsome than he was before. But I still see the boy deep inside of him every time he gives me one of his famous playful grins.

Right now, though, he's shedding his skin, growing into a broody man in front of me. His youth disappears like snow in the sun, showing me the Reign he has become over the years. This Reign is all man. All alpha. All *Wolfe*. His piercing gaze makes it hard to breathe, while his hand keeps a firm grip on my thigh that makes me want to press my lips against his.

"You're going to hold that against me forever?"

"Maybe," I whisper, too puzzled to voice it fiercely.

Before I can blink, he's even closer, his hand moving to twist my head so I have to look at him. The demanding energy coming from his body is moving through me in waves, fueling the desire to rest my hands on his biceps. To feel his muscles under my palm while his mouth is pressed against my neck as he trails kisses up and down my skin.

He lets his vacant eyes fall to the table. "Foster care changed me. I needed that time in New York."

"I don't want to hear it, Reign." I shake my head. He could've explained years ago, but he didn't want to. Now it's too late.

"One day, you're going to listen to me, *baby*." He hovers above my mouth, and I'm seriously wondering what I will do if he closes the distance and covers his mouth with mine. Only, this time, the use of his nickname has me raising the corner of my lip in a sneering way.

"Don't call me that," I breathe against his lips, snarling. "Don't pretend it makes me special when I wasn't *special* enough to come home for." Done with this little power play, I push him off me, grabbing my purse.

"Where are you going?" He grinds his teeth, yet doesn't stop me.

"Home." I slide out of the booth, putting on my jacket while avoiding eye contact.

"Sit down, Sienna. Just talk to me."

I give him a smile that doesn't match my eyes while buttoning up my coat. "What is there to talk about, Reign? You left me, telling me you'd be back in two months. In reality, you ghosted me for another girl and didn't return until a year later. There was a time when I wanted you back, but I'm not some love-struck little girl anymore. I know what I'm worth, and you played with me once. It won't happen again."

"I didn't ghost you for another girl, Sienna."

I give him a mocking frown. "Don't insult me, Reign. You broke up with me over the phone and a girl moved in with you two weeks later."

"It's not what you think." He pinches the bridge of his nose, and a heavy feeling starts to form inside my stomach.

"It never is. Have a good night, Reign."

I spin on the spot, strutting off. Part of me wants him to drag me back into that booth and tell me I'm wrong. To tell me I got it all mixed up and there is a perfect explanation for everything. But I know there isn't. I asked

Killian multiple times, and I know he wouldn't lie to me. Not after all the times he comforted me when I cried my eyes out. I wasn't worth coming back for. It's as simple as that.

"You can't run away from me forever," he calls out behind my back.

"Watch me, Wolfe," I mutter, not loud enough for him to hear, while my heels keep tapping the hardwood floor until I'm outside.

Just watch me.

12

13 YEARS OLD

Sienna

"**G**ood morning, Mrs. Walsh." I look up at Emma's mother with a friendly smile as she opens the door. Her hair sits messily on her head, and she's still wearing her white bathrobe, her typical outfit for a lazy Saturday morning.

"Good morning, Sienna." She gives me the same kind look, as always, though lately she looks more tired. Like something is weighing on her shoulders. "She's upstairs. Go ahead."

With a grateful nod, I move past her, walking up the stairs while she closes the door and retreats back to the living room.

Because our mothers are friends, I've known Emma since we were in pre-school, making her house my second home and vice versa. It's only two blocks from my house and it has been the only house I can go to by myself since I was eight. Ever since, we've been going to the park together every Saturday morning. When we were younger, we would play, pretending we were princesses fighting dragons and other silly stuff like that, but now that we're in junior high, we mostly complain about school and every single clique we're not part of.

"Em? Are you here?" I open the door and she jerks from her bed, wiping the tears from her eyes. "Hey, what's wrong?"

I close the distance between us, wrapping her in a tight hug while she buries her face in my shoulder. I just hold her as she sobs, trying to comfort her with my hand resting on her long blonde hair. "What happened?"

She lets go of me, rubbing her eyes until she notices her bedroom door still open. With a startled look, she quickly trots away, slamming it closed with a loud thud.

"Don't ever leave the door open." There is anger in her voice as she gives me a vicious look. It's a side of her I've never seen and I just blink, a little shocked by her sudden change of demeanor.

"Okay." I nod, like a scared little puppy. Emma has always been the bold one out of the two of us. The one who will tell the boys on the street to go fuck themselves when they are bullying us, even though she's a head shorter and only twelve years old.

"What's wrong, though?" I cautiously take a seat on her bed, not sure what to make of this.

Fearful I might fuel her rage more, I stay still, waiting in anticipation. Luckily, her gaze softens, and she pulls a tissue from her nightstand to blow her nose, then grabs another one to wipe off what's left of her tears before sitting down next to me.

"It's nothing," she tells me. "I'm just tired. I have trouble sleeping."

"How come?"

Her gaze grows vacant at my words, and I can see her slip into another world as her blue eyes darken. She doesn't blink. She just sits there, staring into nothing, the tension forming on her features with every second passing by. I try to swallow away the lump in my throat that seems to swell bigger the longer I look at her. She's scaring me, morphing into a girl I don't know. It looks like the blood drains from her face, her soul leaving her body until there is nothing more left than an empty shell.

"Emma." I hesitantly lay my hand on her leg.

Her head snaps toward mine with a vile look. Her eyes look menacing, narrowing to slits and scaring the living life out of me. I can actually feel my heart freeze for a few seconds while I wait for her to say anything.

"Em," I say again, with more bravery than I feel.

Slowly, she starts to blink, and gradually I see my friend return, giving me a confused look.

"Hey." A frown knits my brows together. "Where did you go?"

As rapidly as her mind left, she puts a smile on her face. "Nowhere."

Well, this is weird.

"Emma, are you okay? You seem... I don't know... *troubled*."

She sighs, keeping her cheerful smile in place. It makes me wonder if I just imagined the last three minutes.

"I'm fine. It's just... it's been a year."

A year?

Not exactly understanding what she's talking about, I cock my head.

"Since *that* day." Her face gives me a knowing look, but the ball still won't drop. "Declan."

It comes out as a whisper, and my mouth flies open, though no sounds come out.

"Yeah," she drawls, bringing her gaze to the floor.

It was a bad day. A day that has been hanging above our heads ever since. We are still young, but I think that day forced us to grow up a little, realizing nothing is forever. I didn't know Declan, other than I knew that he was Emma's boy next door. But that day changed life for everyone.

"Do you miss Reign?" I didn't know Reign like Emma did. They went to the same middle school, a different one from mine, and they've been friends ever since. But to me, he was nothing more than the boy I had a crush on. I know she's changed since Reign was put into foster care and moved to a different state. I felt sad when I heard he left, but it didn't break me like I feel it did Emma.

There is surprise in her gaze before she agrees. "Yeah, I do. And Killian." She pauses. "It's just different without them. I worry, wondering where they are. If they are okay."

The words that leave her mouth make sense and I'm sure deep down she feels that way. But there is a weird glint in her eyes that makes me wonder if she's telling me the whole truth. That feels like she's holding something back.

Feeling silly for not trusting my friend, I wrap my arm around her shoulder, tugging her against me. "I understand. Hopefully, we'll see them soon and everything will go back to normal."

"Yeah." She smiles.

"You wanna go to the park and gush about all the skater boys?"

She chuckles, her weird mood from a minute ago completely gone.

"That's a wicked good plan."

13

14 YEARS OLD

Sienna

"**D**id you hear?" Emma walks into the parlor with a beaming smile, blocking the TV with her body, her hands on her sides.

"Hey! I was watching that!"

She glances over her shoulder, her blonde hair following her.

"Really? You're watching some kind of reality show again? You know that's all fake, right?"

"Who cares? It's fun." I try to look past her, moving my head to the side.

"Killian is home."

Instantly, I snap my gaze back up, my brows moving to my hairline.

"No-suh!"

"Ya-huh!" Her grin couldn't be stretched any wider, and her eyes are sparkling with joy.

"What about Reign?"

She gives me a taunting look with narrowed eyes.

"Sienna Brennan, do you still have a crush on him?"

I press my body a bit deeper into the couch, avoiding her gaze.

"No," I lie, mumbling while I feel my cheeks heating up.

"Ya-huh! You still have a crush on Reign Wolfe."

"Whatever."

"I just ran into Connor at Dunks. He told me Killian came back home a few days ago. He's at the park. You wanna come?" She points her thumb over her shoulder.

"They don't mind?"

"Nah, Killian is cool. Come on." There is a glimmer in her eyes when she mentions his name, and I give her a suspicious look, but keep my mouth shut. Maybe I'm not the only one who has the hots for a Wolfe boy.

"Sure."

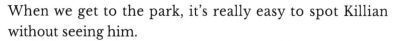

When we get to the park, it's really easy to spot Killian without seeing him.

A group of kids are circled around an edge of the skate ramp, and when we get closer, Killian is sitting on the steel border with a cocky grin plastered on his handsome face.

All the Wolfe boys are attractive. They all have the same piercing green eyes, sharp jaws, and smiles that make almost every girl weak in the knees. But from what I remember, they are also very different. Connor is the intimidating one, the kid you don't want to fight with because you'll probably end up in the hospital. Word on the street is he has a wicked temper. Reign, well to me, Reign is the cute one. He has always been sweet and charming, and even though the last time I saw him, he was twelve, just a kid like all of us, I still remember the occasional wink he would throw at me. It always resulted in a shy look from my side and a bucket load of butterflies. Franklin is the oldest and since I only know him as the adult of all four of them, in my head, he's the one that radiates authority. But Killian? Killian is smooth. Cunning. The one who will make you hand over your marbles to him and make you believe it was your idea. Since the first day I met him, he's been living in a leather jacket and seems like today is no exception. His brown hair is styled in a messy crest and the sly look in his eyes shows how much he's enjoying being back in Boston.

"Looks like he's a freakin' celebrity or something," I hiss as we get closer to the pile of people.

"Well, considering his brother is quickly becoming the biggest criminal in the city, I guess he kinda is."

"You sure you wanna–" My words are interrupted when Killian looks over his shoulder and catches us with a side-eye.

"Little Emma, is that you?" He gets up, dismissing the people around him by waving his hand in the air before he makes his way over to us. I look at Emma, whose eyes seem to light up when he sees her, and she eagerly crashes her body against his. His eyes shut and he breathes her in, the little display of affection making me giddy inside. Seems like that crush might be mutual.

"You're definitely not little anymore." He keeps a hold of her arms when his eyes shamelessly move up and down her body, his tongue pressing against his teeth.

He's right. Emma grew up in the last two years and her natural curves are proof of that. In fact, I'm slightly jealous because I'm still rocking my kid body, looking like a plank.

"Neither are you, *James Dean*," she purrs.

"James Dean?" He chuckles. "Babe, I'm Killian Wolfe. The one and only."

She playfully pushes him back. "Don't be so arrogant."

"I can't help it," he says with a smug shrug before he moves his gaze to me and Emma introduces me.

"Kill, this is—"

"Sienna Brennan. I remember you. You had a crush on my little brother."

I want to sink through the ground and avert my gaze while I feel like my head is turning as red as a tomato.

"Don't be shy." He gives me a brotherly smile, lifting my chin with his fingers, then gives me a wink. "He had a crush on you too."

"What?"

He brings his face closer, and I can smell the wax in his hair as he whispers, "Don't ever tell him I told you."

14 YEARS OLD

"I heard you got into a fight with Brady Johnson today."
I look up at Aubrey from my bed, standing in my
doorway with a skirt that should be at least three inches
longer. Her brown curls frame her face that's caked with
make-up. Red lipstick stains her usually rosy-pink lips.

Last year, her body matured. When I met her, she was a
young girl pretending to be a full-grown woman, lacking
curves and still wearing a little girl's face. A troubled little
girl, but she was still little either way. But now, her female
features show curvy hips and breasts that greet you from
under her deep cleavage. I wish she would cover herself up
a bit more. Stop looking like the whore they want her to
be. I've told her she's pretty without all the make-up and

skimpy clothes, but every time she thanks me and then wears the same shit the next day.

"He was mocking my accent." I scowl before turning my attention back to my homework.

She teases me about it. Says there is no reason for me to keep my grades up because it's not like I'm going to college. She's probably right. But that's the only thing I got if I ever get out of this hellhole, and I want to make my brothers proud.

"Why? Did he ask you to bring some *Dunks* from the Pike?" She chuckles with the worst Bostonian accent I've ever heard.

"That makes no sense. Do you need anything?" I give her a dull look, then point my pen at my textbook. "Because if you're just here to piss me off, I'd like to finish this."

She stays quiet for a brief moment, and I bring my attention back to the text.

I feel for her. And I care for her and Nova, but Aubrey can be a real bitch. She has a vile mouth like her dad. Her mom barely says a word, just sits around high all day, letting life pass her by. But Aubrey paid attention to her dad's behavior, and the older she gets, the more she becomes bitter and mean. I meant what I said; one day, I will get her out of here. I will do my best to give both of them a better life as soon as I get the chance, but part of me wonders if it's gonna be too late for Aubrey.

"Your brother is here."

My chin snaps up. "Why didn't you tell me sooner?" I glare, throwing my pen down as I get up.

"I'm telling you now," she tells me, a sly smile on her lipstick covered lips.

"Yeah, and now you wasted a whole minute of my time with my brother." I move closer, peering down at her. She might have matured, but I've grown in length, and I'm now a head bigger than she is.

She turns around, not giving me a second glance. "You'll get over it."

I push out an aggravated breath, my fists balling before I take off to the living room. A relieved grin splits my face when I meet Franklin's eyes, and his does the same.

He looks older, more grown up every single time he visits, and today is no different. His long pea coat brings out his broad shoulders, and his brown hair has a sophisticated crest.

He looks like a successful man, and pride fills my chest.

"Hey, man. What's doing?" He wraps his arms around me, and I take him in while mine circle his back. I might be bigger than Aubrey, but I'm still not bigger than my older brother.

"Yeah, I'm alright."

He takes my face into his palms, the warmth of his hands giving me a comfortable feeling while he examines my face. His deep green eyes narrow, worry dripping from them.

"Are you sure?"

No, I'm not sure. Every day I wonder if this is my last, praying I won't get beat up until I don't wake up. Every day I hope this day will be better than the one before, but it never happens. *No*, I wanna say. *No, Franklin, I'm not okay. I haven't been okay since the day they locked you up.* But instead, I lie.

"Yeah, I'm sure," I offer with a tentative smile.

"Good." He looks over my head to Jefferson, sitting like a sack of potatoes on the couch. "I'm taking him out for a few hours."

Jefferson brings his head up in agreement, a glare directed our way.

I can feel Franklin's aggravation toward the man, radiating off him in waves, before he tugs my neck. "Come on, let's go."

Eager to get out of the house, I grab my coat and walk through the door as quickly as possible. "Where are we going?" I question while putting my coat on.

"Let's go to the park nearby. You look like you could use some fresh air."

"Okay." My feet take me to the black car parked in front of the house.

The truth is, I don't care where we're going. We could be sitting in his car for the next few hours, and I'd still be content knowing my brother is here.

Franklin picks me up as much as he can. Taking me out for a few hours at least once a month. I know he's still working to get custody over Killian and me, but social services is making it hard for him. Since I got rid of whatever bullshit they got against him, it should be easy to do, but they keep looking at our family history, bringing up domestic violence. It's funny because when my mom went to the police, begging them for help, there was nothing they could do. And now, they are bringing it up to keep me living with the Brady Bunch from hell. It doesn't help that Franklin doesn't have a real job. He works hard, but not in the way the U.S. Government would like to see.

"Business must be wicked?" I beam, opening the passenger door of the Lincoln Town Car. The smell of new leather greets me, and it's a welcoming change from the nicotine filled air I'm used to.

"Business is flourishing," he confirms with a grin as he drops his body behind the wheel. "Let's grab some burgers to go and then later, I got a surprise for you."

I nod, suddenly realizing how hungry I am, and he drives us to the nearest burger joint while we chat about the easy stuff. He asks about school, tells me about all the ventures he's setting up, and he shows me a picture of the big mansion he one day wants to buy for all four of us. It fills me with hope and grows my determination to hold on and stay strong for my brothers.

For Franklin.

When we arrive at the park, we get out of the car and eat our burgers on the nearest bench. The sun warms my face, and I enjoy the soft breeze that's giving me a whiff of the blossoms on the trees. It's comforting to have Franklin sitting beside me. At least on the occasions I see him, I'm reminded of what family really is. That good people still exist. Like my brother. He might not earn his money the way that is considered normal, but he's no murderer. He doesn't sell his daughters for money. He doesn't hurt people or treat them like stock.

My brother has always treated me as an equal, even though he's almost eight years older than me. He's always showed me that I matter.

I might be stuck in hell for the foreseeable future, but Franklin shows me I can survive this. I need to keep fighting every day, just like he's fighting for me.

"Any news about my case?" I ask tentatively, taking a bite from my burger.

With his mouth full, Franklin shakes his head, an apologetic look in his eyes.

"The next hearing is in six months. I'm doing my best to bring it forward, but that social services bitch is doing everything she can to work against me."

Six months. That means at least six more months living with the Bradys.

"Don't worry, Reign." He grabs my neck, forcing me to look at him. "I'm not giving up. I will get you out. You will come home. To *us*."

I see the emotion etched on his face, his jaw ticking as he tries to keep it together.

"I have a surprise for you." A smile slides in place.

I push my worry away, straightening my body as I chew the last bite of my burger quickly, then gleam at him with excitement.

"Me." The voice entering my ear makes my heart drop, and I startle, before snapping my head back to look at whoever is standing next to me.

I gasp when I look into the green set of eyes that I haven't seen in two years. The same eyes we all got, but these are the ones that I used to spend most of my days with.

"Kill," I shriek, shocked.

He's peering at me with a smug grin, specks of joy dancing around his eyes. He's taller than I am, his face still not sure if he's a child or a man. He's wearing a black leather jacket and his hair sits slick and stylish on his head.

"No-suh!" I cry out before throwing my arms around my brother's neck. When I feel him embrace me, the emotion overwhelms me, and tears start to stream down my face as I sob on his shoulder.

"Ya-suh!" He chuckles, though I can hear how he's affected by his cracking voice.

"I missed you!"

"I missed you too, little brother." He sighs into my neck, gripping me even tighter. "Sienna says hi! And Emma, of course."

"You saw her?" I let go of him and meet his grin as he nods. "Is she okay? How does she look?"

"More beautiful every day."

Hearing that about the girl I've been crushing on since the first day I saw her makes my heart jump until I wonder where he saw her.

"I don't understand. Franklin took you to Boston?"

The look on his face changes, as if what I'm asking is heavy on his heart. He glances at Franklin, and I follow his gaze.

"I got custody over Killian. Now that he's sixteen, they are a bit more cooperative." There is a tight smile on his face, as if he expects his words to hurt me. They do. And they don't.

I'm sad that now I'm the only one who's still not home, but my heart fills, realizing Killian is no longer separated from our family.

"That's wicked pissah, Kill," I push out, playfully shoving him.

"Thanks, man." He shoots me a big smile, then his eyes turn serious. "You'll be home soon, Reign."

"I know. It's all good. I came this far. I can survive a little bit longer." A grin splits my face, and I mean it. There is nothing that's going to tear me down until I'm reunited with my brothers for good.

"That's my boy." Franklin ruffles my hair, then points at a man approaching us from the path. He's big for a teenager, his muscles almost popping out of his shirt like he's in the NFL, but I recognize his blond hair and the brooding look from a mile away.

"Connor!" I run toward my other brother like I'm two, jumping into his arms. He wraps one arm around my waist, holding up a backpack with the other.

"Hey, tool. How are you holding up?"

I slide down his body, beaming at him with happiness.

"Much better now that you guys are here."

"Good. Because we need your help." He walks us back to the bench, then opens the backpack.

"With what?"

Connor pulls out a laptop, holding it out to me.

"We need you to find some people for us, Reign," Franklin says.

My eyes roam over each one of them, a silent conversation forming between us. I'm pretty sure whatever he wants me to do isn't legal, but looking at my brothers, I know it doesn't matter. I'd do anything to help them.

"Of course." I take the laptop from Connor's hand, then take a seat and get to work.

15

I rub my face, walking out of the restaurant, trying to catch one last glimpse of her with my phone pressed against my ear. My instinct wants to yank her back, drag her to my condo, tie her to a chair, and force her to listen to me. Then kiss her while she's still tied up, until she finally gives in, and I can worship her like I've been dying to since the first day I set foot back in Boston. But I know that could very much blow up in my face when her Italian temperament bubbles up to the surface.

"What's up, tool?" Killian answers with a bored tone, and I let out a sigh.

"She bailed."

He stays quiet, and I can almost hear him roll his eyes.

"You stupid fuck. You finally got her to go to dinner with you and you fucked it up. Did you at least eat?"

"No-suh. She ran out on me after her first glass of wine."

"What did you do, you idiot?"

"Called her *baby*," I say, guiltily.

"For a fucking whizz-kid, you are wicked-stupid half of the time. Why would you do that? You know it ticks her off when you call her that."

"I know!" I cry out. My neck stretches, trying to see which way she headed, but when I can't see her, I make my way to my condo a few blocks out. "It just happens, okay? It just rolls off my tongue out of habit." I pause. "She just drives me nuts, man. I've been holding back for weeks now, trying to get her to loosen up around me. But the minute she does, I take another step, and she backs up. I know she still has feelings for me. I can see it in her eyes. But she's stubborn as fuck."

"She's Italian," Killian replies, as if that explains it all.

"What the fuck has that got to do with it?"

"They are stubborn."

"Gee, thanks for this mind-blowing revelation. Any more useless comments, Kill?"

I hear him chortle through the phone.

"Look, she's a proud woman. You broke her heart and stomped on it the moment you decided to stay in New York for Callie."

"I didn't stay in New York for Callie," I snap. "I wish everyone would stop saying that."

"I know that. But she doesn't."

"If she let me speak for two seconds, I could explain it to her. Instead of her jumping to conclusions all the time."

"Oh, yeah. This sounds familiar." His tone is judgy, pissing me off.

"What's that supposed to mean?"

"You know exactly what I mean," he retorts with a sharp voice. Killian hinted more than once that I should talk to Franklin. Ask him what happened that night he killed Declan. But every time I find the nerve, something happens, and Franklin pisses me off all over again.

"Look," he continues when I don't reply, "if she was any other girl, I'd tell you to fucking put her on the spot and tell her what the deal's gonna be. We ain't got time to pussyfoot around women. But this is Sienna. She's had a thing for you since you were twelve."

He just stops after that, knowing that's enough. This is Sienna.

I've loved the girl since I was sixteen, and I've never stopped. Yeah, I pushed her away. Left her while I was walking the streets of New York with some other girl, but that wasn't because of her. It wasn't because I didn't love her anymore. I never stopped loving her. After Franklin got me out of foster care, I was happy most of the time, but I was lost. The things that happened in Providence that last night. They haunted me in my sleep. New York was a change of scenery I didn't know I needed until I got there, and the only thing I regret from staying was losing Sienna in the process. But I didn't have a choice. It was me or her.

"I know," I finally concede.

I hear Killian push the air from his lungs.

"So, you got two options. You can either be a damn chucklehead about it and keep pushing her to forgive you. Or you can do it at her pace. I don't know, maybe try to become her friend again first. She doesn't trust your stupid ass."

He has a point. Even though I can still feel the chemistry that sits thick between us every time we are in the same room, she doesn't trust me. And frankly, I can't blame her. I wouldn't trust me either.

"Since when are you the wise one?"

"Always. I just never bother to share my opinion."

"You're a real asshole, do you know that?"

"Ya-huh." The tone of his voice isn't even slightly fazed, totally owning up to it, and I shake my head with amusement.

"Did you tell Franky about the roses?"

"I did. He told me to look into it."

"Did you find anything?" I walk into my building, then press the button for the elevator.

"I did, but it's a dead end. I went to EPS, found out their routes to check the driver. There were no packages delivered today."

"No-suh." I get on the elevator, watching the doors close before it moves up.

"Turns out the guy doesn't work at EPS. I need you to check if you can find more, pull the street cams, see where he came from."

"I'll do that now. I just got home," I tell him right before the doors open again.

"Wicked. You wanna..." he trails off, and a frown creases my forehead until I hear him mumble, "What the fuck."

"What's doing?" His quietness ticks me off. "Killian?! What's wrong?"

"Nothing." It comes out with a grunt, and I expect him to still explain.

"Right," I drag out, skeptically. "Random, but whatever."

"I'll tell you later. You gonna watch the game?"

"Yeah, you wanna come over?"

"Might as well, since you are definitely not getting laid tonight." I hear his words, but my body goes rigid when I reach my door. The blood leaves my face, and I snap my head around the hallway, looking for anyone around me.

"Ay, are you still there?" Killian calls out when I keep quiet, my heart stuttering.

"She was here, Kill."

"Who? Sienna?"

I shake my head, though he can't see me.

"Aubrey."

"What? Aubrey is dead. Drowned herself in the river in Providence, remember?" I can hear the slight distress in his voice.

I remember. I couldn't forget if I wanted to. I checked for records. Her body had been laying in the water for a long time, her face eaten by the fish. The rings on her fingers were all that could identify the body as Aubrey Brady's. But something tells me someone is trying to impersonate her to get to me.

"Then why is there an origami swan sitting in front of my door?"

16

15 YEARS OLD

I t's Saturday night.

The most dreadful night of the entire week. It's weird because as soon as the night falls and the doorbell rings, it's like you can feel the energy in the house shift. It's always wicked tense, but as soon as the door opens and the first customer comes in, it's like the house goes from a solid temperature to stone cold. The lights are on, but the house feels completely dark until the next morning, and we all pretend it never happened.

I have my headphones on, listening to a Nicki Minaj song, just praying I'll fall asleep soon and this night will be over before I know it. It always takes me a while, though. I don't think I've ever slept well living here, but on Saturday nights,

I rarely fall asleep before five. Always listening until the front door slams shut for the last time.

They have a system. The foster girls are forced every weekend, except the last one of the month. The last Saturday of the month, it's either Aubrey's or Nova's turn. It's Nova's turn tonight, and it's the night I always struggle with the most. Just the thought alone of her in the basement with whatever bastard walks through that door has my stomach filled with a ton of bricks. I always stay in Aubrey's room when that happens, not wanting to be alone. Not trusting I'll be able to stay calm if it's just me inside the four walls of my room.

Turning my head, I look at Aubrey, folding her origami swans like she always does when it's not her turn to go to the basement. There is a content smile on her face and it always makes me wonder what goes on through her head. I have a hard time blocking anything out when it's Saturday night, but she can put her headphones on and just calmly disappear into her own world.

I don't think I would've survived in this place without her. She's not my sibling. She's not my friend. I'm not even sure what we are. But I care about her. And I know she cares about me, even though she is a vicious girl every now and then. If she hadn't been here to save me from Jefferson's fists on a daily basis, or to warn me about the rules, there is a big chance I'd be dead right now. Aubrey calls it the hero syndrome. *"If you could, you would save everyone,"* she says. I don't even know if it's a real thing. But she's not wrong, I guess.

But it's what I was taught from a young age. I grew up in a household where my mother and brothers were my father's favorite punching bags. I got hit, but not nearly as much as everyone else. Every single one of my brothers always protected me as much as they could. My mother always shielded me from my father every chance she got. It showed me what was right. They gave me the example to protect those who need your protection, and it's been stabbing my soul that I can't help Aubrey and Nova the way I want to. The way they deserve to be saved.

As if she feels my gaze on hers, she glances at me, her mouth curling up into a sweet smile.

"What?" she mouths, and I shake my head, shrugging my shoulders.

My eyes stay stationed on her, a comforting energy forming between us until a gut-wrenching scream reaches my ears over my headphones. Aubrey's eyes widen in terror, telling me she heard it too, and we both pull off our headphones.

"What was that?" There is panic etched in her voice.

"I don't know." My head wobbles, turning toward the window. "Maybe it was outside?"

"Yeah. Maybe."

It's a stupid question, because we both know it's not from outside. For most kids, the outside is the scary part. The part where bad things can happen. But for us, it's always been the other way around. We're safe when we walk out the door, but doomed under this roof.

We both exhale loudly, settling for that answer, when another raucous scream echoes through the entire house, followed by hysterical howls. We both jump up, Aubrey running through the door before me as I follow her tracks as fast as I can. The parlor is empty, the door to the basement open, staring at us like the black hole leading to Hell itself. Aubrey holds still in front of the door, her chest heaving as she stares into the dimmed light downstairs. The sound of glass breaking is followed by her mother's vicious voice.

"You did this!" she cries, desperately, her words acting as a start to get my feet moving, darting past Aubrey down the stairs.

"Reign, wait!" Aubrey bellows behind me.

I snap my body toward her, giving her an incredulous look.

"What?"

"What if–? What if–?" Her eyes grow vacant, and for a second, it feels like she's about to lose consciousness. I take a few steps back up, shaking her body in my hands.

"Snap out of it! Nova is down there!" The name of her sister seems to pull her from her trance, because she pushes me aside, almost tossing me to the floor, and descends down at a fast pace while I follow behind her.

When we reach the bottom of the stairs, the smell of blood attacks my nose, almost knocking me out while my eyes frantically look for Nova. First, they land on a guy who's bleeding out while Mrs. Brady presses a piece of glass farther in his throat, even though he's clearly dead as a doornail. Her face is malicious, a frantic look in her eyes as she clenches her jaw. It's the first time I can see the resemblance between her and Aubrey.

Jefferson sits next to them on his knees, staring into the room with a blank expression on his face, and I follow his gaze until my heart stops.

Aubrey's piercing cry raises all the hairs on my skin before she runs past me, throwing her body on the floor next to an unconscious Nova. She starts to pull and push her little sister, ferociously looking for a pulse. My eyes widen, horrified, while the world around me seems to spin. Everything around me darkens, except Nova's face, now looking peaceful, as if she's sound asleep. She looks smaller than normal, as if her innocence has returned in her slumber, but deep down, I know she's not asleep. I know she didn't pass out. Her cheeks are rosy, but the cold feeling showering my body tells me they will be pale soon.

Slowly, I shuffle my feet toward her small body, dropping to my knees next to her while my eyes roam over her. Her underwear still sits around her ankles, and I swallow hard, finding any courage left inside of me, before I carefully move it up to cover her private parts. Her skin is still warm as I graze it with the tips of my fingers, pulling down her t-shirt to cover the rest of her body. Tears are falling down my cheeks with every move, a lump forming in the back of my throat while Aubrey sobs against her sister's chest. My hand lands on Nova's face, my thumb stroking the freckles on her soft cheek as I grind my teeth. Then realization hits me like a fucking hurricane.

She's gone.

17

Sienna

I storm through the door with a thundercloud above my head and my mother gives me a puzzled look from the couch.

"What happened to you?"

I can only glare, taking off my coat without giving her an answer. Shoving off my boots with aggravated, impatient motions, I drop down on the couch next to her. She has a glass of white wine in her hand that she silently hands over with pursed lips.

I grab the stem from her hand before downing the entire glass in one go.

If only he could just take this slow. When he asked me to dinner, I was hesitant, but the teenager in me was also excited. The last week has made me realize I've missed him like crazy. More than once I've been lying in my bed, debating whether I should give him a chance or not. When I finally gave in today, I felt giddy inside, eager to spend time with him.

But he had to go and ruin it all by calling me *baby*. It's not that I don't love the roll of his tongue. I do. But it also reminds me of that girl that cried her eyes out for two weeks. The one who vowed to herself to never fall for Reign Wolfe's lies ever again. Or any other man's, for that matter.

"Rough night?" I twist my head to my mother, automatically narrowing my eyes at the smile haunting her face.

I push out all the air in my lungs, not even sure what to tell her because something is nagging at me for leaving. It started off as a good night. Sitting next to Reign in that booth felt comfortable, relaxing even. It felt like home, and all I kept wanting was to scooch closer and feel his body against mine. I can't help the feeling that it's my own fault I'm sitting next to my mother instead of Prince Charming right now.

"Things didn't go well with Reign?"

"How did you know I was with Reign?"

She gives me a mocking glare.

"Come on, Sienna. There is only one person who can get you this worked up. It's not hard to figure out." The tone of her voice is calm, but I can hear the slight irritation etching through. "What did he do now?"

I bring my gaze to the floor, crossing my arms in front of my body like a toddler.

"Called me baby."

My mother stays quiet while I can still feel her eyes boring through me like lasers. My mother is never the one to keep her mouth shut, so I'm bracing myself for the preaching I know is coming my way in a few seconds.

"Please tell me he did more than that."

I close my eyes in response and hear her huff next to me.

"What the hell is wrong with him calling you baby, Sienna?"

"Nothing!" I cry out before my voice lowers. "Everything."

How can a simple word, a simple nickname, hold so much emotion? I feel like the word represents the confusion in my heart. Part of it is dancing every time he calls me that, desperate to hear it again while he makes love to me, while the other part is running for the hills, hiding for the heartbreak that comes with it. It's scaring me more than I want.

"It just reminds me of how he broke my heart," I explain with a sigh.

"Did you ask him why he broke your heart?"

"No." I never can find the nerve to hear what he has to say, fearing he might tell me something that will break whatever is left of the damaged heart inside my chest. Besides, when I asked him at the time, he wouldn't tell me.

A warm hand lands on my thigh, and I turn my head to my mother. She's looking at me with the same brown eyes as mine, giving me a consoling look only a mother can.

"Have you ever considered he broke his own heart as well?"

My eyes roam over her face, taking in her words, but she doesn't wait for a reply.

"Maybe it wasn't about you. Maybe it was about him."

There is a little judgment in her tone, even though it's also filled with comfort. I feel a quiver in my stomach as I move my hair from my neck. My mind goes over the time before he left New York, remembering the troubled look that traveled his handsome face every now and then. I ignored it, respecting his decision to not wanna talk about what happened those four years in Providence, but I knew it was there. I always felt in my gut how it was eating him from the inside as the months passed. How he grew angrier with everyone around him, even though I was never the subject of his rage.

I rub the itching skin on my hands.

"There was someone else, Mom."

"You don't know that. You never asked if she was there before or after he broke up with you. Isn't that the root of the problem anyway? The fact that the two of you never really talked it out?"

Why do mothers always know exactly what to say to make you feel guilty as fuck and question everything you know?

"I don't know if I'm ready to hear it," I confess as my eyes well up. In a way, I've always felt relieved he didn't want to talk to me about what happened to him. I want to know, but I'm scared to find out what happened to him. It won't be a happy story.

"It doesn't matter if you're ready." She shrugs. "If you care about him, you let him explain what he went through and then maybe, just maybe, the two of you can start over. If not, at least you know and you can move on."

She says it with ease and part of me knows she's right. Guilt pulls on my shoulders when I wonder what my part in this is. If I could've done more, if I made him feel alone, unintentionally driving him away with no one to confide in.

Maybe my mother is right. Maybe this was never about me. Maybe this was always about Reign.

18

15 YEARS OLD

M y head rests on the pillow as I stare at the ceiling, my thoughts going all over the place. Aubrey's head lays against my chest while my arm is draped around her shoulder. My thumb strokes up and down her back. This is what we have done every day after school since Nova died. We don't cry. We don't talk. We just lie here. I have no clue what goes through Aubrey's head, but I just hope time flies by faster if I just lie here with her.

Jefferson fed the cops some bullshit story about a burglar killing Nova. Since they bought it, they ruled her mom killed the "burglar" in self-defense. I wanted to tell the cops everything, but Aubrey reminded me we would be put in a different foster home if I did. I didn't care, because it couldn't be worse than this. But the fearful look in her eyes made me go along with whatever they wanted. For *her*. I was all she had left.

The last few weeks, my head has been spinning, wondering how we can get out of this hell faster. I thought about calling Franklin. Telling him everything. But I know if Franklin ever finds out, he will go crazy. He will beat the shit out of Jefferson with the chance he won't wake up after that. I can't do that. Not after everything he's been working for.

Part of me wants to just put a bullet through Jefferson's head and call it self-defense. But I don't think I can. I don't think I can kill someone in cold blood.

"I will get us out of here," I whisper against her hair.

She glances up, catching my eye. "I know."

The look in her eyes is sad, but for the first time, it holds a sparkle of hope. Normally, she just snorts and rolls her eyes, not believing a word I'm saying. But this time, it's different. This time, she believes me. I can see it.

Before I can say anything else, Jefferson's grating voice reverberates through the house.

"Reign! Get your ass out here. Your brother is here!"

Surprised, my eyes widen, and I press a kiss on her hair.

"I'll be right back."

She rolls off of me, and I stroll toward the living room to find my brother waiting for me with a beaming smile that splits his face. There is a lightness in his eyes that I haven't seen in a long time, and a pang goes through my chest.

"I didn't know you were coming!" I cheer.

"Neither did I." He pulls me into a tight hug, a sigh of relief fanning my neck.

"Pack your bags," he whispers.

"What?"

"Pack your bags, Reign."

I look him in the eye, not having to strain my neck anymore since now I'm the same height. The confusion is set on my face, but he just keeps looking at me like he just won the lottery.

"What do you mean?"

"I won."

"Wait? What?" My mind is running a hundred miles an hour wondering what he's talking about. Did he really win the lottery? What else could he have won? Suddenly, a light bulb pops on in my brain and my head starts to shake frantically, unable to utter a word.

No.

No, that can't be it.

"I won," Franklin repeats, holding my gaze to show the importance of his words. "*We* won."

I gasp. My chest heaves as I try to wrap my head around what he's telling me.

"No-suh," I croak out. Tears are stinging in the corners of my eyes as a shiver moves up my spine.

Franklin tilts his head, gripping my shoulders. "Ya-huh."

Finally realizing what he's saying, I swing my arms around his shoulders, my sobs now getting free rein. We stay like that for a while, my big brother holding me on my feet until Jefferson's bitching pulls me out of it.

"Can you just take the damn freeloader and get the fuck out of here?"

With a glare, I snap my head toward my foster parent from hell, desperate to give him the black eye that's long overdue. I charge forward, but Franklin grabs my arm, holding me back.

"Don't," he says, his penetrating gaze trained on Jefferson with a look that matches the devil himself. "His time will come." He brings his gaze back to me, nudging his chin. "Go. Get your things. I'll wait here."

I suck in a lungful of air, knowing he's right. Without giving the asshole a second glance, I give my brother a smile that finally matches my eyes before I get to my room to collect my stuff.

My hands are shaking when I grab my backpack, and I steadily start to put in the things I want to keep. To be honest, there is not much here other than some ragged clothes and my schoolbooks.

"So, you're leaving?" I twist on the spot, my eyes locking with Aubrey's. She's standing in my doorway, her arms hugging her slender body while she stares at me with anger flashing in her gaze.

"My brother got custody. *Finally*," I explain.

"Good for you. I guess he finally bribed enough people to get you out, huh?" The corner of her mouth curls, but her eyes are shooting daggers.

"Why would you even say that?" It stings to hear her talk about my brother like that, but it doesn't surprise me. She never liked him. She always looked at him in contempt, yet she always refused to tell me why. "Aren't you happy for me?"

The features on her face relax a little, and she forces a coy smile.

"I am. I really am." She pauses. "I'm just gonna miss you."

My heart falls realizing what this means, and I grab her neck, tugging her against my chest.

"I will come back for you," I whisper against her hair. "I promise. This is not how your life is going to end." I hold her tight, the sadness overwhelming me.

I don't want to leave her behind. With Nova gone, she only had me to lean on. The other girls in the house come and go every month, and she's never allowed herself to become close with them. Nova and I were her constant. We were each other's constant. Now, with me gone, she has no one left.

"I'll be fine, Reign." Her words are muffled as they vibrate against my chest. I lower my knees, holding her face in my hands to look her in the eye.

"I mean it. I'm coming back for you. Don't give up, okay?"

A tear rolls down my cheek while she offers me a tight smile. She nods her head, but the look in her eyes grows more vacant by the second. Cold. As if she's slowly dying inside, her beating heart the only thing that keeps her going.

I take her back in a tight hug and we stand there for a few minutes, knowing this is goodbye. At least for a little while. When Franklin calls out my name, I press a long kiss on her forehead.

"Don't give up, Aubrey."

I let her go, and my heart feels heavy, conflicted.

She doesn't follow me back into the parlor and the guilt grows with every step I take.

"You ready?" Franklin beams.

"Yes." I conjure a smile, then twist my attention to Jefferson, who's glaring at me. I've grown over the years, and even though I'm not as huge as he is, I still manage to cower above him. "Scum like you shouldn't be allowed to have kids. Let alone foster them. Treat her right," I tell him, referring to Aubrey, "because one day, I'll be back to save her from the hell she was born into."

A devious chuckle comes from his disgusting mouth.

"She can't be saved, boy. You failed to see that from the first day you arrived."

I feel Franklin's hand landing on my shoulder.

"Come on. We're going," he orders, pulling me back with his eyes locked with Jefferson's. His entire stance seems to grow bigger. "If I ever see you near my brother again, I will kill you."

The hairs on the back of my neck stand up by the ominous sound of his voice.

"Whatever," Jefferson sputters. "Just take the son of a bitch out of here."

Gladly, I turn around and walk out the front door with a relieved feeling. I went to school every day walking out of that door, but this is the first time I can feel the sun warming my face, bringing me comfort after years of cloudy days. As if all my senses are turned on now that I know I'm walking out of this shithole forever and not just for the day.

We make our way to the car waiting for us, and when Franklin slams the door behind him, I look back one more time. The paint is still chipped. The house still looks haunted. It's as if I'm going back in time. Going back to that first day. Nothing has changed. But *I* have changed. This house changed me, and I'm not sure yet in what way.

Franklin walks toward me before mimicking my stance, looking up and down the house.

"You're never going back, Reign." There is a promise in his words. One that pushes the air from my lungs. "It's over."

I give him a grateful smile, before we both turn around and make the final steps to the car. I throw my bag on the back seat, then open the door to get in the car while Franklin gets behind the wheel.

He starts the car, the engine vibrating underneath me while I keep my eyes peered at the front door. Feeling like lightning hits me, the door flies open, and Aubrey stands there with a big scowl sitting on her face.

My heart jerks when I see the disappointment in her eyes as they narrow, her lips pursed. She is mad. Dread fills me while our eyes stay tangled. The car starts to move forward, and I stare at her as if breaking our connection means giving up on her until I can't see her anymore.

When she's disappeared out of sight, I press my fingers into my eyes to hold back the tears pricking to the surface.

"Are you okay, man?" Franklin's hand drops on my leg with a comforting squeeze.

"Ya-huh," I push out. "It's just—it was hell, man." The confession makes his gaze troubled, dripping with worry.

"Tell me about it?"

I shake my head.

"It's over now. I'm just happy I'm going home. To you. To Con and Kill. I missed Boston."

"Yeah? What is the first thing you wanna do?"

I think about it for a moment because really there is a lot I wanna do. But there is one thing that sticks out.

"Can we go to a Bruins game? All four of us?"

Franklin shows me his teeth. "I'll make it happen."

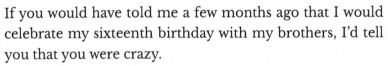

If you would have told me a few months ago that I would celebrate my sixteenth birthday with my brothers, I'd tell you that you were crazy.

But here I am.

My eyes focus on all three of them, singing happy birthday from the top of their lungs, along with a dozen other people, while Franklin holds up a big chocolate cake. On top sits a bear topper that's supposed to be me wearing a Bruins jersey and holding up a laptop. It looks ridiculous, but I still love it.

Living with the Brady bunch, I never celebrated my birthday. I didn't even tell anyone when it was. Not even Aubrey. Living in hell doesn't make you want to celebrate life. But seeing my brothers beaming at me reminds me I'm still alive.

"Dear Reign—" they drawl out my name, before singing the last line. "Happy birthday to youuuuuuuu!"

"Make a wish!" Killian calls out and I take a step forward, blowing out the candles before Franklin tries to smack it against my face.

"Ay!" Before he can reach me, I dodge the cake, pushing it away from me, straight into Killian's face. My jaw drops to the floor, the whole room now silent as fuck, while Killian blinks at me with chocolate cake in his lashes.

"You tool," Killian huffs, a little stunned.

I press my lips together to hold back my smile, but when Connor starts to snort, unable to hold back his laugh, I feel my belly shake as laughter ripples from my throat.

Franklin joins with a guffaw coming from his chest and the entire room falls into laughter while I grip my stomach to control the amusement. My body shakes and I almost drop to the floor, wheezing, while I look at my still glaring brother.

A smile cracks through his chocolate-covered face before he charges at me with a mischievous grin.

"You think this is funny?" he challenges, grabbing a piece of the cake with his bare hands. Like a punch of electricity hits me, I dart out of the way, running around the kitchen table, pushing everyone aside while I continue laughing to the point of crying. My years' long tension seems to release while my brother chases me and tears of pure joy run down my cheeks. He surprises me when he jumps on the table, lunging for me. Not responding quick enough, he grabs my arms, and I let out a playful shriek.

"No! No! Kill! It's my birthday!" I laugh.

He rubs his hand over his face to gather even more frosting before he wipes it all over mine and I cry out.

"I know." He smiles. "Happy birthday, *tool.*"

"Thanks, asshole." I let out a chuckle, grabbing the towel from Franklin's extended hand while Killian does the same.

I look around the room, feeling lighter than ever. Half of these people I don't remember, and most of them are people who do business with Franklin, but everyone makes me feel like this is a special day and it feels good. Like living in hell wasn't all for nothing.

"Well, if anyone wants some cake, Killian is your man to be," Connor bellows through the room as he tosses the ruined cake into the sink. "Ladies, if anyone would like to kiss the chocolate off my brother's face? Now is the time to do it."

"That is a wicked good idea!" Killian's teeth are showing through the chocolate, making him look like a madman.

I throw my head back, not even trying to hide the amusement coming from their comments as the party goes back to normal. The room is filled with murmurs while music is played in the background, and I just keep wiping the cake residue off my cheeks.

"Hey, Reign." I turn my head to the sweet voice, my towel still rubbing my cheek. A grin splits my face when I look into a set of big brown eyes. She has her head tilted, showing her shyness, while my best friend is making encouraging faces at me from behind her.

"Hey, Sienna."

"I hope you don't mind. Emma asked me to come," she says as my eyes roam over her pretty features. Her black hair frames her face perfectly, bringing out the few freckles on her nose. Being one of Emma's friends, I've known her since we were all little, but now that she's grown over the years, she's even prettier than I remembered.

"Of course not. I'm glad you're here."

We both stand there in silence, not sure what to say. She bites her lips, shuffling in nervousness and my mind can't think of anything to say until Emma takes a step forward, saving us both from the awkwardness.

"Sienna needs a tutor. She thought that maybe you could help her with her computer science class." I cock my eyebrow at my blonde friend, giving me a smug grin that has my eyes narrowing in suspicion.

"No-suh?" A lopsided grin forms on my face, totally seeing where this is going.

"Ya-huh." Sienna's eyes snap back up. "I'm wickedly failing. Got a D. My mother was not happy."

"A D is not good," I muse.

"Do you think you can help me?" Her lashes flutter.

A warm fuzzy feeling forms in my chest, and I tilt my head toward her.

"Sure."

She hugs her body, looking at me with hooded eyes. "Maybe you can show me some stuff? Like right now?"

"Right now?" I parrot, surprised. Emma is silently dancing behind Sienna's back, clearly claiming her victory already. She's nuts, but she's my oldest friend and I love her.

She nods, and a chuckle leaves my lips.

I like Sienna, I really do. But after what I've seen for the last couple of years, I don't want to make her uncomfortable, even if she's the one who's initiating this.

I move a step closer, cupping her cheek before I put my mouth close to her ear. My lips part, a tingling feeling sparked while touching her skin.

"You're gorgeous, and if you want to come up with me to hang out, the answer is *yes*. I'd love to. But"—I pull back, looking into her eyes—"if you want to do anything more than that, I'm going to say *no*. Not because I don't want to, but because I want to get to know you first." I watch how she swallows and wait for her response. Her eyes stay locked with mine, and I'm scared to move, not wanting to give her the feeling I'm rejecting her.

"Is that okay?" I ask.

Her lips are pressed together, and she smiles, followed by a small nod. I sigh in relief, letting my head hang for a second, then bring my gaze back up.

"Let me just freshen up for a minute and then I'll come get you, yeah?"

I let go of her face, shooting her a wink, then stroll out of the room and up the stairs while my smile stays in place. Bringing myself to the bathroom, I wash my face, then put on a clean shirt, thinking about the pretty girl downstairs.

Over the last couple of weeks, my life has changed so much. I'm a sophomore in a high school where people talk like me instead of making fun of my accent. My stomach never roars in hunger. I see my brothers every day. I got my old friends back. The whole of Southie seems to be happy I'm home, waving at me when I walk the streets. I'm happy for most of the time. Relaxed. But there is always that feeling that one chip is missing. That feeling that sucks me back into my dreadful memories, hollowing me out from the inside.

Aubrey's face flashes before my eyes, and I frantically start sucking in short breaths, feeling like I'm suffocating.

Quickly, I dart out of the bathroom to open the door to my balcony, then step right outside before filling my lungs with the brisk air of the night. I close my eyes to prevent my head from spinning, dropping my body onto one of the two chairs in front of the window. My focus goes solely to my breathing, trying to control the panic that surges through my veins, until finally I seem to calm down.

Frustrated, I rub a hand over my clean face, then through my hair, letting out a grunt.

Franklin has been looking for a way to get Aubrey out, but since she's their biological daughter, there isn't much we can do other than report it to Child Protective Services. I don't want to do that, because it would mean she'd go into the system like all those other girls her father pimps out, and who knows where she'll end up then? She doesn't want that. I know the chance of her getting a nice family who will take care of her until she's eighteen is greater than her ending up in a worse family than her own, but I can't risk that. She'll never forgive me if it doesn't play out in her favor.

Franklin says I need to let it go. To let her go. *"She'll be eighteen soon and if she wants, she can leave. But we're not even sure she wants to leave,"* he told me.

I didn't tell him about the brothel. Or Nova. He doesn't know all the ugly parts, so I guess he's right. But she still haunts me at night. She still runs around in my head more than I want.

I startle when a knock sounds on the window and I twist my neck to the sound, almost spraining a muscle.

"You alright?" Connor gives me a wary look.

I exhale loudly, nodding. "Yeah."

He steps outside, then leans his back against the railing while he crosses his arms in front of his body.

"You sure? You've been up here for half an hour."

My brows furrow in confusion. "I have? *Shit.*"

"What's going on, Reign?"

"Nothing," I huff, trying to plaster a smile on my face.

"Bullshit. I can see it on that pale face of yours. So, unless you ate too much cake, which is impossible, I call bullshit."

I bury my face in my hands, hunched forward as I rest my upper body on my knees. After a few moments, Connor's palm lands on my back before he drops down to his heels.

"Hey, you know you can talk to me, right?" I can hear the uncertainty in his voice, not knowing what to do about my current state.

Connor is rough. He has a no-nonsense mentality, and he would rather punch away his problems than talk about it. But to me, he's always been different. He always takes his time to show me he cares, ever since I was little. He doesn't say much, but he's there when it matters.

I lift my head, looking into his green eyes. They're vibrant, lit up by the moonlight. A familiar set of eyes like the rest of my brothers, bringing me more comfort than they'll ever realize.

"I know." I pause, offering him a tight smile. "I just don't want to talk about it, you know? It's too much."

"I get that. Do you need anything?"

"No." I shake my head. "I just need a few minutes and I'll be fine."

"Okay, I'll see you downstairs."

I hum in agreement as he walks back into the room before popping his blonde head out one more time.

"Just don't take too long. There is a girl waiting for you downstairs."

A chuckle reverberates from my lips, suddenly remembering Sienna.

"I'll be right there."

19

Sienna

I feel the pebbles of the circular driveway underneath the tires of my car before I park it in front of the mansion. For some reason, it looks bigger than I remember, more impressive.

When I get out, I tug the skirt of my skintight dress, then aim my steps to the front door while holding a bottle of red wine in my hand. The moment I can ring the doorbell, the door flies open, showing me the same brooding man I left in that bistro two nights ago. I expected him to call me, to text me, to find a way to talk to me. But there has been nothing but radio silence. At first it annoyed me, but now I'm happy with it, because it makes it that much easier for me to keep my distance. It gave me some time to reflect on our past and even though I still have a hard time with this, with letting go of the hurt, I want to see if we can at least be civil. If we can be friends. Maybe even have fun together.

"Sienna." His jaw ticks, as if he's still angry, even though his eyes hold a spark of happiness. "I didn't know you were coming."

I give him a confused look, pointing at the doorbell.

"We have cameras. I saw you drive up here."

"I see. Your brother invited me." I hold the bottle up. "I brought wine."

"Aah, Sienna. Glad you could make it." Franklin prances into the hallway, ignoring his little brother to give me a kiss on the cheek in greeting. When he pulls back, he shoots me a wink, silently telling me he's trying to piss off his little brother. "You brought wine?"

"It's from my family in Italy."

"You didn't have to do that." He takes the bottle from my hand, then softly pulls my elbow to guide me into the house. I hear Reign growling when we walk past him, followed by the door slamming shut, and a smile tries to creep on to my face.

"What did the door do to you?" Connor walks down the stairs with a little boy sitting on his hip and Franklin stops us, letting go of my elbow.

My eyes catch Reign rolling his eyes, shooting both his brothers a vicious glare.

His beauty is both striking and terrifying, making my fingers twist and my panties grow damp.

"Hey, Sienna." Connor fixes his gaze on me.

"Hey, Con. Who's this?" I give the little boy a beaming smile, even though I heard about the rumors of a little Wolfe around town.

"This is Colin. My son."

Colin crawls against his father's shoulder in shyness, a sweet smile appearing on his half-hidden face. He's blonde like Connor, and so damn cute, but it's his eyes that have me hypnotized. They are forest green with gold specks dancing around his irises, and even though he's only a few years old, they are just as compelling as any other Wolfe's I know.

"He's adorable." I smile, rubbing my finger over his bubbly cheek.

When Reign approaches us, Colin's body jerks up, a full grin now stretching his cheeks.

"Uncle Reign!" Immediately, he makes long arms, demanding his uncle to grab him and Reign does so with a loving gaze.

"Hey, little man! You wanna go and see if your mommy got some cookies we can snatch?" The way he looks at his nephew has my ovaries singing in unison.

I'm in trouble.

Reign with a baby flashes in my eyes, creating a dreamy fog in my head that I shouldn't feel as he walks toward the kitchen with Franklin following their trail.

"What's doing, Sienna?" I hear Connor's voice, but it takes a moment to register it completely, and when I rear my head back, he's looking at me with an amused grin.

"Good," I push out on a breath, the corner of my mouth curling as I try to settle the tingling feeling inside of me. "You have a handsome little boy. He'll be a real charmer when he's older."

"Yeah, the kid's got moxie. He's crazy about Reign."

"I can see that."

"Reign is crazy about him too. He's wicked good with kids."

I just nod, staring at the kitchen door until I feel Connor's suggestive eyes on me and I meet his gaze.

Connor has always been huge, bulky. The one Wolfe you don't want to go up against in a bar brawl. He has a scarred lip that makes him look even more vicious, but like with all these Wolfe boys, he's never scared me. If anything, I always felt like they would protect me if they were nearby.

"Reign told me you walked out on him at dinner," he says with an amused look.

I roll my eyes, though playfully.

"He keeps thinking we can pick up where we left off. We can't. *I* can't."

"I understand. I just don't think he's going to let you walk this time."

"That's not his choice to make."

"Hey, I'm just enjoying the show. Come on." His hand falls to the small of my back. "Let's see if dinner is ready."

"Do you cook like this every day?" I look at Lily with my palms spread out on my stomach, feeling like I ate an entire cow. Dinner was amazing. Connor's girl got some serious skills. At first, I was nervous, because I knew Connor and Franklin's girlfriends would be there too. I had no clue if they knew about my history with the Wolfes, and it felt awkward walking into a home that was theirs, but part of my past.

But in reality, they are both really sweet. Lily welcomed me with a freshly baked cookie and a glittering smile that matched her baby boy's, and Kendall literally welcomed me with open arms. We've been talking about how they met during dinner, and I listened to their stories with enthusiasm, while the oldest brothers tried to keep up an indifferent stance. But the light in their eyes when they look at their women says it all. They love them fiercely. It's a look I once recognized in Reign, one I no longer search for every time he glances at me. Scared it might actually be there.

"Oh, no. If I did that, we'd all be too fat to walk down the stairs." Lily chuckles. She runs a hand through her long blonde hair before getting up.

"Boys, can you clear the table? I'm going to check on Colin for a minute."

Instantly, Connor and Killian get up, piling the plates.

"Hold up, hold up." I bring my hand up in the air. "You big lugs are cleaning the table without as much as an argument?" I taunt, wanting to see what I can get out of them.

"I really want her to suck my dick later, so I'm picking my battles." Connor shrugs like the unfazed dickhead that he is, and I let out a big burst of laughter while Lily swats his arm.

"Connor!" She scowls.

"Fuck, bro. Too much information," Reign whines, looking up at the ceiling.

"What is your excuse?" I nudge my chin toward Killian.

"There is still cream pie in the kitchen." He shrugs.

Franklin lets out a chuckle. "I'm going to make a call. We're going back to the office in ten minutes, Kill. I need you to go over some papers." He gets up, tucking Kendall behind him. "You coming, pretty girl?"

"You just said you're going to the office in ten minutes. What do you need me for?" she questions, even though she stands from her chair.

"There is a lot we can do in ten minutes, baby." He keeps a straight face, though I see a playful spark in his eyes that makes me raise my brows. I have known Franklin for a long time, but never have I seen him this mischievous. It's weird and heartwarming at the same time.

Kendall shoots me a sweet look, her cheeks turning a pink shade.

"Thanks for coming, Sienna." Franklin finds my eyes, and I give him a small smile.

"Thank you for the invite. I had fun." With a slight nod, he drags his girlfriend out of the dining room while Connor and Killian leave with a pile of plates in both hands.

Suddenly, I realize I'm alone with Reign, and I awkwardly give him a side-eyed glance.

The air thickens with tension, a toxic combination of familiarity and anxiety, followed by a whisper of longing. Longing to be able to talk to him like we used to. To kiss him.

No, Sienna. Don't kiss him. Don't even think that.

"You wanna go outside for a minute?" Reign's voice has a sultry edge, and when I turn my head, he's staring at me with a pleading look in his eyes.

He's confusing me, and I hate it.

My common sense tells me I should keep my distance and make sure he stays at an arm's length, but my heart keeps melting whenever he says the right things or gives me one of those smoldering looks.

"Sure."

He takes my hand, and we both get up before he escorts me to the patio. His hand keeps mine hostage, and though it still feels somewhat awkward, it also feels completely normal. As if our bodies being linked makes sense.

"I'm glad you came to dinner." He rests his hip on the white stone balustrade, never letting go of my hand. His thumb brushes the skin on my palm as he thoughtfully makes scorching circles. It makes it hard for me to breathe and keep my head on straight.

"Me too. Lily and Kendall seem lovely. Franklin's really changed."

He looks at the house. "They are. And he is. She really changed him. Made him less moody all the time. Since Kendall is around, Franklin and I aren't butting heads as much. She softened him a little."

"I noticed that." The silence forms between us, and I look at him while his attention stays focused on our linked hands.

"I like having you around, baby." His eyes move back up, giving me that pleading look again, pushing the air out of my lungs. Even though I feel the flame of his touch burning me up, I shake my head. Then I pull my hand away, trying to create some distance between us, and his face falls.

"Don't call me baby." I can barely get myself to reject it this time. A blind person could see that I'm lying if I were to say I don't want anything to do with Reign Wolfe, but Reign is asking me to run a marathon with two broken legs. I want to see if we can still be friends. If there is any way I can forgive him for breaking my heart like I was one of his old toys. But he won't give me any time to adjust. One minute, I think we're slowly building a foundation again, and the other, I feel like he's ready to put a bow on it and tell the world we're back together by calling me baby.

To anyone else, it might seem I'm overreacting, but to me, that nickname means something. It's what he's called me since the first day I was his, and it's the one word that speaks to my heart. The one that told me I was special. The one I don't allow any other man to call me.

Now it just reminds me of the hurt he caused me and makes me realize that as *right* as this might feel that I need to be cautious. I came here with an open mind, but he needs to do this in baby steps for me.

A mix of irritation and confusion travels across his face, and I can see his jaw tic when his gorgeous green eyes darken. He takes my breath away when he changes to this full-grown man, pushing his boyish grin aside. It makes me wonder if I should forgive the boy, leave him in the past with my broken heart, and give the man a chance to mend what is still left of it.

"I will call you baby whenever the fuck I want to call you baby. Just because you don't want to hear it, doesn't mean I won't use it. You are my baby, whether you like it or not. You can fight it, but it doesn't change a damn thing, Sienna." His tone is harsh and turning me the fuck on while also feeding my anger. "Go ahead, scowl at me all you want. But it won't change a thing. You are *my girl*. You are mine until the day I take my last breath. Even if I'm not yours."

I shake my head again, tears pricking my eyes. "Don't say things like that."

"Stop telling me what to do," he snarls.

I sigh. Deep down, I've always known we were bound to have this conversation someday. I thought I was ready, but every single fiber in my body is scared to push through. Scared of what he will tell me and how I might not be able to overcome it.

"I don't want to keep fighting you, Sienna." He sounds tired, but I refuse to look at him, knowing I will break. "Just let me explain. It's not what you think."

"I don't wanna hear it, Reign. You hurt me too much."

He jumps up, aggravated, running a hand through his brown hair.

"You've always done this. You don't even wanna hear me out," he yells.

"Pot. Kettle, boy." Like he is any better.

"Oh, here we go."

I finally bring my gaze up to him, my eyes now fire-blazing.

"Have you ever asked Franklin what happened with Declan?" He gives me a pained expression, his shoulders slugging. "I don't think so. Don't accuse me of jumping to conclusions if you do the exact same thing, Reign."

"That's different."

"No-suh," I scoff, "it's exactly the same. You're just being wicked stubborn. Like you have since the moment you found out Franklin wasn't innocent." He's not the only one who is hurt and scornful about what happened over the years. What happened to Declan formed all of us. It might not be me who went into foster care, but I still remember how life changed when the Wolfes got split up and my best friend became more depressed and closed off from the world every day. But I know Franklin didn't kill Declan for fun.

Franklin is ruthless, but he's not a killer for the hell of it.

The motherfucker deserved it.

"What do you know?" His eyes grow to slits.

"Nothing you want to hear."

His nostrils flare as he pulls his shoulders back, clearly tempted to ask me what the hell I'm talking about. I want to tell him everything. To scream at him what a fucking fool he's been for years, but I know it's not my story to tell and his brother made me swear I'd keep my mouth shut. Franklin wants Reign to ask himself. To force Reign's *"stubborn mind to communicate"* were his exact words. It's their egos keeping them from fixing their issues, if you ask me.

"Look, I don't want to fight you anymore either," I tell him with a soft and pleading voice, "but I'm not ready, okay? Not yet. I'm not ready to hear what happened in New York. But I'm trying to get there." I close my eyes to not break down when I look at his worried face. It's laced with understanding, even though I can see the sadness in his gaze. He carefully closes the distance between us, resting his hands on my hips. I let him.

"Just give me some time," I say, peering up at him. A strand of his brown hair dances in front of his forehead, making him look cuter than I want him to. "Don't push me and I promise you, I will let you explain. That's all I can give you right now." I bring my attention to his chest, unable to handle his eyes boring into me, like he has the ability to look right into my soul.

His fingers move up, gently lifting my chin to force me to look at him.

"Fine."

His eyes roam over my face, searching for anything else with a deep frown on his face, and I just hold still in anticipation.

"Yo!" Killian pops his head through the door, looking amused, yet he doesn't mock our intimate position. Reign's fingers drop to the front of my neck, cupping it as if he doesn't want to break our connection while we both look at Killian.

"I'm heading back to the city with Franky. You wanna watch the fight at my place after?"

"Yeah, sure." He turns his head back to me. "You wanna come?"

I think he notices the discomfort running through my body because he quickly adds, "As friends. Not me pushing."

We used to watch every Bruins game together. Reign, Killian, Emma, and me. We'd bring the snacks, and the boys would get the drinks, which basically means they would ask Franklin to buy us some beers, then all four of us would curl up on the couch as we watched the game. They hold some great memories. I miss those days. I slowly turn my head toward Killian, silently asking him for his opinion.

His eyebrows move up in encouragement, and I let out a deep sigh.

I just promised Reign I'd give him a chance. That I would do my best to make sure we can rebuild some of the friendship we once had. I guess right now is the best time to start.

"Okay." I nod, and a wide grin stretches Reign's lips.

"Wicked."

20

16 YEARS OLD

REIGN

When I arrive at the park, it doesn't take me long to spot Emma sitting on one of the benches around the skate park. I wave at her, but she doesn't notice me and I just keep sauntering toward her. The closer I get, the more I become aware of the deserted look in her eyes as she keeps her gaze trained on nothing. She seems in a trance, her cheeks pale like the blood is drained from her face. The blank expression makes me uneasy, and I slide next to her on the bench with force in an attempt to cheer her up.

"Hello," I sing. "Is it me you're looking for?"

My eyes widen in surprise when she startles with a horrified look, almost dropping off the bench. I quickly grab her arm to keep her from falling, and I can see the fear in her eyes until she notices it's me.

"Are you okay?" I ask with worry.

"You scared me. I'm fine." She puts on a smile to comfort me, but the heaving of her chest tells me I wasn't the only thing that scared her.

"Are you sure?" I frown.

"Yeah. I was just lost in thought."

I don't believe her, but her fake smile tells me she doesn't want to talk about it. When I was younger, I'd push her to tell me, nagging her until she would finally let it out, but nowadays I have a few secrets myself, so I decide to not dig any further.

Instead, I pull out the small box out in the pocket of my jeans. "Look."

Her gaze drops to my hands and her eyes light up in excitement.

"You bought it?"

"Ya-huh!"

"Show me, show me!" She waves grabby hands at me, her sad mood completely gone, and I put the green box in her hand. She lets out a cooing moan when she opens the box, revealing the wolf-shaped pendant.

"Do you think she'll like it?" It's rose gold, delicate and petite, because I want to give her something graceful like her.

"Are you kidding me? She will love it." Emma looks up at me. "I'm really happy for you two, Reign."

"I would assume so. You're the fucking matchmaker of it all."

"Oh, please. As if you haven't had a crush on her since middle school. You big softie."

"Emma," I hiss jokingly, "not so loud. You'll ruin my street cred."

"Your street cred?" She laughs. "You sound like Killian now."

"Well, yeah, we're Wolfes, you know? We've got a reputation to uphold."

"Sorry, *Prince Charming*, but Killian is more intimidating than you."

"What?" I screech, indignant. "How come?"

"You literally just showed me a necklace you bought for your girlfriend." She holds up the jewelry box with a dull look. "Killian's form of affection comes in orgasms."

I frown, narrowing my eyes, mockingly. "And how would you know?"

"Pff, it's common knowledge if you're from Southie."

I shrug. Can't disagree there. Killian is a player, and he doesn't even try to hide that. He has a *fuck me or get lost attitude* that has many girls crawling around him before he kicks them to the curb with tears in their eyes. They all want to be special, but no one ever is.

My eyes catch Sienna's black hair as I look past Emma, and I snatch the box out of her hands, putting it back in my jeans. "She's coming. Act normal."

"Oh, shit." We both plaster smiles on our faces as we wait for Sienna to close the distance between us. She gives us a wary look, with a ghost of a smile.

"Hey, you," Emma says with a double meaning that has me rolling my eyes.

"I said normal, you idiot," I hiss from the corner of my mouth through my teeth. "Hey."

I look up at Sienna, and my chest swells. Her fair skin is slightly blushed, and her honey brown eyes are shining at me like diamonds. Her black hair gives away her Italian roots, making her look like a classic Mediterranean beauty with a hypnotizing smile.

"Hey, what are you two doing?" She moves her gaze between Emma and me.

"Emma was about to go find Killian."

"I was?" She turns her head in confusion, and I give her a glare as I push my elbow into her side. "Yeah, he's waiting for you at the packie, remember? You need to help him with something."

Her mouth widens in realization before she turns her attention to a frowning Sienna.

"Right! I had to help him with something, uh—" she trails off. She sucks at lying, really. "School!" she shouts with one finger in the air.

I rub a hand over my face, then give her a reprimanding look, silently telling her she's screwing this all up.

"Killian graduated." Sienna blinks in suspicion.

"Right." Emma purses her lips, giving me a questioning look.

"Just go." I shake my head with a smile tugging on my lips.

"Okay! Bye!" She darts off and Sienna looks after her before giving me an incredulous look.

"What was that all about?"

I hold out my hand and tug her onto the bench next to me when her hands land on my chest. I turn my body to face her, our knees touching. Without hesitation, I move my hand to her hair, bringing her lips closer to mine until they fall into my own. Holding still, I enjoy the warmth of our mouths connecting, letting it linger before I press my forehead against hers. She sucks in a breath when we break loose, as if I kissed the air from her lungs. We've been stealing kisses and hugs here and there over the last few weeks, but never in public. Never for everyone to see. It makes me feel as if this is our first kiss. The first one to finally make it official. To finally give in to the butterflies that seem to drive me nuts every time she's close.

"I got you something." I let go of her and pull out the box from my pocket. Her eyes grow big when I put the green box in her hand, and she snaps her gaze up at mine.

"What is this?"

"Open it." I rest my hand on her neck, slowly brushing her skin with my thumb.

When she lifts the lid, she gasps, followed by a swallow as she pulls out the necklace.

"A wolf." It's a statement, but I can hear the question in her voice and when she rears her head back to look at me, the corner of my mouth curls.

"I want the whole city to know you're mine." I lean in, bringing my lips only a few inches from hers. "Sienna Brennan, will you be mine?"

21

Sienna

"**W**here do you need me to put these?" Killian walks in with a big box in his arms.

"What is it?"

"Wicked heavy shit."

I pull a face at his obvious contribution as he puts the box on the bar, then I peek inside and start clapping like a seal.

"Oh, the new tumblers! Look how great they've turned out." I hold up the crystal tumbler that's engraved with the name of the bar.

Killian blinks, staring back at me with a dull look.

"You don't give a damn."

"A glass is a glass." He shrugs.

"This is not true. Can you put them in the extra dishwasher in the stockroom?"

"Sure." I continue what I'm doing, listening to the radio until a few minutes later, Killian walks back out again.

"The other night was fun," he says, with one tumbler in his hand.

"It was."

He grabs a bottle of Royal Blue Whiskey and pours himself a glass before leaning his back against the workstation.

I shake my head. "Do you ever drink water?"

"No." His tone is firm, clearly not in the mood to discuss his drinking habits. "It felt like old times." I can hear the suggestion in his voice, and it's really starting to irritate me. It's confusing enough that Reign is slowly trying to lure me into his grasp, so I don't need Killian pushing me in the same direction as well.

"Where are you going with this, Kill?" I don't look up and just keep putting the clean glasses on the shelf one by one.

"Nowhere. I'm just saying."

Bullshit.

"Saying what?"

"We should do it more often."

"Maybe." I loved sitting between those two boys on the couch, hearing them scream at the TV with beers in their hands like old times. It felt comfortable, and it made me relax, something I haven't been able to do in a long time. But as soon as I headed home, the worry came back in full force. All night I tossed and turned, thinking about how I can't handle a broken heart at his hands again.

"Reign told me you're going to hear him out."

Of course, he told his brother that part. "Did he also tell you I need time?"

"Why, though?" I rear my head back and he's looking at me with a questioning expression. "I know deep down you're dying to know what happened. Why he didn't come back."

I purse my lips, the temptation to ask Killian tugging on me. "I'm assuming you know."

"Come on, Sienna. It's Reign. He tells me everything."

I turn my body, mirroring his stance with my arms crossed in front of my body.

"Are you never fed up with always ending up in the middle of everyone?"

He frowns, as if he doesn't follow.

"You know why Franklin killed Declan." We all know, except Reign, because Franklin swore us to silence.

"Ya-huh." He brings his drink to his lips, looking at me over the rim of his glass.

"Yet you don't tell Reign the truth."

"Not my story to tell."

"And you know why Reign stayed in New York for *Callie*." I speak her name with disdain, like it's acid on my tongue, because to me, she's part of the reason why Reign and I broke up.

"He didn't stay for her," he argues with a smug grin.

"But you won't tell me why he did."

He licks his lips with amusement sparking his eyes. "Do you want me to tell you?"

"No." Yes.

"Look, Sienna, he's never just been the romantic boy with the grand gestures. He's still a Wolfe, capable of things he can't even grasp if he thinks it's the right thing to do. He's both." I lift a brow at his cryptic description of his brother. "His soul is tortured since he went into foster care, and he can live with it for the rest of his life if he has to. It's you who's torturing yourself unnecessarily. He hurt you. He's an asshole. He has done shit he's not proud of. You kinda knew that when you started running around with us Wolfes at sixteen. Just hear him out." He offers me a gaze filled with sympathy.

"Why are you playing matchmaker? I thought you were the ruthless one."

He snorts. "You want me to tell you with a knife to your throat?"

"Funny."

He throws his drink down his throat, pushing himself off the station, then places his glass in the sink.

"I know I don't scare you. Stop killing yourself over this, Sienna. I'll see you tonight." He shoots me a wink, then carries his feet toward the door.

"See you tonight." I watch him walk away, leaving me alone with my thoughts while I glance around the bar.

Killian plays on my curiosity and the bastard knows it. I do want to know. As much as I'm scared the answer will hurt me as much as Reign leaving me behind, I still want to know. And the more time I spend with him, the more I wonder if I'm ready to find out what really happened in New York.

22

16 YEARS OLD

Sienna

"Where are we going?" We get off the elevator and he holds up a piece of black silk fabric.

"I need you to put this on." His eyes are sparkling with joy, an infectious smile tugging the corners of his mouth up.

"Why?" I drag out the word, my eyes narrowing in suspicion.

"Just trust me, baby."

Reluctantly, I sigh, and he moves behind me to fold the soft fabric around my head. He takes my hand in his, then throws his arm around my shoulder before leading us down the hall. I hold on to him close, taking in the citrusy notes of his cologne, trying to figure out where we are going. I can still feel the carpet underneath my feet until I hear him open a door. The air changes, our movements echoing through the area.

"We're going up the stairs," he tells me, and I place my foot up, slowly putting it down until I reach the first step. Carefully, he leads me up, and I realize we're going to another floor.

"This is not some kind of joke, right?"

"What do you mean?" I can hear the amusement in his voice.

"Well, you know. Like those videos on YouTube where they blindfold people, telling them they are going to bungee jump when really, they're falling in a lake."

"We're on the eighth floor," he says, mockingly. "I'm strong as fuck, but I can't throw you all the way into the Atlantic from up here."

He has a point.

"There could be a pool?"

"No pool." He chuckles when I hear him open what sounds like a push bar on the door and instantly the hot summer air hits me in the face. I feel a soft breeze flow around my body while the din of traffic sounds somewhere far away.

"No-suh! You're not going to let me bungee jump, right?" I abruptly hold still, too quick for him to stop me as I pull the blindfold from my eyes.

"No, don't!" he cries until his body slumps, and he gives me a slight scowl with a ghost of a smile. "You stubborn little girl."

I gasp when I look past him, bringing my hand up to cover my gaping mouth. Tea lights are lighting up the entire rooftop, with torches placed to create a path that leads to the edge of the railing. The floor is covered in rose petals, and I slowly take steps forward in complete awe.

"You did this?" I whisper as I walk past him. I slog my way farther, taking in every single detail. At the end lies a mattress, surrounded with lanterns, while beside it stands a cooler with drinks and a picnic basket with a box of Dunks on top of it. It's the perfect outdoor setting, one you only see in movies. One of those scenes where they look upon the stars while holding each other. I can't believe he did something so special for me.

I squat down, running my fingers over the soft fabric of the blanket on top of the bed, then twist my head back to Reign.

He's still standing where I left him, his hand in his pockets, looking at me like I'm the most amazing thing he's ever seen. There is love in his eyes. I know because I can feel it radiate from his green retinas, just like I feel it radiate from mine when I look at him.

"How?" I shake my head in disbelief.

He shrugs, putting his feet in motion. "Killian helped me a little. I wanted to give you the best view of the city."

I heave myself back up, turning to take in the view. It's dark, but when my eyes follow the river, I can see all the way to Admirals Hill. On the left side you have a perfect view of all the boats, docked at the wharf, but it's the lights of the rest of the city that make it breathtaking at night.

"One day, I'll be living here." Reign's arms wrap around my shoulders, pulling me against his chest as he rests his chin on my hair.

I rest my palms on his arms, holding him tight. "This is where you want to live?"

"Ya-huh. At least for a little while. I like to see the boats sailing into the harbor, to watch the city come to life while I relax on my balcony after a long night."

"What is it that you're going to do?"

"Work for my brothers," he answers in a matter-of-fact tone, like there is nothing better to him than becoming part of the empire his brother is building. "Make love to you." The words make my belly flutter and I smile as he presses a lingering kiss on my cheek, turning my head to find his lips.

"Is that a hint?" I taunt with my lashes beating softly.

"No, baby. I can wait as long as you want. But eventually, when you're ready, I want to." The gentle look in his eyes encourages me to give myself to him. To show him I'm ready to give him everything I have. My heart, my body, and my soul. It's his. All of it.

"I'm ready," I tell him, with a shred of a whisper.

I see the wonder in his eyes as he searches mine for any doubt.

"Are you sure?"

I nod, then amplify my answer by brushing his lips in an affectionate kiss. I can feel his desire growing when he lowers one hand to my stomach, tugging me against the hard bulge in his jeans. I turn around in his arms while his hands desperately slide into my hair, our lips moving at a slow and thoughtful pace as he moans against my throat. Our breaths mix in an intoxicated combination, making it hard to not melt into his touch. When his tongue gently pushes against mine, I groan against it, my fingers slipping under his shirt to feel the warmth of his skin on my palm.

Suddenly, he jerks, breaking our connection, and I give him an incredulous frown.

"I didn't do all this to get you naked. I mean"—he brushes his nose against mine, never letting go of my face—"I want you naked. But only if you're sure. We can just hang out and watch the stars if you want to. That was my plan anyway."

There is an awkwardness in his tone that makes me giggle against his lips before I press my forehead against his.

"I want this, Reign. I want *you*."

"Yeah?" His voice breaks, then he clears his throat to steady himself. "Don't do it for me."

"I'm not. I promise." Satisfied with that answer, he crushes his mouth against mine once more, with demanding yet comforting strokes every time he pushes against my tongue. We get lost in each other, every move delicate and passionate, until I push him back and he looks at me with a quizzical look. I can feel his hesitation to take the next step, not wanting to make me feel uncomfortable. But the truth is, I don't think Reign can do anything to make me feel uncomfortable. I want to feel him inside of me, to be the one to break down my walls for the first time.

A seductive smile travels up my face as I push him toward the bed, and he falls down, keeping his body up by his elbows.

"I want you, Reign." I take off my top, exposing my cream lace bra. His lips part as need flashes in his piercing gaze and he nods as if he finally realizes this is really what I want. He reaches out his hand, and I eagerly take it, then he yanks me onto the bed with a chuckle. He lowers his body, pressing another scorching kiss on my lips. The tips of his fingers migrate down to my jeans, unbuttoning the denim with ease before I pull his shirt over his head.

"You're the most beautiful thing I've ever seen."

He peppers my skin with a trail of kisses along my collarbone, then moves up to the sensitive area on my neck while his hand starts to rub the lace of my panties. A tingling feeling moves through my core, growing when he lowers himself more with every kiss, shifting down my body until he reaches my breast. Tenderly, he pulls one out, taking a nipple in his mouth while massaging the other and I arch my back to undo my bra, then throw it next to me.

"Are you okay?" He smirks up at me, clearly appreciating my relaxed stance while I surrender to his touch.

With my lip tucked between my teeth, I bring my head up to cup his cheek.

"Keep going." I nod.

He licks his lips and I gasp when he pushes his fingers inside the hem of my jeans, slowly peeling it off my hips. Bringing my knees up, I help him get rid of the fabric before he does the same with my panties. He takes a moment, staring at my wet center with parted lips. His gaze moves up to mine with devotion, never breaking our connection as he wets two of his fingers. Our fixed look intensifies when he slowly rubs his fingers through my folds, and I gasp for air. Immediately, my hips move up, wanting more, as he smoothly starts to glide them up and down my slit.

"Oh, whoa," I croak out in amazement.

"Does that feel good, baby?"

"Yes! So good." The desperation is audible in my voice, and I close my eyes, enjoying every second of his touch. Every move makes me squirm underneath his hand, every stroke more scorching than the other, and my moans grow more frantic with each passing second.

You read about sex in books. You see the passion in movies between two people. But never would I have expected it to feel this good as his fingers rub my core.

When I feel my eyes roll to the back of my head, he stops, and I bring my chin to my chest to lock my eyes with his. His piercing green eyes are staring at me while his mouth is hovering above my sex. He licks his lips with a hungry smirk and my lips form a silent O, then snap shut when he presses a kiss right above my clit. He moves down, with a series of open-mouthed kisses along my folds until he reaches my opening and dives his tongue in.

A longing screech falls from my tongue while he starts to move up until he takes my clit into his mouth. He plays with it at a blistering pace, filled with gentle moves and small sucks, alternated with flicks of his tongue. The feeling that starts to form in my lower abdomen is like a drug. A high that is slowly working to its peak, and all I can do is lie there, in complete submission to the boy responsible for it.

"Oh my God," I huff. Desire flushes my face, and it feels like my brain is no longer functioning, completely enjoying my moment on Cloud 9. Part of me is anxious, a little fearful about what will happen when he pushes me into ecstasy, but the other part suddenly realizes why people go crazy over sex.

"Come for me, baby," Reign whispers against my dripping wet entrance, the vibration of his tongue causing a shiver to fall down my spine. "Let go. Let me show you how much I love you."

My head can hardly wrap itself around the words he's giving me when I feel his tongue enter me again, and his fingers start to rub my sensitive nub at a fast and steady pace. Within seconds, my body begins to vibrate with liquid fire, and I cry out in pleasure, my legs shaking next to his head. With my back arched, I look at the dark sky, staring at the stars while I ride out the best wave of euphoria I've ever experienced, until it simmers down and my body goes completely limp.

I grip my heart with closed eyes, panting, as I hear the sound of Reign's belt fall to the floor with a loud thud. When I look up, he's standing in front of me, butt naked, looking at me in a way that steals my breath. His chest is toned for a sixteen-year-old boy, and the thirsty look in his eyes shows me the man that he really is. He makes me feel like the most gorgeous girl in the world when he looks at me like that and the rerun of his words hit my brain.

"Did you just tell me you love me?" I glance down at his cock, bobbing against his stomach, stiff and impressive, and I can't help but swallow at the sight of it.

He's rolling on a condom and a smirk moves up his face before he lowers himself on the mattress, crawling on top of me until I can feel his tip push against my center.

His hand moves into my hair, his lips hovering above mine while his eyes search my face.

"Are you sure? We can still stop if you want to."

I rest my palm on his cheek, softly brushing my thumb over his skin with a loving smile.

"I don't want to stop. I want to feel you inside of me."

He nibbles my lip, pressing his forehead against mine while I feel him slowly push his shaft inside of me. My body needs some time to get used to the penetration, and he goes slow, never dropping his gaze from mine to make sure I'm comfortable. At first, it feels tight, burning, and when he reaches my wall, he holds still for a moment.

"Are you okay?"

I nod. "Yeah, keep going."

Gently, he starts to thrust inside of me, dropping his face against my neck as he lets out a desirable grunt with every move he makes, fueling my want for him. After a while, the tight and stiff feeling is replaced by an addictive one as he pushes against my wall over and over again.

"The answer is yes," he huffs against my neck before he pulls back to look at me while he keeps his pace of forward motion steady.

"What answer?" I gasp in needy agony, barely able to keep my head on straight while I enjoy his weight on top of mine. I feel completely one with him, grateful that he's the one who's taking my virginity while I get all of him in return. It's all I ever wanted since the day he asked me to be his, to feel completely in sync with the boy I felt so madly in love with.

"I just told you I love you." He holds still, waiting for my reaction, and my eyes widen. "I love you, Sienna. And I know we are young, but I will never stop loving you. I can feel it in my gut."

I take his face in my hands, doing my best to cherish this moment, wanting to remember it for a cloudy day.

"I love you too, Reign Wolfe."

23

17 YEARS OLD

"Hey, aren't you supposed to be in class?" Killian asks when I walk into his room.

"I'm skipping class."

He nods his head, shrugging his shoulders with a look that says *fine with me.*

"I need you to do something for me, and it might get us in trouble." I drop myself on Killian's desk, and he turns his desk chair toward me. He holds still, his tongue darting out to lick his lower lip as he takes in my words before a smirk forms on his face.

"You know I live for trouble." Without asking any more questions, he gets up, grabbing his leather jacket hanging on the door. He puts it on, then holds up the set of keys he pulls from his pocket. "You coming?"

I shoot him a grateful look, rubbing my legs before I get up and follow him downstairs. Of all my brothers, Killian truly is my partner in crime. It was like that before we all got split up and I feared that might've changed when I got back. But since the moment I stepped through the front door of our new home, he and I have been as thick as thieves. With him literally being one. Apparently, he learned a few skills in his foster family, making him the star pickpocket. Franklin is pretty pleased about his skills because, from what I understand, Killian has been getting more involved in the business lately.

A few minutes later, we sit in his black-on-black Audi, cruising downtown.

"I can't believe Franklin gave you a brand-new car." My hands move over the sides of the leather seat, my face beaming as I suck in the new car smell.

"It's wicked, right? I bet he'll give you one when you graduate." He glances at me, his fingers wrapped around the wheel, his foot pressed heavily onto the throttle. "So, where are we going?"

"Providence."

He takes his foot off the throttle and quickly the car slows down as he gives me a slight scowl. "Reign."

I know the preaching that is ready to fall from his tongue. I know every word of it. My brothers have talked to me about it more than once. They tell me to focus on Sienna and ask me if I'm happy with her. And I am. I'm so wickedly happy with her it's insane. But every time I drop Sienna off at home, I feel guilty. Not because I love her, but because I'm happy while Aubrey is still trapped in the fire pit of hell.

"I just need to see her, okay?" I explain with a pinched expression. "I just need to know she's okay. I promised her."

"You didn't leave her behind. She's their daughter."

"I know." But it still feels like that. It keeps me up at night, tossing and turning, wondering how she's doing. If she's still forced to "work" on Saturdays. I hoped I would be able to let it go, but I can't. My happiness is overshadowed by the aching worry I feel for her, and I just need to know she's okay. That she'll be okay until she turns eighteen and she can do whatever she wants.

"Look, I get it. I understand *why*, and if I were in your shoes, I'd probably feel the same." He gives me a piercing look, emphasizing the why because he knows now. Everything that happened. I told him a week ago when he found me on my balcony, staring blankly into the night.

Again.

Killian can be brutal as fuck if you push him and there is not much he's impressed by. But when I was done telling him about the last four years of my life, he just focused his gaze on the floor, staring into oblivion. We haven't spoken about it since, but it felt good sharing it with him. As if the burden is lighter now that he knows, and I'm not alone with my nightmares.

"But this can go wickedly wrong," he continues. "If things go south with her father, I won't hesitate to kill him, Reign." He lifts up his shirt, showing the gun tucked into the hem of his jeans. The look on his face is serious, and I know he's only saying it to make sure I'm making a well thought out decision about this. But I have thought about it. I know this might be a stupid plan. I also don't care. I *have* to see her.

"I know, Kill."

It's almost three when Killian and I stand in front of the public high school with our asses leaning against his car. It feels weird to be back here. Almost like another lifetime, but really, it's a little over a year ago when I still went to school here every day. When the bell rings and heaps of kids swarm the school grounds, my eyes roam the entire area, not wanting to miss Aubrey. Fully focused, I peer through my sunglasses, looking for her curly brown hair. Within a few minutes, the crowd is thinning out and a renewed wave of worry enters my body.

"Maybe she got detention," Killian offers. "Or some after school shit."

"She doesn't do after school shit."

She doesn't do anything other than go to school. She's a girl who never fits in and doesn't really participate in school activities. Why the fuck would she? It's not like she's going anywhere after graduation.

I exhale loudly, rubbing the back of my neck, when a girl with ash blonde hair walks by us while eying Killian.

"Damn. Nice car," I hear her say, making me twist my head. Her lashes flutter, her focus on my brother. She gives him a flirty look, moving a step closer.

I remember her.

"Hey! You're in one of Aubrey's classes. Tara, right?"

Her face falls, a bit shocked when she puts her attention on me, a pinched mouth now sitting on her lips.

"Reign."

"Yeah! Have you seen Aubrey?"

She gasps, her eyes widening before they close, and she drops her head.

After a few seconds, she looks back up with a gloomy expression. "You don't know?"

I frown. "Know what?"

She tries to keep a straight face, but her excessive swallowing tells me the emotion that must be sitting in her throat.

"She died."

Two words. Two words that make my head spin and my knees weak, causing me to drop my ass on the hood to prevent myself from hitting the ground.

"What?" Killian blurts.

"She died a few months ago."

I shake my head.

"How did she die?" My voice breaks while pressing my fingers into my eyes to literally push back the tears.

"She drowned in the Seekonk River. Suicide. Witnesses said she walked right in without a second thought. Her clothes were still on. It was about a week after her mother left."

"Her mother left?"

She nods. "A few weeks after you did."

Pebbles trickle down my skin, an uncontrollable itch mocking me as the words reach my ears. It feels as if thousands of ants are pacing up and down my limbs, eating me alive. My head frantically starts to waggle in complete disbelief.

"I'm sorry," she offers, wiping a tear from her cheek. "I know you two were close. She's buried at Saint Francis Cemetery at the edge of town."

"Thank you for telling us," Killian tells Tara. She gives a tight nod, followed by a short wave before she continues her walk, leaving us alone. When she's gone, tears roll down my cheeks, the grief tainting my already black heart.

I feel Killian's hand land on my shoulder. "Are you okay?"

"No," I answer honestly.

It's not fair. She deserved to live. To experience more than the hell she grew up in. She deserved to be saved, but instead she's dead. I didn't save her.

"It wasn't your responsibility to save her," Killian says, his voice quiet.

Did I say that out loud?

"She was already doomed by the hell she was born into. It's not your fault." He wraps his arms around me, pulling me into his chest.

"I should've taken her with me. I should've fought for her," I sob.

"You couldn't, Reign. You're just a kid. What exactly could you have done? Franklin tried to get her out, but we don't have that kind of control yet. It was a battle to get you out when he did." I listen to his soothing words, but all they do is fuel my anger. My grief. The heavy feeling that's been sitting on my chest while I enjoyed being home is now being replaced with something that feels like the weight of the world.

I pull myself out of his grasp, wiping my tears away with the back of my hand. "Take me to the cemetery."

A troubled expression travels his features. "You sure?"

"Positive."

"Kill?"

We're sitting in his car in front of the Brady family home. It's now ten PM and after staring at her grave for a few hours, I just needed another glance at the house. To feel the shit I no longer have to deal with. To see the house I left her to die in. I failed her. I know I did. I promised I would save her, but as soon as I got home, I got caught up in picking up my life again, too selfish to make her a priority.

"Yeah?" He brings his gaze up from his phone.

"I'm going to kill him." The tone of my voice is flat, almost as if someone is speaking for me, yet I mean every word. I thought I wasn't capable of it, but right now it feels like it's something I'm meant to do. I'm going to kill Jefferson. Simply because I can't sleep knowing he's still out there being a predator to innocent girls.

No.

I can't have that. I can't live with that knowledge. Jefferson is the epitome of what's wrong with the system, and I'm going to take out the error. Even if it will destroy me inside. I owe it to Aubrey. I owe it to Nova. And I owe it to every girl that has come before and might come after.

Killian blows out a breath, running a hand through his hair.

"I'm not going to stop you, Reign," he confesses. "But you have to be one hundred percent sure." He twists his head, locking his gaze with mine. His green eyes grow dark, showing me his true form. Even at eighteen, Killian is a killer. He won't hesitate to end someone's life if he believes it's for the greater good. I'm scared to ask him if he has killed before, because I don't have to hear him say it out loud to know he has. Same with Connor. It's Franklin and me who are different. Less ruthless when it comes down to it. It should scare me that two of my brothers are capable of things that can't see the day of light.

But I'm not. I trust their hearts. Just like I trust mine. I have to. That's all I got.

"I am," I reply firmly.

A silent conversation takes place between us for a beat until he grabs the gun from his side and hands it over.

"I'll be right behind you."

Scraping every ounce of courage inside of me I can find, I feel the weight of the gun in the palm of my hand, take a deep breath, and then exit the car. The adrenaline starts to pump through my veins, sounding like an ominous drum in my ear.

When we reach the front door, I wiggle the doorknob, only to realize it's locked.

"I got it." Killian pulls a bobby pin from his pocket, then squats down in front of the lock. In three swift moves, a click is audible, and I raise my eyebrows in awe.

"Foster care?" I whisper.

"My foster brother taught me some skills." He gets up with a smirk on his face before he opens the door.

With my heart feeling like it's in my throat, we slowly step in, waiting for any movement. The parlor is dark, the light of the TV dancing through the room. Jefferson sits on his recliner, passed out, his mouth agape with a beer still in his hand. His belly peeks out of his shirt and he looks like he hasn't showered in days. Smells like it too. It's disgusting.

"That's your foster dad?" Killian hisses with a scrunched-up nose.

"The one and only. Though he shouldn't even be allowed to be a parent. Let alone take care of anyone else's children."

My eyes roam around the house, chills moving up my arms when my mind goes back in time. As if Killian notices my vacant expression, he gives me a quick elbow.

"Hey, look at me." I rear my head toward him. "This is not your life anymore. Blow a bullet through the tool's head and we'll be on our way home, okay? Your *real* home."

I swallow, bringing my gaze to the floor while my fingers grab the gun even tighter. With a few big strides, I quickly but carefully move myself in front of Jefferson, who hasn't got a clue we're even here. We could rob his entire house empty with the state he's in.

I could make it easy on myself and just pull that trigger right now, without him ever knowing or realizing. But I want to look him in the eye one more time. I want him to know who's giving him a one-way ticket out of this world.

"Ay! Wake up, asshole." I kick his shin, and he jerks awake with a loud snort, looking at me with confusion written on his face. He blinks, his mind slowly waking up, and when he finally does, he shows me a lopsided grin.

"Well, well, look who it is. You've grown up in the last year. You missed me, boy?" His taunts have me grinding my teeth, and I lift the gun, pointing it at his face. His smile falls and panic glints in his intoxicated eyes.

"What are you doing?" he croaks out, now completely frozen in his chair. There is terror written on his face, and I hope it's the same terror all those girls felt when they were forced to go into that basement like one of his whores. I hope he feels what they had to feel every single weekend, knowing there was no one who would be there to rescue them. I want him to feel regret right before that bullet pierces through his brain.

"Ending you," I inform him as I pull the trigger without any second thoughts and his head jerks back, his eyes still open wide.

I expected to hear him grovel. To plead and admit his wrongs. But when he opened his eyes, I realized I didn't want to hear another word from him. I just want him to be gone.

A perfect red wound sits on his forehead, almost looking fake on his lifeless body. There is still tension in my fingers, an anger boiling inside of me that wants to pull the trigger a few more times, but Killian comes beside me, placing his hand over the gun.

"He's gone." He softly pulls the weapon from my grasp, then gives me a slight nudge to get my feet in motion. "Let's go. Before anyone calls the cops."

Realizing what I just did, my mind wakes up and I quickly dart out of the house with Killian following my tracks. We jump in the car, the gas pedal to the floor as we drive away. I stare out of the window, waiting for the pain to arrive. The pain that will gut me because I took his life without even blinking, but instead it feels like the weight is lifted from my chest. The only worry that flashes through my head is the one about getting caught.

"Shit. I killed him, Kill," I huff, a bit shocked by my own actions. "What if the cops find out it was us?"

"Don't worry about that, man. I will take care of it."

"They could've seen your car!"

He snaps his head toward mine, moving his gaze back and forth between the road and me.

"You know we don't have regular jobs, right? Franky? Connor? *Me?*"

I nod.

"I will fix it, Reign. Don't worry about it." His look is serious, penetrating through me as if he wants to make sure I understand every word he's saying, and for a second, I feel like a little boy again. The one that relied on the protection of his big brother. But I also feel older. As if whatever was left of my innocence is now gone forever.

"Don't tell them."

"Who?" Killian questions.

"Connor. *Franklin.*"

"Why not?"

"I dont–I don't want them to know. Can we keep this between you and me?"

"Okay. I won't tell them. Are you okay?"

Am I okay? My eyes are moving back and forth, as if searching for the answer, and a hundred thoughts are going through my head. I can't make sense of everything, but there is one thought that's the strongest. One that stands out. The one that tells me I did the right thing.

"I'm not sure," I reply honestly, "but I think I will be."

The sun is about to disappear behind the horizon, and I close my eyes to enjoy the warmth of the last rays of the day. We're propped on one of the lifeguard chairs and Sienna sits on my lap while Emma sits on the steps of the other one, with Killian on top.

I fill my lungs with a heap of salty air, feeling content for the first time in a very long time.

I thought killing Jefferson would bring me nightmares, that he would hunt me in my sleep, but I have never slept better with the knowledge he can't hurt another innocent child. It's when I'm awake that I question myself. It's when I'm awake I realize what I'm capable of, and it makes me feel like shit. I don't regret it, but every single day I wonder if I'm evil for feeling relieved, and what it says about me being content since that bastard took his last breath.

I might have killed for a good reason, but it doesn't make me any better than all the other people who take someone's life.

That night, I vowed to never kill again unless I have to. Not unless it's in self-defense.

"Is it true, Em?" I glance down at her blonde hair, pushing my gloomy thoughts away.

"Is *what* true?" She keeps her eyes closed, taking in the warmth of the sun with her feet laid out in front of her.

"That you and Ryan are going to prom together?"

"What? No," she blurts, looking up at us. "I don't like him."

I frown. "You don't? Because you were all over him at lunch."

Her gaze turns troubled. "I don't. And I don't want to talk about it." The tone of her voice quickly turns angry, and she gets up, stomping off to the shoreline.

"What did I do?" I ask, incredulous.

"I'll go." Killian jumps off the chair and runs after her while I turn my head, confused, to Sienna.

"Seriously, what did I do?"

"Nothing." She smiles. "But apparently, Ryan said something that upset her. She ignored him when we got out of class later today. I was surprised she even hangs out with Ryan. For the last four years, she's done her best to avoid all boys."

"Really?" I press my cheek against her hair, folding my arms around her body.

"She changed, you know."

"What do you mean?"

She shifts on my lap, making sure she can look at me with her honey brown eyes. They radiate a sense of comfort. The only sets of eyes that can make me forget about the war raging inside of me, nurturing me with peace when I get lost in them. Her skin is flawless and free of make-up. Her black hair frames her face, showing off her Italian roots. She's the prettiest girl I've ever seen.

"When you left, she changed."

"How?"

She shakes her head. "I don't know if it was you or something else. But she isn't as open as she was in middle school. Not as happy. She can stare at something, completely lost for minutes without hearing a word. I asked her about it a few times and she says it's nothing. She doesn't want to talk about it. But something nags at her mind, I know it does. When you got back, I thought you'd be able to bring her back too. Spark her back to life. But as the time passes by, it feels like she's crawling more and more into her own world." She pauses. "Your brother even tried to talk to her."

"Killian?"

"No, Franklin."

"He did?" I twist my head so I can look at her face to face.

"Last year. Emma and I got into a fight at a party because she didn't want to do anything. She'd rather stay at home watching a movie. I was getting a bit desperate to get my friend back. Franklin walked in, spotted us, and took Emma to the side for like half an hour before he went off with one of the seniors who lived there. Emma reluctantly stayed with me at the party. We had fun. Not sure what he said, but it worked. For a while."

A smile creeps onto my face. "That's Franklin. He's one of the good guys."

I say it with pride because I know I can never live up to the bar Franklin set for me without him even knowing. He's not just our big brother. He's the alpha, the leader, because he deserves the title. He takes care of all of us with a clear conscience, and I respect him even more for it.

She brushes her mouth against mine, and I eagerly close the distance. Her warm lips melt against me and a jolt of happiness moves through my body.

"You think very highly of your brother."

"I do. He's my big example." Now more than ever. I'm not worthy like him. I took someone's life. As much as I don't regret what I did, the guilt pressing on my shoulders will be a constant reminder of that for the rest of my life.

She settles her head against my chest, and I press a kiss against her head before resting my chin on her black hair.

"I didn't know," I confess.

"How could you? You weren't here."

"I know. But she's my best friend. We used to tell each other everything before... well, you know."

Her soft hands land on my cheeks. "I'm sure it will be fine, Reign. You're here now. You can become her best friend again. We can all be best friends."

She looks cute with her vibrant eyes and sweet smile. I secretly had a crush on her when we were younger, but now that she's all grown up, that crush is growing into a love I can't seem to control. I want to touch her all the time.

I bite my lip, smiling. "I don't want to be *your* best friend, though."

She grips her heart, scoffing. "Why not?"

"Because I want to be your boyfriend."

"You already are." Her confession is followed by her mouth pressing against mine, and I tug her even tighter against my body.

"I wasn't going to let you go anyway." I smile against her lips. "You're mine, Sienna Brennan."

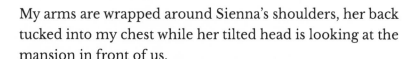

My arms are wrapped around Sienna's shoulders, her back tucked into my chest while her tilted head is looking at the mansion in front of us.

"I can't believe your brother bought a mansion," she says in awe.

"It's wicked, right?" I stare up at the brick building that I now get to call my home. White arches and pillars make it appear stately, though the white windows and door give it the homely feeling I've always longed for. "The inside is even better. You wanna see?"

"Let's go to the party first. Then later, you can show me the rest of the house." She turns in my arms, bringing her chin up. "And your bedroom."

"You wanna see my bedroom?"

"Actually," she purrs, running the tip of her finger along my chest, "I was hoping I could stay the night?"

My hands dive into her hair as I dip my chin. "Sounds like a great plan."

I press a bruising kiss on her plump lips before grabbing her hand to tug her behind me.

"Come on. Let's go to the others."

We walk toward the back of the insanely big gardens that surround the entire mansion, where Killian set up a bar next to the fire pit. Music sounds in the background while people are laughing, sitting around the fire with drinks in their hands. Franklin said we couldn't have a housewarming party inside, thinking a bunch of teenagers would trash the place within the hour, but he did allow us to have a party outside.

"You want a drink?" I glance over my shoulder.

"Beer, please."

I lead her to the bar before pushing the hired bartender to the side with a cocky smirk. An indignant frown forms on his face until he sees who I am, and he steps aside while I grab two beers out of the mini fridge. We then find a spot near the fire pit, hanging out with our friends. A few hours later, we all have a nice buzz and the boys start mocking each other with our macho behavior.

"Sometimes I wonder if you were born in that leather jacket, Kill." Killian gives Thomas, one of his former classmates, an incredulous look.

"Don't mock my jacket. We can't all look as good as me, you tool. You just wish you had the Wolfe genes. Sorry, man." Killian gives me a fist bump with a smirk.

"As far as I know, the Wolfe genes come with a whole lot of trouble. I'll pass," Thomas adds with a laugh.

"Watch out. Before you know it, Franklin will blow a bullet through your brain for insulting his little brother." We all drop our attention to Jimmy sitting next to Thomas, both now chuckling like they are Beavis and Butt-head.

My brows knit together, his smirk fueling my annoyance. "Franklin is not a murderer."

Everybody grows awkwardly silent, their eyes all focused on me as if they have a big secret I don't know.

"What? Franklin didn't kill Declan. He's innocent."

"Yeah, he did," Patrick argues. "Emma saw him. She got questioned by the police."

I twist my head to Emma, who gives Patrick a frightened look. The blood seems to leave her pink cheeks and she blinks.

"Emma?"

She shakes her head while the rest of her body goes rigid. Without a word, she gets up and trots off, Killian following behind her.

Feeling confused as fuck, I get up to follow them.

"Kill!" I call behind his back. He keeps walking and I pick up the pace before I'm being halted by Sienna, hanging on to my arm. A breeze blows a strand of her black hair in front of her face, moving over the troubled look on her face.

"Reign, wait. It's true."

I search her face. "What do you mean?"

She cautiously glances up at me, offering me a sympathetic look. "Emma told me."

"What did she tell you?" I grind my teeth as my anger grows.

"She saw Franklin kill Declan. It's why she can't sleep. She's been having nightmares for the last few years because she still sees his face. It's why she's depressed. It's why she's in therapy."

I move my eyes up, looking over her head into the huge garden of the mansion while my head starts to spin.

"Emma saw him?" My mind can't seem to process what she's saying, but I'm trying to.

She nods.

"No, he's innocent." There is doubt in my voice, and I hate it. "Isn't he?"

Her silence says it all, and I stomp off back to the Mansion.

"Franklin!"

Like a raging bull, I storm back into the house with my feet on fire. Sienna's right on my heels, trying to calm me down as she keeps tugging my arm.

"Reign, calm down."

"I don't want to calm down!" I shout, shrugging her off. My nostrils flare as I stomp through the hall. "Franklin? Where the fuck are you?"

"The kitchen."

I follow the sound of Connor's voice with Sienna still on my heels. "Reign, please!"

Ignoring her, I push the swinging kitchen door, and it flies open. Connor and Franklin both have their backs pressed against the counter, beers sitting in their hands.

"Reign." Franklin frowns. "What's wrong?"

"You killed Declan?" My tone is vicious, and I watch as his face slowly grows stern. There is a hint of regret in his green eyes, though I don't know if it's because of the answer he's about to give me or the fact that I found out. Our eyes stay tangled, the tension rising.

"Answer me!" I bark, slamming my hand on the white marble of the kitchen island.

"Yes." The word flies out with a deep sigh, and it's like a gust of wind knocks me in the face at the same time. I feel like my world is falling apart, questioning everything I believed for the last five years of my life. My stomach clenches, and I suck in a breath to get rid of the light-headedness I'm experiencing.

"What the hell," I mutter, in complete disbelief as I try to keep on my feet while my knees grow weak. "All this time I thought you were innocent when really, you're a goddamn murderer?"

I can see the hurt of my words flare his face, before he purses his lips.

"He deserved it, Reign."

"I bailed you out, Franklin. I tampered with evidence to get you out," I whine. Frustrated, I run a hand through my hair, then ball them into fists. I want to hit him. I want to hit something, but I'm doing my best to keep things at bay.

"Reign, it's not what you think," Killian tells me when he walks through the door.

"No!" I bark. "I went through hell for four years thinking you were innocent! And now it turns out my brother is a murderer?"

Franklin gives me a pained expression, putting his beer in the sink. "It's not that simple."

He takes a step forward to come closer, but I raise a hand to make sure he keeps his distance, not sure what I'll do to him with all this anger surging through me.

"You killed Declan?"

He exhales slowly, then raises his chin with a straight face. "Yes."

"Did you intend to kill him when you went to see him?"

"Yes."

I scoff. "Seems pretty simple to me, Franky! Did you know Emma saw you?"

"Yes." His answer gets me riled up even more, now that I know he's the reason for her depression. The reason she disappears for days. Can barely concentrate and is failing her classes. All because he gave her an image she can't get out of your head. A trauma she can't overcome. I don't know how to help her. I don't know how to erase it.

"She is scarred for life because you decided to play God and kill the boy next door!" I roar.

This time, his face transforms, and I can see the anger building in his gaze.

"Decided to play God?" he snarls.

"Yes, an arrogant asshole thinking he can play God! Thinking he can decide who lives or dies!" It's no secret Connor and Killian have less of a conscience than I do. But up until now, I thought I wasn't alone in that. I thought Franklin and I were the same. I thought Franklin, of all people, would understand the pain that comes with taking someone's life.

"There is more to that story, Reign." Connor takes a step forward, scowling.

Franklin raises his hand to command Connor to a halt. "No, let him."

The regret in Franklin's eyes is now completely replaced by rage, matching mine.

"I looked up to you, Franklin," I sneer with a desperate tone. "I thought you were different. That you danced with the law, but you were nothing like the other gangs in this city. That you were–" I trail off, letting my head hang.

"That I was what, Reign?" he grates, his fists balled alongside his body.

"That you were smarter than that!" I shout. "Better. Honorable. A businessman. But it turns out, you're nothing more than a criminal." I break my own heart when the words come out faster than I expected and part of me regrets it the second they are spoken. But they have to be said. I have to let them out. I also thought my brothers and I had morals, and ever since I killed Jefferson, I questioned my own. It was Franklin who made me believe I do. Just looking at him, seeing how he runs our businesses and how he grows our empire bit by bit. He's been my example, and I knew he always did the right thing. That's my big brother. But that was nothing more than a lie. He walks, talks, and looks sophisticated, standing out against the other criminals in this city. But really, we're all the same. Including Franklin.

And *me*.

"I'm out." I throw my hands in the air in defeat, then spin on the spot, carrying my feet to the door.

"Reign," Killian pleads, trying to grab my arm.

I pull away. "No. I don't want to hear it."

"Let him go," Franklin booms with an authority filled voice.

I give him one last glare, followed by a mock salute with a smile that doesn't match my eyes, before I disappear through the door.

24

Sienna

I walk around the bar to check everything is ready for tonight, when I hear someone whistle behind me. Curious, I twirl on the spot and my happy mood grows when I look into the wide grin of Reign. His eyes light up when he sees me, making my knees grow weak.

He looks so good.

After my conversation with Killian today, I decided to put on a brave face and give Reign a chance. To see if I can find the courage to try and mend my once broken heart.

"Damn, you look breathtaking," he bellows theatrically enough to make me blush while his gaze moves up and down my body. He closes the distance between us, cupping my neck in a dominating way that makes my breath hitch before he pushes my chin up with his thumb.

There is surprise in his eyes when the usual scowl doesn't appear and a lopsided grin relaxes on his lips.

"You're not slapping my hand away. That's a win."

I move my gaze to his chest to avoid his hypnotizing eyes.

"I meant what I said the other night, Reign. I don't want to fight you anymore. I don't want to fight this." I move my finger between the two of us.

"This?" he asks, amused, keeping his palm over my pulse. "And what is this?"

"I honestly don't know. But I'm trying to figure it out." I pause, looking up at him. "I'm trying to find the courage to work this out between us. If that's what you want too."

"It's all I want, baby." He abruptly shuts his mouth, carefully waiting for my reaction when he realizes he slipped out the one thing that's made me snap.

I exhale loudly, closing my eyes for a brief moment to push away any irritation that comes with it.

"Don't hurt me again, Reign." It's a plea; my way of showing I'm going to try and trust him, while my heart pounds out of my chest.

When I open my eyes again, I watch how his teeth are dragged over his lower lip in the sexiest way. He gives me a tentative look, as if he's waiting for me to tell him anything more. Then his hands move up to cup my face, and I rest my hands on his wrists when he moves his face closer. I can smell the fresh mint on his breath as he softly presses a scorching kiss on my jaw. His lips linger there before he moves them flush with my ear.

"I'd rather die than hurt you one more time, baby."

He presses his forehead against mine, our noses touching.

The small space between us feels electric, fusing us together.

"I want to kiss you so badly," he says with desperation.

"Then why don't you?" I breathe out, unintentionally sultry as fuck. I'm surprised by my own words, but I mean it. My lips are dying to be touched by his, to feel his warmth melt into mine. To find out if kissing him is just as toe-curling as it was in the past. If it will be better after all those years of absence.

"Because if I kiss you now, I won't be able to stop."

"Ooh, you two finally kissed and made up?" Killian's voice sounds from behind Reign's back with clear amusement and is followed by a chuckle when Reign snaps his head toward his brother moving past us. "Took you long enough."

My head falls against Reign's chest as I try to push the embarrassment aside, even though it's just Killian. Reign presses a kiss on top of my head before he lets go while his hand lingers on my hip.

"This conversation is not over yet." He shoots me a warning look with a ghost of a smile, and I can't help but snicker at his silly face before he follows his brother who's disappeared into the stockroom.

The party is a great success and I'm proud to say everyone is enjoying themselves. I've been mingling for about an hour after everything seemed to be under control until I joined the girls at the bar. Facing the shelves, I let my eyes roam the different spirits while glancing over my shoulder to Reign, every now and then.

"Girl, stop. You're making me all giddy." I turn to Lily, giving her an incredulous look while stirring my

Manhattan. I'm sitting on one corner of the bar while Kendall and Lily sit on the corner next to me.

"What? Why?"

"Oh, please," Kendall chimes in with an amused grin splitting her friendly face. "We see your secret glances at Prince Charming over there." She nudges her chin to Reign, who's talking to one of the real estate moguls of the city. He catches my eyes on him, giving me a wink, and I feel my cheeks grow flush. I do my best to keep a straight face when I move my attention back to the girls. I like them. Since we first met, they have been nothing but nice to me, making me feel like we've been friends forever. It reminds me of Emma. She has been my one and only best friend, and I've never found a friendship like that since.

"I'm happy for you." Lily takes a sip of her martini. "You two look good together."

"We're not together." I shake my head, pushing back the flutter that ignites at the sound of the word *together*.

"It won't take long, though." Kendall gives me a knowing look, and I let out a deep sigh.

"I don't know." I want to give Reign a chance. But that year, that summer, Reign changed because of what happened, and I felt him slipping away within just a matter of months. I still remember the excruciating pain of loneliness like it was yesterday, and I have a hard time letting that go. I needed him as much as he needed me, but he decided to leave.

I look up when Kendall's hand covers mine, giving me a tentative look.

"He really hurt you, didn't he?

I nod. "He did."

For me, Reign Wolfe represents a time when I was happiest in my life, but he also represents the time when

I used to cry myself to sleep, feeling like I had no reason to get up in the morning."

"I don't think he would hurt you again," Lily offers. Her long blonde hair is up in a classy ponytail, her lips painted a soft pink. She looks like an angel, but her little black dress suggests otherwise.

"Me neither. But a Wolfe in pain can be lethal. And let's be honest, as much as Reign's eyes sparkle, they are laced with pain." Kendall takes a sip of her drink, glancing at Reign over the rim of her glass.

I follow her gaze once more, my thoughts running overtime when they land on the man in question. He's the sweetest man I've ever met, thoughtful for as long as I can remember. He made me feel special every day of our time together. Like I was the only thing that mattered. Until he turned cruel and treated me like nothing. Something inside of me feels like he can't be both men, and I want to believe he's still the Reign I fell in love with. But the facts keep rearing me back to a frustrating point of hesitation.

"I always knew his brothers could be brutal and ruthless, but until we broke up, I never considered Reign to be. Working with them for the last few weeks made me realize they are more alike than I first thought. Sometimes I wonder if that's what's bugging him."

"His brothers?" I lock eyes with Kendall.

"Mostly Franklin. He had put his brother on a pedestal until... until he didn't. I think that's when he first really started to change more and more every day."

"What happened between those two anyway?"

They both look at me in anticipation and part of me wants to share everything I know. I want to tell them exactly why those two have issues, secretly wishing they will tell Reign the truth. But I promised Franklin.

I point my glass at Kendall, holding it up in the air. "Your man swore me to secrecy. If you want to know, you have to ask him. He'll probably tell you. He loves you." I finish with a smile, hoping to lighten up the mood a little.

"Ugh, he does," Lily agrees. "I swear Franklin can be scary, but when you're around, the man lights up like a Christmas tree."

That giddy look flashes in Kendall's eyes again, and her scoff is loud. "You make him sound like a puppy."

"Well," I pitch in with a grin traveling up my cheeks, "I've known the man for a decade, and I've never seen him as light-hearted as when you're around."

"Except for when you want to go out." Lily chuckles.

"Oh, yeah, he goes all angry Wolfe on me then." Kendall rolls her eyes with amusement.

I can smell him before I feel him wrap his arm around my shoulder, tugging me into his side as he presses a lingering kiss on my hair. "What's doing, ladies?"

Franklin slides his arms around Kendall with that relaxed smile we've just been talking about as he connects his lips with her neck, and Lily and I give Kendall a knowing look.

"Having fun, pretty girl?" Franklin asks as he watches Killian step behind the bar, walking toward our side.

Kendall nods, and he spins her on her stool, locking their lips as soon as she's facing him.

"Good." He smiles, before he glances over her head to me. "Thank you for tonight, Sienna. It seems to have been a great success."

I raise my glass in response while I feel Reign's lips tickling the skin underneath my ear.

"I still want to finish that talk."

"What talk?" I whisper, feigning innocence. I hold still, swallowing, scared to move my head, knowing my lips will link with his if I do.

"Hmm, don't play all coy. I'm going to kiss you tonight, Sienna. The question is *when*, not *if.*" His breath caresses my neck, and I have a hard time not giving in to his touch and letting him kiss me, right now, just as he wishes. But I close my eyes, leaning into his body instead.

Luckily, he straightens, his hands resting on my hips as he looks around at the rest of us.

"Let's go out. Kenny, are you in?" Reign asks, trying to rile Franklin up, no doubt.

Kendall shrugs. "Sure."

"What?" We all put our focus on a now scowling Franklin. It's clear he's trying to keep his calm, but when he locks eyes with Reign, they are shooting daggers. His jaw clenches, and I keep my mouth shut while I feel Reign silently snicker next to me.

"I don't think that's such a good idea, baby." Franklin cups Kendall's cheek in the most endearing way, as he gives her a pleading look.

"Come on, Franky. I'm with your brothers."

"Yeah, that's what worries me," he mutters, glaring at them over her head.

She holds his gaze with gooey eyes, then flashes him a sweet smile.

"Fine." He pushes out the word with a growl, and she gives him a kiss in reply.

"Kill?" Reign looks at his brother. He's leaning against the back of the bar, amused, glancing between Kendall and Franklin with his glass of whiskey in front of his chest.

"Ya-huh."

"What about you, Lily?" Reign twists his head to Lily at the same time Connor presses her back against his chest, wrapping his arms around her neck and whispering something in her ear. A playful smile tugs on the corner of her pink lips and she shakes her head.

"We're going home. Check on Colin and stuff."

"And stuff," Reign deadpans. "You mean fuck like bunnies?"

"Reign!" I swat his stomach, though I can't help but chuckle when Lily shamelessly shrugs her shoulders.

"Pretty much," she beams.

"You're coming." I look up, wondering who he's talking about when I realize he's talking about me the moment I catch his gorgeous green eyes.

"What?" I huff, indignant. "You're not even going to ask me?"

"You don't have a choice. You're coming."

"What if I don't want to?"

"I don't care," he discloses before he leans in, mixing his breath with mine. "I almost tasted your lips today, and I'm not going to bed before I feel your lips on mine."

"It's funny, before I met you guys, I didn't think a possessive man was romantic." I look at Kendall who may as well have hearts coming from her eyes. She gives me a swooning smile with her head in her hands, while Franklin gives her a dull expression.

"And now?" Reign chuckles.

She glances at Franklin with a side-eye, then clears her throat. "I'm pleading the fifth. I don't want to encourage this behavior."

We all fall into laughter while Reign tightens his grip on me, and I realize how comfortable I feel. Like I belong. It's a nice feeling, one I haven't experienced in a long time, and

I hold still while the brothers discuss how much security is going to be tagging along. They throw banter back and forth, though you can see how much these brothers love each other and form a union. They have their differences, but even Franklin and Reign would go to war for one another.

"Are you okay?" Reign whispers in my ear, making me look up at him, my lips close to his sharp jaw. It's tempting to press a kiss on it, the action feeling completely natural, but instead I just nod with parted lips.

"Good," he says, showing me that boyish grin that has me melting on the inside. "Let's go."

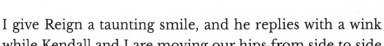

I give Reign a taunting smile, and he replies with a wink while Kendall and I are moving our hips from side to side on the dancefloor. The boys are watching us from one of the standing tables on the edge of the club, and I can't help glancing back at Reign every time I feel his eyes on me. His green retinas peer through the strobe lights like a beacon, acting like my lighthouse in this crowded club.

Kendall and I have been dancing for the last half hour, and I haven't had this much fun in years. There is just enough alcohol surging through my veins to loosen me up, and I boldly move to the rhythm of the beat, my skin damp from the heat.

"When was the last time you went out dancing?" I yell at Kendall over the blasting music. The strobe lights flicker over her blue eyes that are sparkling with joy, and her smile seems glued to the corner of her lips. It's contagious, and I have a feeling she hasn't been much of a party girl over the last few years.

"Forever! I don't even remember!" She twirls on the spot, looking like a happy little schoolgirl as the skirt of her skater dress flares around her. "You?"

"Same! I'm not really a party girl."

She nods in understanding, then moves her mouth close to my lips.

"Let's get some drinks." Without waiting for my reply, she grabs my hand, tugging me behind her as we move through the crowd. I quickly twist my head to Reign, who immediately gives me a questioning look that is accompanied by a small scowl. I motion to him that we're getting drinks, and he gives me a reluctant nod. When Kendall catches his scowl, she rears her chin over her shoulder. "I swear, Prince Charming is so cute, acting all overprotective over you."

We reach the bar and both place our elbows on the cold, wet surface.

"Not always cute when you're on the receiving end, you should know that." I chuckle while she places our order with the bartender.

"It can be a pain dating a Wolfe," she agrees with a smile when he takes off to make our drinks. "But my ex was an abusive criminal, so I ain't complaining about my man wanting to keep me safe. Even if it drives me nuts sometimes."

"I heard you dated Emerson Jones. The man was a creep."

"You know about that?"

"Boston may be big, but Southie isn't. I guarantee you every Southie will be able to tell you who's an enemy of the Wolfes. Emerson was their biggest."

"I forgot you're from Boston."

"Born and raised." There is pride in my voice. I love this city. It's part of my roots, and who I've become. I love how the seasons change and even though I'm not really into sports, I love it when I see people wearing a Bruins jersey or a Red Sox baseball cap.

"Hey." She nudges me in my side. "What happened that year between you and Reign? What made him leave you?"

I push out an awkward breath, looking into her interested gaze. Goosebumps pebble my skin when I think about that dreadful day, my mouth turning dry as I do my best to keep breathing. It's an image I will never be able to erase from my mind, and every now and then, it still haunts me in my sleep. That day changed everything.

"Our best friend Emma..." I pause. "She died," I croak out, offering her a tight smile. Her baby blue eyes grow wide while she just blinks, stunned, clearly not expecting that answer. "After that, he grew angrier every day until finally he left for New York. He was supposed to come back after two months. But he didn't."

"Oh my God. What happened?"

"She killed herself."

25

18 YEARS OLD

"Emma, are you ready?" I walk into her house and toward the parlor, knowing her parents are still at work. "Come on, Sienna and Killian are waiting for us at Dunks."

The house is silent, igniting a grim feeling in my stomach. "Em? Where you at?"

When she doesn't reply, I walk up the stairs, thinking she's sitting in her room with her headphones on or something. Sauntering to the end of the hall, I knock on her door before softly opening it.

"Em?" My eyes scan the empty room and I close the door with a frown while walking back until I reach the stairs to the attic. Covering my mouth with my palm, my heart literally stops beating when I register the sight in front of me, blinking. For a brief moment, it feels like I'm leaving my body, my brain not really registering what I'm seeing. As if I'm floating between reality and a nightmare.

Emma hangs in the stairwell of the attic, a brown rope tied around her neck. My lungs try to suck in short breaths when I glance at the blonde hair covering her lifeless face.

"NO! NO! Emma!" I run to her, trying to lift her up in an effort to save her, but when I register her cold skin, I know it's useless. Dread fills me, trying to mentally pull me under, but I keep fighting to keep her up, obsessed by the tiniest spark of hope inside of me until my muscles turn sour. My mind I make a few more futile attempts while the desperation seems to swallow me whole until finally I give up.

Defeated, I fall to my knees, looking at the horrible sight of my friend. Her eyes are bloodshot, her arms hanging alongside her body. I bring my hand up, feeling her fingers in mine. Her once rosy skin is now gray, feeling weird and rubbery, reminding me of the night Nova died.

My phone rings in my pocket and on autopilot I pick up, but the massive lump in my throat keeps me from voicing anything.

"Reign? Are you there?" I hear Killian bellow over the line when I stay quiet. "Where are you at? Did you pick up Emma?"

I try to swallow, doing my best to find my voice.

"She's dead." I stare at her face, a tear slowly running down my cheek.

"What? What are you talking about?"

"She's dead," I repeat.

"Who's dead?"

"Emma. She's dead." This time, my emotions get free rein and tears flood my eyes.

"What? Where are you?" As if my voice stops working, I stay quiet, unable to speak. "Are you at her house?"

I manage to let out a confirming grunt while I press my fingers to my eyes, trying to get rid of the heavy feeling on my chest.

"Stay there! We'll be right there!" Killian shouts, and the line goes dead.

My skin tingles in the most agonizing way, forming a dizziness in my head that I can't settle. It feels like a ton of bricks sits in my stomach and I press my back against the wall, my head resting against the wallpaper. I sit there for I don't know how long, when I hear Killian downstairs calling my name before he runs up the stairs, followed by one more set of footsteps behind him.

"Reign, where are you?" There is panic in his tone, and I close my eyes, trying to gather the strength to face him. "Reign!" I feel him fall to his knees in front of me, shaking my shoulders. "Reign!"

I open my eyes with a pinched mouth and welled-up eyes. I hear Sienna gasp behind him and Killian slowly turns his head to my right, his eyes growing wide when he sees our friend hanging in the stairwell.

"What the—" His mouth agape, his gaze fills with horror.

"Kill? Killian, where are you?" Franklin's voice booms through the house.

"We're up here!" he calls back, his focus never diverting from Emma.

Franklin and Connor storm up the stairs, pained expressions on their faces until they're replaced by shocked ones when they look into the stairwell. Franklin's eyes lock with mine, and I know all he can see is hurt.

"This is your fault, you know that, right?" My words are filled with disdain as I get up.

"Reign," Sienna whispers with a breaking voice. I bring my hand up, ignoring her, then point my finger at Franklin.

"You destroyed her when you killed Declan in front of her eyes." I want him to snap. I want him to punch me, to replace the pain I'm feeling inside with actual pain in my body. But he just stares back at me with a straight face, looking like the authority he made himself in this city. His shoulders are squared, his arms hanging beside his coat covered body, as if he's bracing himself. As if he's willing to take whatever I'm throwing at him.

"Reign," Connor reprimands.

"It's your fault!" I shout, not giving a damn that everyone wants me to shut up. It's the truth. Franklin showed himself as being better than the rest. But he's just like them. Like all of us. He killed a guy and traumatized Emma with no regard for the consequences.

"It's your fault she's dead! She couldn't live another day because she couldn't get rid of that image in her head!" My voice is raging, my fists balled. There is this boiling anger inside of me that is dying to get out. To punch and trash everything and everyone around me. I want to bore my fist into my brother's cheek, but something holds me back.

"I hate you!" I spit instead, before I storm down the stairs. The world around me seems to collapse. I need air. I need to get out of here. I need to get away from my brother.

26

I left New York a different man, knowing the world around me had changed.

Specifically, Boston changed.

My hometown would never be the same again, for the simple reason the woman I loved with all my heart had me on top of her shitlist. I tried to lay low for a few days, finding the courage to go see her, but instead she found out I was back and came marching into the bar below Franklin's penthouse. As soon as I noticed her prance into the room with her black hair waving around her gorgeous yet scowling face, my heart stopped, taking in her beauty that only magnified over the previous twelve months. With an attitude she rarely gave me, she slipped into the booth next to me, giving my brothers a sweet *"hey, boys"* before she slapped me in front of the entire bar. It was fierce, it was burning, and it was deserved. I hurt her more than I could ever grasp, and I knew the sting on my cheek wasn't even comparable to what she felt when I broke her heart. As quickly as she came, she stood back up, but not before I grabbed her wrist, holding her still. Foolishly, I didn't see the second slap coming, but it made my head turn with a deafening crack.

"Don't you ever touch me again, Reign Wolfe. You're an asshole, and you'll be sorry you lost me for the rest of your life." She was livid, and fuck me, I knew she was right. Not a day has passed by when she didn't cross my mind, regretting how I handled that entire year.

But now she's here. With me. Dancing with a beaming smile on her face that I've missed something fierce. I catch her eyes glancing over at me, and I can't help the grin on my face as I give her a wink every now and then.

"You really gotta stop smiling." Killian gives me a taunting smirk, bringing his glass to his lips.

"I can't." It's true. In the last few years, I had to control my longing for her whenever I would run into her, feigning an indifference I never felt. Now that she's letting me show her how I feel without a scowl coming my way, I want to stare at her forever.

"Have you kissed her yet?"

"No." I glare with pursed lips. "Because my tool of a brother has fucking bad timing."

He chuckles. "Sorry about that."

"But I guarantee you my lips are on hers within the hour."

"Don't fuck it up, Reign." I twist my head toward him, just in time to catch the knowing look he's giving me.

"I won't. Not again." She can fight me all she wants, but I'm not going to give her up this time. Something tells me she wants me just as much as I want her, though. She feels the everlasting pull between us, one that hasn't died down over the years, even though I'm sure she hoped it would. It was easy to pretend it wasn't there when she would only see me every few months for a minute, but it's difficult when we are in the same room like we have been over the last weeks. With my luck, there is a big chance I will piss her off again, but this time, it's different. I will fight for her, stalk her for all I care, anything to make it impossible for her to ignore me.

My gaze moves back to the bar, watching the girls order their drinks, until it falls to the girl sitting on the other end of the bar. Her gaze is fixed on Killian with an intensity that makes me raise my eyebrows. Being a Wolfe comes with a lot of women falling to your knees and Killian has always been one to completely indulge in it, but with her black jeans and black t-shirt, this one seems different from his regular skimpy-dressed hook-ups.

"There is a girl staring at you from the bar."

He takes a sip from his drink, not even following my eyes. "I noticed."

I bring my brows to my hairline, wondering why he's still sitting here. "You gonna do anything about that?"

"Yeah, why not." A wolfish grin meets my gaze as he knocks down the rest of his glass. He gives me a mock salute, then saunters off.

"Wrap it up, man." I call behind his back. "You don't want to get any cooties."

"Shut up, you tool."

I chuckle, my gaze heading back to where Sienna and Kendall are still stationed at the bar. Relieved, I sip on my bourbon while I keep an eye on them.

I'm glad she's getting along with Kendall. I knew it must have been awkward for her to have dinner at the mansion the other day, knowing it would stir up a lot of memories. But the girls welcomed her with open arms, and I'm grateful they did. It helped her loosen up to me, and God knows I can use all the help I can get right now.

Curious, I fix my gaze on Killian talking to the girl at the bar. He's looking like the cocky motherfucker I'm used to, resting his elbow on the bar counter while his knees almost cage her in, giving her the attention most girls would die for. But she doesn't look like she's waiting for a place in his bed. If anything, she looks annoyed, sassy, like she has a bone to pick with him.

When his eyes land on mine, I move my fingers in a clawing motion, taunting him with a vicious meow. I can see a smile haunting his stoic gaze as he flips me off behind her back, then puts his focus back on his newest conquest.

Laughing by myself, I look at my glass, swirling the contents around before I bring it to my lips. My glass hangs mid-air when I don't see Sienna and Kendall at the bar anymore. My senses instantly go on high alert, and my eyes go back and forth to scan the area for the two dark-haired girls I'm looking for. When I can't find them after a minute or so, my pulse starts to race through my veins, and I snap my head to Killian.

I let out a growl when he's no longer sitting at the bar, cursing him on a mumble.

"For fuck's sake."

27

Sienna

K endall is looking at me in shock, her drink dangling in front of her face. Her lashes flutter in a slow but steady pace, showing the disturbance in her eyes.

"Whoa, that's heavy, girl. How did Reign take it?"

"He left for New York and broke up with me a few months after," I reply with a straight face before I fix my gaze on my glass. As much as I don't mind telling her, the words are always followed by a sense of embarrassment. Feeling the rejection all over again, like an old doll thrown in the trash.

"Right."

"He blames Franklin," I explain, as I take a sip of my drink. "Say it's his fault she was depressed because she was there when he killed Declan."

"But?" She gives me a questioning look.

"But he doesn't know the full story."

"But you do?"

"Don't you?"

She shakes her head. "He told me he killed Declan. I asked him if he deserved it. He said yes without hesitation. I know they are criminals and they do a lot of shit in the dark corners of this city that I don't want to know about. But after dating a sadistic sociopath, I learned real quick that the Wolfes are different. They might not be all good. But they have morals. Values. I have yet to hear about any of them killing without reason."

I know she's right. In the last few years, they've taken over the city by storm, and I could feel their presence everywhere. But they also do a lot of good things for the city. They help the communities. They help start-ups. I've heard about the gruesome things they've done to people, sure, but I've never heard of them hurting anyone innocent.

"It's true. There is more to that story, but Franklin won't let us tell him. Reign hurt him when he lashed out, and he's too stubborn to tell him the truth now. Say he wants him to figure it out himself."

"They are stubborn, aren't they?" Kendall lets out a cynical chuckle.

"For as long as I can remember."

"It's stupid, really. I can see how much the two of them love each other." A sadness washes over her face, and I give her a tight smile. I know what she's feeling, because I feel exactly the same. As soon as Franklin and Reign are in the same room, I'm confronted with a tension that fills the air, but it's heartbreaking to know it's completely unfounded. A cold war going on for too long based on nothing but misunderstandings and lack of communication.

"I know." I push out a breath, not wanting to ruin my night. "I'm going to the bathroom for a minute."

"I'll come with you." We both slide off our stools, our drinks in hand, as we make our way through the crowd. My skin still feels damp, moving past all these dancing people and fan my hand in front of my face to try and cool down when we get to the hallway that leads to the restrooms.

"Can you hold this for me?" I hold my drink out to her. "I'll be right out."

She takes my glass and I stride into the restroom while she stays in the hall. I welcome the fresh air of the air conditioning with a moan, glancing at myself in the mirror before I do my business in the bathroom stall. My sticky skin makes it hard to smooth my dress back on my body when I'm done, but after a minute, I step out to wash my hands. I glance up in the mirror, giving the blonde coming out of the stall next to mine a coy smile in acknowledgement while I feel the cold water on my wrists cool me down a little.

"You're beautiful," she offers as she finds my eyes in the mirror. She smiles, but it lacks sincerity, and I feel goosebumps trailing up my arms when her ominous eyes scan me. They are amber-colored and laced with something I can't decipher.

"Thank you." I smile politely.

"It's true what they say, isn't it? The prettiest are always the dumbest."

My smile slides off my face, and I twist my head to face her. "Excuse me?"

She crosses her arms in front of her body as she leans her hip against the sink, a devilish grin cracking her face. I narrow my eyes, mimicking her stance as I glance up and down her body. She's wearing a bordeaux dress that hugs all her curves but barely covers her ass, accompanied by a set of black stilettos that can only be described as hooker heels.

"You know, running with The Wolfes will get you bitten in the end?" My lashes flutter with irritation at her question, suddenly understanding her interest. Not willing to let some trashy girl talk crap to me, I press my tongue against my teeth, the corner of my mouth slightly raised.

"Only if you're not a part of the pack."

She laughs. It's joyless. Mirthless. Like the villain in a bad movie.

"And you're part of the pack?" she taunts. "Please."

"Who are you?"

She steps closer, ignoring my question.

"Let me give you a piece of advice. A warning." She pauses until she's completely in my personal space. I feel my muscles tense and my heart thudding in my chest, but I keep my chin high, refusing to give this bitch the satisfaction of my discomfort. "Walk away. He's going to rip your heart out. Like he did the first time."

It's hard to hide the surprise in my features when she brings up my past.

"I can take care of myself." I try to keep my face straight.

Within a split second, her bitchy glare flashes with hate and she grabs my neck, roughly pushing me against the wall behind me. Her eyes darken until they are almost black while I try to pull away her fingers that are tightening around my neck. Her grip grows stronger as I try to kick her off, but she pushes her entire body against mine, locking my hips in. A gasp leaves my lungs, the lack of oxygen slowly fogging my mind.

"Let me rephrase that," she growls against my lips. "Stay away from Reign Wolfe. Or you'll be the next on his list of dead girls."

She pulls me back before forcefully slamming my head against the wall, causing a sharp pain to run through it. When she lets go, I collapse to the floor, coughing for air while I grip my head in agony. My vision is blurry, looking at the patterned tile around me as I hear her heels trotting away, but the fire in me can't help but yell with a croaking voice. "You bitch!"

She doesn't reply, and when I'm left alone in the restroom, I rest my back against the wall, staring up at the ceiling while I rub the muscles on my neck.

What the fuck?

I close my eyes for a second, taking deep breaths to calm myself down, doing my best to soothe the pain away that's still running through my scalp, when I hear Reign's voice coming from the hall.

"Sienna? Are you in here?"

"I'm here!" I shout.

As if he can hear the distress in my voice, he storms in, followed by Kendall, a worried look written all over his handsome face. His eyes quickly flash with rage when he sees me sitting on the floor.

"What happened, baby?" His tone is demanding, and he squats down to my level, cupping my cheek.

"Are you okay?" I look up at Kendall, her cheeks flushed and eyes wide.

"Who did this?" Reign presses. I notice Killian enter the restroom from the corner of my eye, a worried and pissed frown creasing his face.

I swallow to get rid of the sourness of my throat, then grit out, "Some girl."

"What does she look like?" Killian grunts. I can see the anger seeping through his composed stance, his hands balled into fists.

"Where were you?" Reign gives him an incredulous look, not having realized before that his brother walked in, but Killian keeps his angry eyes locked with mine.

"What does she look like?" he repeats, a command in his tone this time.

"Long, platinum blonde hair. Red dress." Before I know it, Killian turns on his heels, pelting out of here with a thundercloud hanging above his head. If he finds her, she's screwed.

Happy he's here, I offer Reign a coy smile, wanting to simmer down his concern. He replies by pulling my head against his chest, resting his chin on my head.

"I got you. You're okay." We stay like that for a minute before I break loose, looking up into his green eyes. They bring me comfort, knowing he's there, and for a second, I don't know how I could've lived without them for so long.

"She knew about Emma," I tell him.

His face falls. "What?"

"Told me to stay away from you, or I'll be next on your list of dead girls." I watch him grind his teeth, his jaw tensing at the movement. "She wanted to hurt me, Reign."

He sighs deeply, his nostrils flaring, before he wraps me into his arms once more.

"No one is going to hurt you. I'll keep you safe." His lips connect with my hair as he rubs my arm to soothe me. "Come on, let's go home."

28

I put Sienna in the SUV waiting for us with one of our men sitting behind the wheel.

"Give me a minute, yeah?" Her reply is a coy smile, as she wraps my lammy coat tightly around her body. Her own coat is draped over her legs, and when she rests her head against the headrest, all I feel is relieved. The red skin on her neck makes me furious, knowing someone hurt my girl, and when I saw her sitting on the floor like that, it made me want to turn the entire club upside down to find whoever was responsible.

I turn around to Killian and Kendall, who are both waiting for me on the sidewalk.

"I want you to check the feed for me," I grunt. "Find out who that girl was."

He nods, but it's followed by a shrug and an expression that says it's going to be useless.

"Could've been any girl with a history with you, though. You're not a saint." He's not wrong, but it still pisses me off how he throws it in my face.

"I haven't slept with any girls in months, and the only remotely blonde I slept with is Callie Reyes," I argue with a growl as I rub my face.

"It can't be her?"

"Don't be fucking stupid, Killian. She's my friend. Besides, she's a Carrillo now. She doesn't have a thing for me."

He doesn't push it, because he knows the relationship I have with Callie, making his question ridiculous.

"So any blonde one-night stands you can remember?"

"None," I reply, honestly.

He slaps my shoulder, giving me a reassuring look. "We'll figure it out. Go home. I'll take Kendall home."

I watch her gorgeous face while I play with the strands of her silky hair. Her eyes are closed, the fatigue settling into her body. When we stop in front of the building of my apartment, Sienna looks up, taking in her surroundings before giving me a questioning look. I could've been selfless, asking her if she wanted to go to her home, but I'm not willing to let her go. After what happened tonight, I want her close, knowing she's safe in my arms, or at least between the walls of my apartment.

A silent conversation forms between us, while I ask her what she wants with just my eyes, and after what feels like forever, she replies by opening the door and exiting the car. Pushing out a relieved breath, I follow behind her and we make our way to my floor. She saunters in, quickly taking off her heels before walking barefoot to the floor-to-ceiling window, looking over the main channel below.

She's still wearing my jacket, her legs peeking from under her dress while the light of the moon illuminates her black hair.

She's never looked more beautiful.

I can't take my eyes off her as she revels in the view, my hands tucked into my jeans while I stand back. I can't even remember how many times I wished she could see the view, or how I wanted her to be prancing through my living room like she owned the place.

"It's breathtaking," she whispers, barely audible.

"*You* are breathtaking," I counter.

She turns around with an amused scowl. "I meant the view."

"I know." My legs move forward on their own accord, wanting to feel her close. "I like my view better."

I wrap my arms around her shoulders, pulling her back against my chest while my eyes roam over the many lights of the city. "I told you one day I'd be living here."

"You did,' she replies with pride in her voice. "You did good for yourself, Reign."

"I'm just part of the family business."

"You always talk about that like it doesn't mean anything. What would you wanna be doing if you could do anything else?"

It's a question I've asked myself many times, staring out of this very same window with a bourbon in my hand. Every single time I felt like something was missing, I tried to figure out what it was, but I always came back to the same answer; I don't know. I have no clue, but I know it has nothing to do with my brothers. As my level of empathy has a hard time coping with some of the things we do to stay on top, I'm not against it either. I'm proud of the name we made for ourselves. I'm proud of how far Franklin moved up the ladder.

"The same. It took me a while to get there, but I'm a Wolfe. I'm not as ruthless as my brothers, but I'm no saint either. Maybe once I'd like to believe I was able to stay on the right side of the law, but I can't. I'll always want to taunt the lines. Test the limits."

"Like your brothers," she states without any surprise or disappointment.

"Just like my brothers."

She twists in my arms, sliding her hands to the small of my back. Her honey brown eyes peer up at me in admiration, and it makes a pang go through my heart.

"You're more alike than you think, Reign."

My desire for her grows out of proportions when she keeps her gaze locked with mine with complete wonder, looking at me like I'm the best man she's ever met. Considering I broke her heart once, I know I'm not, yet she chooses to see the best in me. We will have a long way to go, but the way she's looking at me now tells me I still have a shot. That she is willing to look past the bad parts that are Reign Wolfe.

"I know." I smirk, licking my lips.

"Why are you looking at me like that?" she breathes, her voice sounding smaller with every word.

"Because I'm going to kiss you, and I'm really hoping you won't slap me for it like you did a few years ago." She chuckles. "It's not funny. I can still feel it burn if I close my eyes," I joke.

"You deserved it."

"I did."

Her mouth curls up in a taunting smile, and she shrugs. "Can't guarantee it won't happen again. You can be a real asshole, you know."

I shake my head at her silliness, knowing she's stalling the inevitable as I push a strand of her hair behind her ear.

"Sienna?"

"Yeah?"

"Shut up," I tell her. And before she can say anything else, my mouth crashes against hers, desperate to find out if she still tastes the same.

29

Sienna

When his lips connect with mine, it feels exactly how I remember. Affectionate. Sweet. Filled with desire that tingles all the way to my lower abdomen. But it's the demand that's new. His dominating grip as he fists my hair to pull my head back, making sure he gets better access to my mouth. It's the force he uses to press his tongue against mine, as if he's dying without my kisses. I moan into his mouth, completely giving in to him. All my senses come to life as if I've been in hibernation, ripping me from an endless sleep I've succumbed to since the day he left.

My hands move up his t-shirt, wanting to feel his skin against mine, and he takes a step back to rip it over his head while his craving gaze never leaves mine. I hold him, feeling the beating of my heart in every vein of my body as I let my dress drop down to the floor. Our longing is forming a thick curtain around us, pulling us together while we both hold still, staring at each other in awe.

I trace the fine lines on his stomach, leading to the happy trail into his jeans. He's bigger. Stronger. The chest of a boy, now completely replaced by that of a man. Half of his chest is completely covered in tattoos, going all the way to his arm and onto his hand. Not horizontal like you'd expect, but vertically. Like a perfect line, splitting his body in half. He looks like yin and yang, the epitome of his own words.

He's right. He's both. One half will always be the Wolfe, the criminal that's feared by the city. But the other half represents the boy I once fell in love with. The one who's empathetic, sweet, kind, funny. For years, I wished that boy would come back to me, but looking at him standing in front of me now, fixed at the black and white of his soul, it makes me realize he has always been there.

Slowly, my eyes move back up, all the way to his heaving chest until they reach his hunger-filled eyes. His gaze has darkened, as if he's the wolf that will rip me apart until my soul is his for the taking. Maybe it's the alcohol, maybe it's the leftover adrenaline rushing through my body, but all I know is that I want him.

When he blinks, our trance stops and I leap myself onto him, wrapping my legs around his waist, and he catches me with his hand on my ass. With bruising kisses, he takes me back to the kitchen while I slowly grind against the bulge in his jeans with my palms holding his mouth in place. With one hand, he unclasps my bra, right before my butt cheeks collide with the cold marble of the kitchen island, and he comes to stand between my legs. I feel his hands everywhere, touching every single inch of my skin.

"I've been thinking about this"—he presses a kiss to my collarbone—"every single day, since the day I left." He takes my nipple into his mouth, swirling his tongue around it as I moan against his touch. The desire between my legs rises as he palms my other breast, kneading and caressing while his mouth moves at a torturous pace. I throw my head back, enjoying his touch until I run a hand through his messy hair. With force, I fist it, pulling his head back so I can look him in the eye.

"Yeah? What else did you think about?" I purr with hooded eyes.

His lips part as his face breaks into a thrilling smile. "Since when are you so bossy?"

"You like it?" I hover my lips above his with sass.

"I love it." He cups the front of my neck, roughly pushing my entire body down while my legs are still hanging off the surface. "But I'm the one in control here, baby. I didn't wait all this time to not do exactly what I've been doing to you in my dreams every night."

I let out a whimper when I feel his lips connect with the lace of my panties, his breath caressing the sensitive skin underneath it.

"You want to know what else I've been thinking about?" He peels the lace off my hips, throwing it over his shoulder in a casual manner that has me smirking up at him. Without warning, he dives into my center, ravishing on my pussy like he hasn't eaten for days, making me cry out in relief. My lashes flutter shut, taking in every stroke, every brush of his tongue as he makes love to my center with his lips.

"Fucking hell," I scream, frantically squirming underneath his face. He holds me in place with his hands firmly on my hips, and all I can think about is how I'm seeing stars even though I'm looking up at a white ceiling. Like the time he made love to me under the night sky, taking my virginity with a wave of ecstasy.

"I've been thinking about this." I feel his tongue dip in, collecting every drop of my wetness. "The perfect taste of your sweet pussy against my lips." I moan as he flattens his tongue, dragging it all the way up to my clit. "How I wanted to feel your muscles tense under the tips of my fingers. And hearing you moan in agony and bliss, because you know I'm the only one who can make you feel like this." His mouth never misses a beat, my moans mixing with whimpers, and I can feel my orgasm building inside of me. "I'm the only one who can find every button. Making you come nice and slow, or make you explode as quick as a bomb going off. Whatever way I prefer."

He's right. I don't have words to argue, because there are none. After all the men that have come after him, he's the only one who can make me feel this good. The only one who can stir up emotions I don't feel with anyone else, and spark nerves alive that I didn't know existed.

"But do you wanna know what I've been thinking the most," he says as he sucks my clit, making me jerk forward at the sensation moving through my sensitive flesh. My eyes find his, a smirk on his now glistening lips, and I give him a questioning look.

"This." He grabs my ankles, yanking me toward him until my ass is hanging off the edge, and he holds me up with his hands. I don't know when he found time to take off his jeans and boxers while he worked me into a frenzy, but I tilt my head to the ceiling when his lips pepper my neck with kisses, and I feel him press his tip inside of me. I cry out when I feel him stretch me wide while I hold on to his neck, connecting my forehead with his shoulder. When he's completely buried inside of me, he lets out a feral growl.

"Shit, I forgot a condom," he mutters against my ear when he slowly starts to thrust inside of me. "Do you want me to stop?"

My common sense is telling me yes. But my body is yelling at me to not even think about letting him slip out of me. Feeling his skin against mine as we become one feels too good to let go of for even a moment.

Unable to fully tap into my functioning brain, I shake my head. "Don't stop," I huff with a raspy voice. "Don't you dare stop."

Settling with that answer, he snickers, then rams his cock inside of me with all he's got, his thrusts claiming me all over again.

"Fuck, you're so sexy." He runs his tongue along my neck, fisting my hair like it's a rein; his way of keeping me completely in place. It burns my scalp, the kind that has you aching for more, as he plows his dick in and out of my body. The feeling of him relaxes me in a way only he can provide as we completely succumb to this. To us.

At this moment, I have no worries. I have no fears. I have no hesitation. The only thing I'm wondering is how am I ever going to come back from this? How am I going to keep living my life without him making love to me every night?

I don't want to.

My mind rushes back to the first night he made love to me under the stars, the memory creating an ache that's not only sensible in my heart, but something that feels palpable in the air. I knew then and there I was never going to feel as much for any man in my life, like I did Reign. I've always known he was my first love, but deep down I also knew he was my last, as much as I tried to push it to the side. It was undeniable now that he was back inside of me in every way and form. With every thrust, he claws himself back into my heart, and every time he crashes against my walls, he reminds me of the addiction I once had for him. It storms through me, guaranteed to make me completely hooked before the night is over.

"Reign, I'm close." Controlling my release, he grabs the back of my neck, pressing his forehead against mine with a tight grip. His eyes stare into mine with a ferocious gaze while our breaths mix in a toxic blend.

"I got you, baby. Give me your fingers." He takes my hand, pushing two fingers into his mouth, and he wets them with his tongue until they're dripping with his saliva. "Now, touch yourself." It's a command, an order. One I happily fulfill. I close my eyes for a brief moment when my fingers connect with my clit, and it amazes me how easily I reach that last nudge as he never changes his pace. I cry out, the desperation audible, as my legs start to shake, pushing me over the edge I've been longing for since that first day at the pack. A sense of euphoria comes over me, raising the hairs on my body as the most delicious shiver runs through my every muscle, until finally, I bring my hand up to cup his cheek while he chases his own release. Enjoying the aftershocks of my orgasm, I hold on to him for dear life as he moves his hips in a frantic pace before he lets out a feral yelp that makes my eyes glint in victory. Knowing his cum is sitting inside of me brings out a raw feeling of possessiveness that surprises me as much as it doesn't.

"Let me get one thing straight," he pants against my lips when his body stills. With our foreheads still fused, I conjure a flirtatious smile on my lips in anticipation.

"I don't care if you want to say it back. Or how much you're going to pretend I'm wrong. I've said it before, and I'll say it again. *You are mine, Sienna.*" His lips connect with mine in a bruising kiss before he pulls back. "You are mine, and there is not a damn thing you can do about it. Never have, and never will be, without me again. Better wrap your pretty little head around that, baby."

I roll my lips, trying to hide my wolfish grin. There is a very sober, mindful voice in my head that's telling him to *fuck off; I'm not his, nor anyone else's.* But there is another voice with a megaphone, blasting in my ear; *who the fuck are you kidding?* Maybe it's the alcohol. Maybe it's my high on his dick. Who knows? Who cares?

My tongue darts out, and I run it along his lower lip, definitely not done with him just yet.

"I'm yours, Reign."

30

REIGN

F or the last eight hours, I've felt lighter than I have in years, like something completed me when her body melted against mine, in my arms where she belongs. The few times my consciousness returned, I breathed in her scent and drifted back to a content sleep while I tugged her back against my chest. I've missed her since we broke up, but I didn't realize how much until she landed in my bed last night while I showered her slender neck with scorching kisses. But like any other time, I feel like life is starting to look up, it passes quicker than I want it to.

I feel her get out of the bed, then hear her grabbing her scattered clothes from the floor, unaware that I'm awake. There is a small fraction somewhere in my body that has hopes she's going to make breakfast, get some coffee, whatever. But when I look through the crack of my eye, I watch her attempt to tiptoe out of here with her boots in hand and her clothes tucked under her arm.

"Sneaking out?"

She freezes, her messy black hair falling in front of her face, before she twists her body with guilt washing her pretty features. A sharp pain hits me in the chest, because I know the answer before it leaves her mouth.

"Reign." She moves her attention to the floor, as if she can't look at me, while her shoulders grow slack.

I sit up, leaning on my elbow with the sheets covering the rest of my naked body. I do my best to keep a straight face, but inside my blood is starting to boil.

"Sienna." There is an edge to my tone, because even though my heart continues to beat for her, she's starting to piss me off more than usual.

"Last night was a—"

"If you're gonna say *mistake*, I swear I'm going to lose my shit."

"Well, it was," she huffs. Her arms fall to her sides in defeat, her hands still holding on to her stuff in a tight grip.

I get out of bed with flaring nostrils, taking the three big strides toward her.

"Why?" I bark, not able to hide my rage. I'm standing in front of her, glaring, my hands at my sides, wearing nothing but my birthday suit. But I don't care. She's not leaving like this.

She does her best to not back down and keep our eyes locked, but the trembling of her lip tells me she's having a hard time facing me.

"Because—" Her voice breaks, hurting me on the inside, but I keep my stern look. "We've already been down this road. It didn't work out."

"We didn't work out because we didn't *work*, Sienna."

"Something wasn't working." There is judgment on her face. "Otherwise, you would've never left."

I press my lips together, breathing in through my nose.

"Tell me, Reign. Tell me what happened." At that, my breath gets caught in my throat and I lock up. She's ready to know, after me basically begging for her to listen to me for weeks. She's giving me the opportunity to explain everything.

I search her face, swallowing harshly, then my eyes drift down her body as my mind swirls. She's wearing nothing more than her panties and bra, her skin glowing from our night together; she's so gorgeous... and *mine*. When my gaze lifts back up to her face, her eyes are blazing at me with fire. A fire that I love, and I know telling her my past will completely snuff that out. I'm scared it will haunt her head like it does mine. The last thing I want is to cause her any more pain.

If I tell her the truth, I could keep her, but at what expense? Will she lie awake at night with darkness hovering over her like I still do sometimes?

But if I don't tell her now, don't give her all of me, she will walk away. I know she will. And I don't think I can continue to live without her by my side.

"See!" she shouts, pulling me right out of my downward spiral. "You expect me to just pick up where we left off, but you can't even tell me what happened! After all these years, you still won't tell me! Don't you see, Reign? This is going to always stand between us if you won't open up to me!"

I rub my hands over my face, knowing she's right. But the tight feeling in my chest makes it hard to tell her what she wants to know. "Sienna."

"You know what, never mind. It doesn't matter." She raises her chin in the air, turning it away from me. "What we have is in the past."

I clench my jaw together, then reach out and grab her face, forcing her to look at me.

"It doesn't have to be."

There is a sadness in her eyes, and it's killing me because I know I put it there. I hurt her, even though it was never my intention. But that's the thing, ain't it? We humans are selfish creatures. I hurt her years ago because it was me or her. And at that time. At that moment? I couldn't handle any more pain. I just needed to live. To feel alive and in control.

"But I *want* it to be."

My hand falls from her soft skin when she turns away from me, her feet carrying her toward the door. Wearing just her underwear, she drops her clothes on my kitchen counter, putting her black hair up in a ponytail. Her lack of clothes makes me want to yank her back into my bed and show her at least a handful of reasons why we still fit like a damn jigsaw puzzle, but I know it won't last long. Sienna's fire is not tamed with kisses. If you want her to stop burning you, you have to earn it.

"Hold up. Where are you going?" I ask. Her clothes are back on, and she pushes a foot into her boot.

"Home, Reign." There is disdain in her voice that's cutting through my heart like she's holding a machete. "Last night, I was stupid to think we could start over."

"You can't go home. Someone threatened you yesterday," I remind her, indignant.

"So?" She looks up, putting on her other boots. "What? You wanna lock me up in your room for safety reasons like Connor did with Lily? Nice try, Reign."

Not a bad idea.

"No, but you need protection." I run a hand through my hair, still standing in the doorway of my bedroom. My rage is replaced by desperation, feeling her slip out of my hands again. Literally.

"I didn't have protection before. I don't need it now." There is a sass in her voice that I've always appreciated, but it sure as fuck is timed badly right now. I glance at my bedroom door, contemplating if I should grab some sweatpants or just follow her tracks, butt naked.

She plucks her jacket from the couch, heading to the front door like her pants are on fire.

"Sienna, don't," I plead, moving right behind her. "Just give me a minute to call someone. It doesn't have to be me. Just someone who can protect you."

"I'll see you at the Pack, Reign," she sing-songs, mocking my worry. Growling, I stomp forward, having every intention of keeping her here until I call Killian to get her home. I know that girl who threatened her was probably just a lowlife skank looking for someone to bitch at, but I don't want to take any chances.

"Sienna, stop!" The door flies open at the same time a delivery guy stops in front of the entrance and she flies past him.

"Sienna!" I shout, with a glare over his shoulder. He follows my gaze with widened eyes before turning to me with a beaming smile.

"She seems pissed."

I reply with a glare before his gaze moves down, looking at my naked crotch. When he realizes the awkwardness of the situation, he plasters on a tight smile.

"Package for Reign?" He holds up the big box.

Ignoring him, I watch Sienna get on the elevator, her eyes avoiding mine at all costs until the doors close and I yank the pen out of his hand.

I sign my signature before I pull the box out of his grip, slamming the door behind me, followed by a muffled, "Good day to you too, asshole."

Shaking my head, I walk back to my room and grab my phone to call Killian while I wait with grinding teeth for him to pick up.

"For fuck's sake, Reign. What did you do now?" He sounds bored and tired, as if he still has his eyes closed, lying in bed with his latest conquest.

"I didn't fucking do anything! She just tried to sneak out on me."

"You must have done something."

"I gave her three orgasms in an hour. Does that count?" I huff like a smartass while putting on my sweatpants.

"Well, maybe that did scare her away. Thinks it's too much work to keep up with your stamina." His grin is audible in his voice, and even though I appreciate my brother's approach to make me laugh, it's not doing shit for me.

"Funny, Kill," I scold as I walk back to the living room.

"Come on, Reign. You must have said something?"

"I swear, I didn't do shit. We had sex. It was great. No, scratch that, it was mind-blowing, and if she tells you otherwise, she's fucking lying." I grab a knife out of the kitchen drawer and start to open up the box. "We fell asleep fucking spooning and this morning she tried to sneak out, thinking I was still asleep."

"That's fucked up."

"Tell me about it."

"She's just scared, you know that, right?"

"Yeah, but I'm really trying here, Killian."

I hear him sigh through the phone. "I know you are. Where is she now?"

"Stormed out." I stay quiet, pushing the knife through the duct tape to open the box. "Can you just do me a favor and check if she gets home okay?"

"Yeah, sure." He clears his throat while I push the lid of the box to the side. "You picked up some pussy last night?"

"Something like that," I hear him grunt when the overwhelming smell of rotting flesh attacks my nose. I gag, squinting my eyes at the sight in front of me. The inside of the box is covered with foil to keep the smell out, while in the box lies a cut off swan's head. The blood is smudged over the dozens of origami folded swans, and my head starts to spin before I gag again.

"Reign? What are you doing?" Unable to say anything at the gruesome contents in front of me, I press my hand in front of my mouth. Then notice the postcard inside of it. Doing my best to not breathe in the vile smell, I pull it out with the tips of my fingers to check what's on it.

My heart stops when I recognize the Seekonk River Bridge in Providence. Aubrey's face flashes in front of my eyes, and I suck in a breath when I turn the card around.

"Reign? Are you still there?" my brother bellows in my ear.

Sometimes those who fly solo have the strongest wings.

"Reign?" Killian yells in my ear this time.

"Yeah," I reply with a vacant voice.

"What's going on?"

"We got a problem," I tell him, trying to breathe away the nauseous feeling lurking in the back of my throat.

"Why?"

"I got another package."

"This is getting out of hand." Franklin scowls at me.

He's sitting behind his desk, slouching a little in his chair with that don't-give-a-fuck look in his eyes. It's a talent how he can appear completely calm and composed when I know there is worry surging through him. I can detect the urgency in his voice. A year ago, he'd probably tell us to keep an eye out and would go door to door to find whoever was harassing us. He would make it his mission, but he wouldn't be worried. He's an authority in his own right and even though we don't really get along, I still respect him more than anything. But now, as our family is growing, there is more to lose, more things to take into consideration, and I know it adds to his stress. I know because it's keeping me up at night to consider Colin or the girls being at risk.

Sienna.

Every time I feel like I'm making progress with her, she freaks out and shuts the door in my face. I don't blame her, but it does make my heart ache, turning me into a brooding son of a bitch. I hurt her, and I understand why she's acting this way, but to see her close off her feelings with a deadbolt, knowing I caused it... it fucks with my mind. Makes me regret every decision I ever made, even though I didn't have a choice at the time.

"How can we not find anything about this–this girl?" Franklin mutters. "Is it a girl?"

"It has to be, right? Disgusting romantic gestures?" I shrug. I've been breaking my head over who it can be. I even checked Providence High, went through the yearbooks to figure out if there was some girl I might have hurt in some kind of way. But I came up blank. I can't remember making any enemies or breaking any heart other than Sienna's. But the swan references tell me it has to be someone who knew both me and Aubrey.

"Unless he broke a guy's heart once." Connor offers with a chuckle. He's standing in front of the window, his arms crossed in front of his body, with his back leaning against the windowsill. He's giving me a smug grin, trying to piss me off, and I pull a face in response.

"Pretty sure there is no one with a bromance in their head."

"I wouldn't be so sure. You're not called Prince Charming for no reason," he counters.

"Bite me, Con."

"You got anything on the delivery guy?" I twist my head toward Killian when his voice sounds in my ear, then shake my head.

"Haven't found him. All I know is I have him walking in Seaport with a little girl. I can trail them all the way to Harbor Street and then they disappear. I'm not even sure it's a guy, though. Could've been a girl in disguise. He wasn't a fat ass like Connor." I nudge my chin toward my brother, and he flips me off.

"Maybe we should check underground," Killian says, taking a sip of his drink. "See if there are blueprints of the area that show any cellars or tunnels."

"Good idea," Franklin agrees. "Connor, arrange that. I want those prints on my desk first thing in the morning. We need to comb out the entire area as soon as possible."

"There is an event this weekend at the ICA. The cops are not going to let us roam the area without getting something in return." Killian gives Franklin a knowing look.

"We pay those tools more than enough."

"We could push it over the weekend?" Killian suggests.

"No. Reign, find some dirt on the officers on duty this weekend. I don't want to wait five more days before we can find out what's underground in the area."

I sigh, not in the mood to argue. "Fine."

"Kill," Franklin continues, "I want you to do another round. See if you can find anyone who wants to talk. Dangle money, dangle your knife, I don't care. I want something."

Killian replies with a nod, downing the rest of his drink.

"In the meantime, I want more security for the girls and Colin. I want three men with them at all times. Reign, what about Sienna?" I look up when Franklin puts his focus back on me, rolling my eyes. I don't really feel like talking about my ex-girlfriend, soon-to-be-girlfriend, or whatever the fuck our Facebook status could be.

"What about her?"

"It would be safer if she stayed at the mansion for a while. Stay under our protection until we find out who's after us."

I huff. "Pff, yeah, doubt she'll go for that."

I'll be lucky if she answers my damn phone calls, so there is no way in hell she's going to stay with me for the foreseeable future. She's a stubborn little thing, and as much as I love her for it, it's fucking inconvenient at times like this. As much as I want to drag her to the mansion and lock her up like Connor once did with Lily, I know she will only grow more furious, and Sienna Brennan on fire is lethal. My memory is still very clear about that.

"Did you screw it up again?" Franklin cocks a brow, giving me a reprimanding look.

"I didn't do shit." Not this time. I thought we were working things out. That we were making progress. "We had sex. She freaked. We fought. She left."

"Story of your life." Connor grins.

"Can't you go piss someone else off, Connor?"

"I can," he replies like the asshole that he is. "But I don't want to."

"Should we send her protection?" Franklin asks, ignoring Connor, who is trying to be funny. We all know I'm the funny one. When I'm not pissed about my girlfriend walking out on me.

"She'll freak out if you do that."

Killian clears his throat, sending me a serious look.

"But we have to, Reign. Remember that girl who assaulted her. If it isn't for this stalker we're looking for, we still need to have someone keep an eye on her for the sole fact that she's being associated with us again. If the city thinks she's one of us, she'll have a target on her back."

I know he's right. It's something that has been lurking in the back of my mind since she sneaked out of my bed. Making use of my skills, I've been tracking her phone, keeping an eye on her. But I can't do shit if someone tries to hurt her and I'm on the other side of Southie.

"Yeah," I concede, rubbing a hand over my face. "Just make sure she doesn't know."

"Alright. We'll send some men to her to make sure nothing happens to her." The comforting look Franklin gives me doesn't go unnoticed, and I swallow to push away the lump that's forming in the back of my throat while Killian and Connor get up to walk out the door.

I hold my Franklin's gaze for a few more seconds, not sure what to say before getting up and following the rest of my brothers.

"Reign." I turn around right before I walk out the door, looking at my oldest brother. There is sympathy in his gaze and even though it would piss me off in the last few years,

I just don't have the energy to fight him anymore. To make him pay for what he did. Now that Sienna has pranced back into my life, it all seems stupid. A waste of time that makes me realize how important my family is.

"Yeah?"

"Have you talked to her?"

"She won't answer my calls." I pause, letting out a heavy exhale. "Or my texts."

"She loves you." It's a statement. Not a question. Not a suggestion. Not an *I think*. He says it like it's a fact, and my brother doesn't say shit like that if he isn't absolutely sure.

"I'm not so sure about that," I argue.

"I am. She'll come around."

31

Sienna

I walk past the Old South Meeting House on Washington Street, when my phone rings in the pocket of my beige wool coat. It's getting colder every day, the winter really starting to kick in, making it impossible to get out of the house without a proper jacket. I reach into my pocket and let out an aggravated sigh as I look at the caller ID.

"Killian," I answer with a scowl as I keep walking.

"What are you doing, *Sienna*?" There is no judgment in his voice, but I know why he's calling, and it instantly fires my irritation.

"What do you mean, *Killian*?" I mock, never missing a beat.

I hear him sigh, and in my head, I can see him rolling his eyes. "Why are you ignoring him?"

"Because—" I start, coming up blank. Why am I ignoring him? Because he won't open up to me? Because I'm scared I can never push away the darkness in his head and he'll leave me all over again? Because I love him, but I'm scared I will never be enough? That he will never love me enough?

"You don't even know," he finally says, a grin audible in his voice. I hold still as my head drops, closing my eyes while I try to ignore the shiver running over my back. Tears are pricking in my eyes, and I press my fingers to them to prevent any from falling while I take a deep breath.

"I'm scared, Killian." Try terrified. He's the only person who has the ability to break me, and I don't think I've fully recovered from the first time. "You know how much he hurt me."

"I do. But I don't think I've seen you as happy as you were with him the other night."

"I've seen you like twice a year in the last five years."

"You've seen *me* twice." He pauses. "Doesn't mean I didn't see you."

I snap my head back up. "Have you been keeping tabs on me?"

"Maybe." I feel the corner of my mouth rising a little. I could scold him for it, telling him he has no right to check up on me like that, but part of me likes knowing there is a Wolfe always keeping an eye on me. Even if it's not the one who holds my heart in his hands, I still appreciate the friendship I have with one of his brothers.

"I was drunk," I mumble in defense, and it's pathetic. I put my feet back in motion, when I notice Lucas standing in front of the restaurant. Sucking in a deep breath, I attempt to plaster a beaming smile on my face.

"Nice try."

"I don't know, okay?" I hiss as I close the distance between my date and me. *He's a distraction* is what I told myself when he asked me to dinner this morning. Nothing more than dinner to keep myself from eating a pint of chocolate chip ice cream while I cry my eyes out on the couch. After my night with Reign, it's clear there is no room for any other man right now, but I can still have fun, right? I'm allowed to distract myself with dinner.

"He's not going anywhere," Killian says at the same time Lucas pulls me into a hug.

"Hey, beautiful." His voice is low and manly, and I know it will not go unnoticed on the other end of the line.

"Where are you?" Killian sounds pissed, like the big brother I never had.

"I have a date," I tell him while I smile up at Lucas in greeting. It feels wrong. Like I'm doing something I shouldn't be.

"For fuck's sake. You're just as full of shit as he is," Killian mutters before his voice grows more demanding. "Don't, Sienna."

It's one word, but it's laced with reasons why I should just turn around, go home and take my chance with that pint of chocolate chip ice cream. The worst part is I know he's right. It's my defiance that's still putting up a fight. She's raging inside of me like a fucking teenager, with a popped hip and arms crossed in front of her chest. She's putting all kinds of crazy shit in my head, like, why isn't Reign here? Why isn't he fighting for you? He never chased you to explain, did he? If he cared, he would just tell you the truth, wouldn't he?

"Why do you care so much?"

"Because," he trails off as if he has trouble voicing whatever he's about to tell me, "the man has been through hell. Literally. His time in foster care was nothing like the stories I told in high school showing off." He pauses and I motion to Lucas that I'll be right in before I watch him walk inside. "He resided with the devil and it broke him. I tried to fix him. To help him. He has always been my best friend, and I was mad at him for staying in New York. I can't remember all the ugly shit I called him when he broke up with you."

I try to swallow away the lump that's now sitting in the back of my throat.

"Then what happened?"

"I let it go," he says with simplicity, easily, and it makes me wonder why it's so hard for me to do the same.

"How did you do that?" I whisper.

"I realized it wasn't about me. It wasn't about you. It was never about *us*, Sienna. It has always been about him."

I feel like a light bulb just got turned on in my head and I don't know what to do. Part of me wants to turn around and run toward the man I love right now, telling him I understand. But that sassy little teenager tells me I will never completely understand if he won't share it all. They are both right, and I'm completely torn.

"I don't know what to say."

"I swear if you ever tell Reign I told you, I will make your life a living hell." His words are followed by a growl, and I can't help chuckling while I suck in another lungful of air to calm my senses.

"I won't." I look at Lucas waving at me from inside of the restaurant. "I have to go."

"Just think about it, Sienna."

32

REIGN

"**W**hat's doing?" I leave my whiskey hanging in the air when my brother takes the stool next to me, and I press my tongue against my teeth in annoyance.

"Not much," I reply, following it up by taking a sip of my drink. I swirl the rest of the gold liquid around my glass while enjoying the scorch as it floods through my body. The only kind of burn I can enjoy right now.

"Not much?" Killian runs a hand through his messy hair, then gestures to the bartender for a whiskey as he points at my glass. "Just sulking like a baby over a meal of whiskey?"

I shrug. "If it works." To be honest, it doesn't work. I've been walking around with a thundercloud above my head for the last two days, and the whiskey just seems to raise my tolerance to deal with people. In no way does it lessen the ache I feel in my chest.

"How did you find me anyway?" I glance at Killian.

"Pff, you might be the hacker, but I still have some skills of my own."

"You tracked my phone."

He nods with a smug grin, picking up his drink. "Yeah, pretty much. So, do you have any clue who's after you?"

I shake my head. "It's killing me. I've never been close with any of the other girls. I don't even remember their names. They just were there until they weren't."

"What about their mother?"

"The woman was a druggie. Something tells me she isn't sly enough to pull this shit off."

Killian rubs the back of his neck, holding my gaze for a few seconds with a pinched expression.

"Are we sure Aubrey is dead?"

I've been thinking the same thing, but I checked every database I could find. The nights I haven't been working at the bar, I've been up all night trying to find out any new information about Aubrey, Nova, or the Bradys in general. I came up empty.

"There are no other records. If they were there, I would've found them. There is just the coroner's report. There was a body wearing her rings and the dental records showed it was her. It *has* to be her."

"We have to be missing something."

"I know," I grunt, frustrated. My eyes trail off, scanning the room as I try to sort my mind. It's eating me up inside that I can't figure out who's messing with me, and having Sienna in the back of my mind is not helping with that. I take another sip of my drink, eager to numb myself, until my gaze stops on a girl sitting on the other side of the bar. She looks young, though her fiery eyes draw me in. Her ivory skin stands out against her chocolate brown hair and leather jacket, and even though she's at least ten yards away, I can see the freckles that are spread over her cheeks. Narrowing my eyes, I wonder why she looks familiar until finally it hits me, and I slap my brother's shoulder with the back of my hand.

"Hey, isn't that the girl from the other night at the club?"

Killian's head twists to follow my gaze, and I hear him exhale in irritation, though he keeps his features drawn in a blank expression.

"It is." He rears his head back, bringing his glass to his lips. "She's been following me around."

"And you've been letting her?" I ask, curious. Killian isn't the tolerant one. His temper doesn't match Connor's, but mess with him and he will make your life a living hell.

"I'm curious how long she's going to keep it up."

"What does she want?"

"She wants to avenge her family. Begged me to train her."

"She had the balls to ask Killian Wolfe for help?"

"I found her at Sullivan's doorstep last week. She was ready to start a kamikaze, stalking in there with a lady gun."

"No-suh!" I chuckle in awe.

"Ya-huh. Stopped her and sent her off before she could do anything stupid. Like get killed."

"She must be really pissed. You know what happened to her family?" I watch how he glances at her, this time turning his body and waiting until she catches his eyes.

"Didn't ask," he replies. She brings her gaze up and there is a slight startle in her stance when her eyes lock with Killian's before she gives him a look of defiance.

"You know how old she is? She looks young."

"Definitely not twenty-one." She boldly throws the contents of her glass down her throat with a taunting glare, then slams the glass on the bar while she never drops her gaze. I can feel the tension rise between the two of them as she slips off the stool, flips him off, and saunters out of the bar like she doesn't have a care in the world. When she's through the door, Killian chuckles, moving his eyes to his glass, but not soon enough to hide the appreciation for her attitude.

"Damn," I bellow in admiration, "she is like you. But with boobs."

He quirks up his brows in agreement.

"Find out a name," I tell him. "I'll run a background check on her."

"Cool. Did you talk to Sienna?"

I drag my hand over my face before running it through my hair. "No."

He shakes his head.

"Why don't you just tell her, man? You've been waiting for the chance, so just do it." The tone of his voice is painful, and I know he means well.

"Because it's dark, Kill. You know how dark. I still have nightmares. You had nightmares after I told you what happened. Don't need to taint her brain with that shit."

"I didn't." He pulls a face, disagreeing with my comment, and I shoot him an incredulous look.

"Fine, I did," he concedes with a whisper. "We agreed to not share that with the world."

Rolling my eyes, I continue holding my glass in front of my face. "I can't do that to her. I'm the only one who should carry that burden."

"Maybe if you shared it with some more people, it wouldn't feel like such a burden anymore."

My glass lands on the wooden bar with a loud thud.

"You really need to stop with the words of wisdom. You're starting to scare me. You're the silent, cunning one. Stay in your lane, asshole."

"Whatever, tool." He waves my words away. "All I'm saying is, don't you think that maybe, just maybe, you would feel better if you didn't carry that shit around like a secret suitcase all the time? You're like Harry Potter going through that brick wall. Except you're too stupid to get through it."

"Nice one." I give him my fist, and he taps it while I nod in respect. "Didn't make any sense, but still kinda funny."

"Thanks," he mumbles with a smug smile before my features turn serious again.

"I've killed people, Killian."

"So what?" he screeches. "We *all* have. Hell, I'm pretty confident Con and I have a wicked long list that doesn't even come close to the handful of people you've killed," he mocks. "You killed people in the heat of the fire. You don't kill for sport."

"I killed one that wasn't." Instantly, my mind goes back to the last night I ever set foot in Providence. If I close my eyes, I can still bring myself back to that living room. Remembering every sound, every smell, and every feeling that went through my body.

"And that son of a bitch deserved it," Killian huffs, a little pissed this time. "You know, sometimes I wish I pulled that trigger."

"What? Why?"

His jaw ticks as he keeps our eyes locked with agony apparent in his.

"Because this has been weighing on you since we walked out of that house."

Sometimes I forget my brothers seem to possess a gene I don't have. How they can kill without looking back, and not lose a night of sleep over it. Sometimes I wish I was more ruthless.

"How do you do it? Kill without remorse?"

He turns his body toward me, his elbow leaning on the bar as he rests his head in his hand with a scowl.

"I don't. I just don't let it drag me down."

"What do I need to do, Killian?"

"Put on your big boy pants and get your girl back. For good, this time."

I can't deny that. This whole stalker shit is weighing on me, but not as much as Sienna's disappointed gaze that's embedded in my vision.

"It's going to be ugly," I warn him.

He chuckles with a look that makes my brows knit together. "Oh, you don't even know how much."

"What do you mean?"

"She's on a date."

My heart drops, and my rage goes from ten to a hundred in a split second. The thought of Sienna with another man doesn't make my stomach clench or all that sappy shit. Nah, there is just a voice in my head saying *hell no*.

She's mine.

"She's on a date?" I parrot back through gritted teeth.

"Yep."

"Right now?"

"Ya-huh."

"Motherfucker," I huff.

I drink the last of my whiskey to get up, ready to find her as we speak. I can hack into every single system in the city. It will take me five minutes to find out where she is and which tool she's with. Getting off the stool, I push my empty glass forward, not even bothering to say goodbye to my brother as I stomp off.

"Where are you going?"

"To get my fucking girl back."

On a date. Is she fucking crazy? She can ignore me all she wants, but the second her lips touched mine the other night, we both knew it sealed the deal. I'm giving her space, but let's not pretend it's anything more than that. Sienna Brennan is mine. And there is no chance in hell she's getting away from me. I'll carry her over my shoulder if I have to.

"Reign?"

"What?" I bark, turning around to face him. I feel like steam is coming from my ears and I glare at the piece of paper he's holding out in front of me.

"What's that?" I curiously stroll back, ripping it out of his hand and glancing at it, finding an address inside.

When I look up, his cocky grin splits his entire face as he downs his drink and gets off to follow me. "Figured I'd save you some time."

I flash him all my teeth. "You've been sitting on this for the last ten minutes?"

He nods, stalking past me, and I trail behind him.

"Asshole."

When our feet move over the threshold and onto the pavement, a rank gust of brisk air hits me in the face, cooling down my whiskey-flushed cheeks.

"Okay, so how do you wanna do this?" When I turn around, Killian is waiting in anticipation on the sidewalk while my feet are already rushing off.

"You're coming with?" I frown, holding still.

"What?" He chortles. "You think I'm going to let you have all the fun? Besides, you think you can just storm in with a scowl on your face. You need a little more than that. Pull out that romantic shit you're so good at."

"You're talking rose petals and a trail of candles?" I deadpan. As much as I'm willing to do anything for her, I don't have time for that shit when she's on a date with another man right now.

"No, *tool*. I'm talking about this." He throws a green box at me, and I hook my fingers around it, pressing it against my chest.

My heart starts to beat faster, and the tendons in my neck grow tight. I haven't seen this in years. Naive as it might seem, I always assumed she kept it, or maybe that's what I wanted to believe. My lashes lower as I try to swallow the tightness in my throat, then search my brother's eyes.

"She gave it to me after you broke up with her," he explains. "Told me to give it back to you." There is sympathy behind his eyes that gives me the encouragement to nod, completely accepting that I can't change the past. All I can do is fix the present and make things better for the future.

Killian strides forward, slamming me on the chest as he walks by.

"Come on, jackass. Let's get your girl back."

33

Sienna

L ucas is handsome. He's half Italian like I am, which is noticeable by his thick black hair and olive skin tone. The scruff covering his sharp jaw would normally turn me on, making me think about how I'd run my fingers through it while I kiss him.

But not tonight.

There is only one man in my head, and I catch myself looking at Lucas's moving lips but not hearing a word he's saying because Reign keeps flashing in front of my eyes. It's turning my already gloomy mood more sour with every passing minute, and I'm seriously wondering if I should fake an emergency and go home.

Killian's voice keeps lingering in the back of my head. *It was never about us, Sienna.*

Deep down, I feel this to be true. I know this. But I'm conflicted. I want to give Reign a chance so badly. For him. For me. For *us*. If we want to move forward, we need to throw all our cards on the table. I If he can't trust me with his past, how can I trust him with my future?

With my lips glued together, I give Lucas a tight smile, leaning against the back of the booth, doing my best to keep my attention on whatever he's saying. I made it past the appetizer, but sticking around for the main course seems like an awfully long time right now.

"You want another glass of wine?" His hand lands on my knee, and I awkwardly glance down, wanting to slap it from my leg.

I open my mouth to politely decline, when I feel the cushion of the booth drop down as someone sits next to me.

"Hey, baby." The sound of Reign's voice rumbles through me, and I twist my head right in time to feel him slide closer to my body. Our knees touch, and he places a possessive arm over the back of the booth behind my neck while I feel Lucas's hand quickly slipping from my leg. The fresh smell of his cologne immediately enters my nose, and I breathe him in.

"Reign," I croak out. "Killian told you." As if on cue, Killian walks past the table to the other side of the booth, resting his elbow at the corner while his mouth twists into a cocky grin.

"Hey, Sienna."

"I hate you," I glare with narrowed eyes, making him shrug in reply.

"What the hell is going on?" Lucas bellows.

"Kinda expected, since it's my brother, right?" Reign pitches in with a smirk. I feel him boldly take a strand of my hair in his fingers before his face turns serious, giving me a dark expression. "You have ten seconds to tell your friend goodbye and walk out the door before I do it for you and make a scene."

My eyes flash open at his possessive words, stirring up a desire that is thundering all the way to my thighs. I squeeze them together with an agape mouth before I scold him. "Reign Wolfe, you do not get to talk to me like that."

The words come out with a vicious wield of my tongue, blurting out his name louder than I intended.

"Really? You wanna throw my name around like that. Do you have a death wish?" His voice is low and ominous, vibrating against my ear. I twist my head a notch, staring into Reign's deep green eyes, our lips now dangerously close.

"Sienna?" I hear the uncertain tone in Lucas's voice, urging me to turn around to comfort him, but I can't untangle myself from Reign's gaze. He's sucking me in with his mesmerizing pupils, compelling me to give in. To do whatever he says.

"Let's go," he growls as his whiskey breath hits me in the face.

"I don't want to."

"And I don't care." He turns his attention to Lucas, glancing past me, and I can't bring myself to follow his gaze. "What's your name?"

"Lucas."

"Nice to meet you, Lucas." There is sarcasm in his tone, and my jaw clenches. "I hope you had a nice meal and a nice first date because it's also your last. Get up, Sienna."

I fold my arms in front of my chest, my chin raised in the air. "No."

"Fine." He gives Killian a short nod, who then pulls out a gun from the hem of his jeans, pointing it at Lucas with that cocky grin still spreading his cheeks.

"No!" I screech, holding up my arm. I scan the rest of the restaurant, hoping no one can see our little situation before I glare at Killian.

"Put that thing away, Kill," I hiss, my eyes shooting daggers at him. He raises his brows with a glazed look in reply, not even moving an inch.

God, these Wolfe boys drive me crazy.

Frustrated, I grunt, then offer Lucas an apologetic smile. "I'm sorry for their caveman behavior. But we have some things to discuss. You better go."

His gaze moves back and forth between Reign and Killian. He's trying to keep an unaffected stance, but I can see the insecurity in his demeanor. There aren't many men to dare the Wolfes in this city, and the conflict in his eyes tells me he's wondering if I'm worth fighting for. I give him a small shake of my head, silently answering his question.

"Come on. Get moving, man." Killian impatiently waves his gun to motion Lucas to get up, and finally he relents, sliding out of the booth.

"Are you going to be alright?" Lucas frowns when he's back on his feet.

"She's going to be great. Get up, *tool.*" Killian pushes him forward right after I give Lucas a reassuring nod, and I watch Killian escort him out. Reign's attention is drawn back to me and I fiercely meet his gaze.

"You're an asshole."

He chuckles, but I can sense the cynicism in his voice. "Yeah, that's nothing new, baby."

"You haven't always been an asshole."

His hand moves into my hair, and it takes everything I've got to not lean into his touch when he brings his face only inches away from mine.

"I have. You just had the privilege of not having to deal with him because you never pissed me off enough. I guess he's at your disposal now. Let's. Go." The last two words fall off his tongue with a growl before he throws a few bills on the table and takes my hand in his. I barely get time to grab my coat and purse as he drags me out of the booth, then has me trotting behind him as he hotfoots us out of the restaurant.

"Is Killian going to hurt him?"

"Don't worry about your new *friend*, baby. Killian is just going to take him home." He glances over his shoulder with a devilish grin, but his eyes tell me he's being truthful.

"I hate you," I huff when we get outside.

"Wicked, you can hate me some more when we get home." He lets go of my hand, and I take the time to put on my coat to protect me from the chilly air of the night.

"Home? Which home?"

"My home."

"What?" I scoff. "No."

He sucks in a breath through his nose and his nostrils flare as his energy turns dark. With broad shoulders, he marches up to me, wrapping his hand around my neck.

"Fight me all you want. But I'm done fighting. This bullshit between you and me?" He moves a finger back and forth. "It ends tonight. Get in the damn car, Sienna, or so help me God, I will throw you over my shoulder and do it myself."

Excitement fuels my body, my growing desire confusing the shit out of me. My heartbeat is pounding in my ears while my fingers are itching to pull him closer.

His eyes narrow as he searches mine, a smile tugging on his lips.

"You want me to throw you over my shoulder," he states.

"No," I lie, even though I don't sound convincing.

"You've always been a shit liar. Get in the car."

34

18 YEARS OLD

I walk into Franklin's office with a bored look on my face before dropping my ass into the chair in front of his desk. Connor leans his back against the window, giving me a slight nod in greeting while I do the same. Franklin glares at me, hating my indifferent attitude, and I answer with a fake smile.

"You summoned me?" I mock.

He's sitting behind his desk like a damn mob boss, the sleeves of his white button-down, rolled up, bringing out his toned arms.

"The Distuccis called. There are a few politicians trying to get out of their grasp," he informs me. "They need help gathering some information. We owe them and–"

"You mean *you* owe them," I cut him off.

"*We* owe them," he growls, unimpressed, "so one of us needs to be there for a few weeks. Help them sort that shit out."

Franklin has always been adamant that it's *our* business. All four of us. But I don't do shit for it other than take his orders, so I like to be an asshole about his choice of words.

He waits for a reply from me as he holds my gaze for what feels like forever, and finally I roll my eyes in surrender.

Sort of.

"Okay," I drawl. "And?"

"We decided you're going."

"What?" I indignantly shake my head. "No. I'm not going to New York."

As much as I don't like being in Boston, I don't want to go to New York either. My life is here, no matter how fucked up it is.

"It's only for two months, and now that you've graduated, there is nothing keeping you here."

"Err, well, I don't know? My girlfriend, maybe?" I huff, sarcastically. "No, I'm not going. Find someone else to do your dirty work for you." I get up, ending the conversation while I hear Franklin let out a deep sigh as I leave the room. Ever since Emma died, we haven't been seeing eye to eye. We have been at each other's throats every single day, and I don't know how to stop it. I don't even know if I *want* to stop it. The respect I had for my brother disappeared overnight, and as much as I try, I can't seem to get it back. Everything he does irritates me.

I hear Connor's heavy footsteps following behind me, creating a rumble in the back of my throat.

"Reign. Wait."

"What, Connor?" I turn around with an annoyed stance, not feeling like receiving a lecture right now.

"Look, things have been tight around here since Emma died. You and Franklin are suffocating the entire place with this cold war going on." Irritation is flashing in his eyes, and for anyone else, this would be the moment they would cower, knowing when Connor Wolfe gets mad, you're in trouble. I don't give a fuck, though.

"Just go to New York," he continues. "Take a break from Franklin. From *us*. Being in a different city might do you some good. But people are seeing the cracks between you and Franky. We can't have the other gangs thinking we have a weak link. Or worse. That you might be able to swing to the other side."

"Pff, they can't swing me for shit." I give him a dirty look, pissed he would even suggest that. I don't like Franklin, but he's still my brother. My brothers mean the world to me, and I would give my life for any of them without a second thought. Including Franklin. I would never betray him.

"I know," he rumbles, drowning out my words as he runs a hand over his face. "But the two of you do need a break."

His eyebrows lift to his blond hair, daring me with a single look. I press my lips together, hating that he's right. I know he and Killian have been walking on eggshells, trying to get Franklin and me to be somewhat civil, and even Sienna doesn't want to be around the house anymore. Maybe he's right. Maybe I need a break from it all. It would be nice to not be a Wolfe for a while, having the time to just be Reign without the expectations of my last name.

"Fine," I concede, forcing a grateful look to wash over my face, realizing this could be a good thing. "When am I leaving?"

He slaps my shoulder with a snort, as if he knows I'm not going to like the answer.

"Tonight."

"Oh, shit."

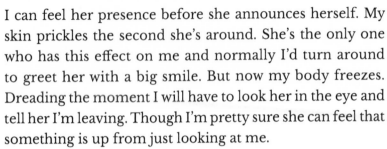

I can feel her presence before she announces herself. My skin prickles the second she's around. She's the only one who has this effect on me and normally I'd turn around to greet her with a big smile. But now my body freezes. Dreading the moment I will have to look her in the eye and tell her I'm leaving. Though I'm pretty sure she can feel that something is up from just looking at me.

For the last two hours, my gut kept telling me that Connor was right. This was for the best. We all needed the time to take a breath and, hopefully, when I get back, we can all start over. And while packing, the idea of leaving Boston had me feeling like I could breathe after a very long time. Like a literal breath of fresh air, it gives me life in the form of a new city. I don't want to leave her, but I also know I can't stay here either. I need to sort my thoughts for a while, and the more I think about it, the more I think it's what needs to happen. I need a change of scenery.

"What's going on, Reign?" Her sweet voice makes me sigh, and I throw my head back, looking up at the ceiling.

"I have to go to New York," I tell her while I keep packing my bag.

"For the weekend?" Her tone is small, hopeful, and I hear her come closer until her hand lands on my back. I can see her looking up at me from the corner of my eye, and I shut them, sucking in a deep breath. Gathering the courage I need, I twist my head toward the girl I love with a pained expression, offering her a tight smile as I open my eyes.

"For two months."

"What?" Her eyes light up like a bonfire.

"I need to take care of something for my brothers. I'll be back before you know it." I know brushing it off is unfair to her, but I can't make this a big deal. I'll break if I do that.

"I don't want you to go." Her voice cracks and my heart breaks along with it, yet she doesn't put up a fight like I'd expected her to.

"It's not forever." It feels like a lie.

"Then why does it feel like that?" I don't know, but I feel it too. I can't tell her, though. I can't tell her that I need a break from everything and everyone in Boston. Including her. I can't break her heart like that.

I take her face in my hands.

"It's not, baby," I reassure her with a coy smile. "In two months, I'll be back. Maybe we can try to find our own place then." I place a peck on her sweet plump lips, then turn my attention back to my bag to hide the despair that's running along my spine.

"You wanna leave your brothers?"

"I think it will be good to not see Franklin every day." I shrug.

"Yeah, maybe."

"Reign!" Connor calls from downstairs. "Time to go!"

"I'm coming! I have to go now." I bring my hand up to cup her cheek, and she shakes her head, her eyes now filled with disappointment.

"You're leaving right now? Can't you stay for a few more days?" I can. I know if I were to ask Franklin, he would let me stay a few more days with Sienna. But I don't want to. Now that we've decided I'm going, it feels like the longer I'm in this house, the less oxygen sits in the air. Like I'm rapidly suffocating, and all I can do is run to try and stay ahead of it.

"I can't, baby. The Distuccis need one of us today. I've graduated now. I need to take my place in the company." I loathe myself for lying so easily to her, but it rolls off my tongue like I rehearsed it a hundred times. Before she can reply and let the tears out that I can see sitting in the corner of her eyes, I press a longing kiss against her mouth, tugging her against my chest with my other arm. I try to take a mental memory of her body glued to mine, breathing in every note of her scent. When I pull back, my forehead aligns with hers, our noses almost touching.

"I'll be back before you know it. I promise." I give her one last kiss. "I love you, baby."

"I love you too." Her voice breaks again, and like the scaredy cat that I am, I bolt out of there as fast as I can, grabbing my bag and throwing it over my shoulder. I can feel her arm gracing mine as I trot away from her, and before I walk out of my room, I hear her release a sob. I grind my teeth together while I descend down the stairs, already knowing that the sound of her crying will haunt me forever.

Like another demon, added to the list.

35

"What am I doing here, Reign?" She's standing in my apartment with her hands on her hips just like the last time she was here, only this time she's a little more clothed. I take in her curvy frame, appreciating every swell of her body, loving the way it's hugged by the silky black dress that touches her knees.

I ignore her, walking toward the kitchen to pour myself a drink first. She's been silent the entire car ride, her raging energy coming at me in waves. I used the time to finally suck it up and decide I will tell her everything she wants to know, but now that we're here, I'm not feeling so sure anymore.

I hear her footsteps reach the kitchen and a small sense of victory sparks in my stomach. With my glass of Royal Blue in one hand, I turn around, leaning my back against the counter while I dangle the necklace between my fingers. Emotion flits across her face and I catch her swallowing hard, staring at the shining pendant in my hands.

"When I gave you this, I wanted something that lasted," I disclose, looking at the wolf shining back at me. "Something that would keep its value over the years, like you do to me. I want you to wear it again. Show the world you're mine." I bring my gaze up, linking it with hers.

"I'm not yours." She pushes out the words on a breath, though I can see the lie in her eyes. She brings out her Italian fire when she needs to, not letting anyone mess with her, but she lacks the ability to pretend. To play a game of make-believe.

"You are, Sienna."

She shakes her head, but her eyes are glassy with unshed tears.

"Tell me what happened." Her voice breaks, and it's killing me inside.

"Sit down."

"No!" She slams her fist on the marble of my kitchen island, shooting me a fierce look. Her black hair falls a bit in front of her face, and her plump lips are dying to be kissed. She's gorgeous. More beautiful than I remembered. The last few weeks made me realize we both changed over the years, and hers only makes me want her more.

"Sit down, Sienna," I reply calmly. "I'm not going to tell you again."

"Or what? You'll tie me up?" she sasses.

"Don't tempt me." A ghost of a smile lifts my lips, making it hard for her to keep up her attitude.

"Killian taught you some tricks?" There is amusement in her honey brown eyes, a taunt that's begging me to get her naked and make her scream my name.

"Just because I'm the nicest of the Wolfes doesn't mean I'm not a Wolfe. I will tie you up if you won't sit down and listen to me."

She drags her teeth over her lips as if she's contemplating what to do.

"Whatever, Reign. I'm out." She shoots me a brash look and turns around to prance toward the door.

"It was a brothel," I boom, my voice never skipping a beat.

That clearly caught her attention, because she twists on the spot while her defiant attitude slides off her face.

"What do you mean?"

I suck in a lungful of air, figuring it's now or never. I don't want her to know, not because I don't trust her. I don't want her to know because I don't want to damage her with the knowledge of my fucked up teenage years. But Killian is right; I need to try to dissolve the permanent cloud residing above my head.

"My foster family. They ran a brothel in their basement with all the kids they fostered." I take a big sip of my drink, hoping it will function as liquid courage.

"No-suh." Shock is slowly starting to form on her pretty features, as if she's starting to understand the meaning of my words with every new beat.

"Ya-huh."

She shakes her head.

"No, that can't be. D-did they…?" she trails off with a stutter, unable to look me in the eye. "Did they?"

"Hurt me? Abuse me?" I finish for her, making her lock eyes with me again.

There is fear in her eyes that's physically hurting me. It was the same when I told Killian. A fear that I'm changed. That I'm damaged goods. *I am.* It fucked me up, but it didn't kill me.

"Yes. No. Not sexually. But I got beaten up weekly. They didn't want me. The only reason they got me was because the agency refused to honor their request to only send girls. They were a corrupt bunch of pigs, and to cover it up, they shoved me in that house to show there wasn't a preference."

"Reign," she whimpers, bringing her hand in front of her mouth while she starts to round the kitchen island toward me.

"They sent their own daughters down. Every other Saturday."

She gasps, horror now written on her face.

"Oh my God." She pauses, her brain taking the time to process. "How old?"

I move my eyes to the floor, swallowing when I think of the first day I met Aubrey and Nova. Aubrey was clearly damaged, her eyes permanently laced with a haunted expression, but compared with her sister, little Nova was still innocent. Still full of life. It wasn't until later that I saw her fire slowly dying, until finally there was no spark left.

"Aubrey was a year older than me, and Nova was nine when she first had to go down."

"Oh my God." She palms my chest, and I let her, but I'm unable to look her in the eyes, keeping my gaze trained on the lines of my gray fishbone floor.

"One day, one of the assholes killed Nova. Choked her a little too hard." A throbbing headache builds in the back of my head, accompanied by aches in my limbs, as if I was freshly beaten up just minutes ago. I keep my glass in a tight grip, scared my fingers will remember Nova's skin underneath them that last time.

"No."

"I still see her lifeless body when I close my eyes." A lump the size of an apple makes it hard to breathe, the welling of my eyes showing the grief that seems to seep from my heart. Like an open wound, cut up all over again.

"Reign." Sienna holds a tight grip on my shirt, as if she physically needs to hold on to stay on her feet while I continue.

"When I left, I vowed to get Aubrey out." I sniffle, feeling my failure ripping through my body all over again. It's the only thing I regret. I don't regret killing Jefferson. I don't regret trying to stick up for Aubrey and Nova when I did. I don't even regret hacking into the evidence bank to exonerate Franklin. But I regret not taking Aubrey with me when Franklin brought me back to Boston. "But I failed. I fucking failed her. She trusted me. I was supposed to get her out."

"What happened to Aubrey?" The tone in her voice is filled with unease. She's scared of the answer that will come from my lips.

"She killed herself." Those three words act like a gate flying open, a dam breaking.

All the tears that have been piled up in the last few years seem to rush out all at once, my cheeks becoming wet within seconds as I put my glass in the sink before wrapping Sienna in my arms. I wallow in the comforting scent of her silky hair, feeling like she's my only hold on the world. The only thing that keeps me going, knowing it's more terrifying to lose her all over again than to face my demons. No matter how dark.

"It's not your fault."

"It is," I cry with my chin resting on her head, my gaze vacantly staring into my living room as I keep her as close as possible while my tears tickle the skin on my cheeks. "I should've fought harder. I should've gone back and taken her with me. But I was too occupied with being home.

Feeling like I belonged. I was finally happy again being around my brothers. With Emma. With *you*."

"It's okay. You're allowed to be happy, Reign. It's not your fault. It's okay," she shushes me while her hand moves up and down my spine. I can hear the emotion in her voice, and I consciously feel the hurt it brings me. I let out my agony, no longer able to push it back down, and she just holds me for God knows how long. The longer she holds me, the more tears seem to pour out of my body, until at some point, I suck in a deep breath. My eyes feel heavy, my body ready for a good night's sleep, but for the first time in years, my heart feels lighter. My head doesn't feel as clouded as always.

Looking up at the ceiling, I take another deep breath before I exhale slowly, then repeat it until I feel my heartbeat slowing down a little. I press a kiss on top of her head, and she looks up at me. I expect her eyes to look at me with pain, grief, *pity*. But instead, they are laced with love, sympathy, *pride*.

"Thank you for telling me."

A frown creases my forehead when I realize what a fool I've been. Why I kept telling myself that she couldn't handle my past, when really, it was me who couldn't handle it all along. Feeling grateful she's in my arms, I crash my mouth against hers, giving her a bruising kiss while holding her face in my hands.

"I'm sorry I didn't tell you sooner," I whisper against her lips.

"I'm sorry you didn't feel like you could." In reply to that answer, I kiss her once more, lingering, vowing to myself I will never let her slip out of my hands ever again. When I bring my head back up, dipping my chin to look at her, I hold her cheek in a firm grip with one hand while the other brushes through her hair. Her eyes well up, a small trembling of her lip shown as she holds my gaze like she's trying to find the courage to ask for more.

"That's why you stayed in New York?"

I nod, pushing her own tears over the edge as regret crosses her beautiful face.

"I'm sorry," she says, her voice shaking.

"What for, baby?"

Her shoulders start to shake as she sobs. "For not giving you the chance to tell me. We just lost Emma and then I lost you. You broke my heart, but I should've dug a little deeper. But I couldn't. I shut you out when I should've given you the chance to explain."

"No. No. I'm sorry I shut *you* out." My heart tightens, regret slicing through me. "I should've never left you in the first place. I'm an idiot, baby. I hurt you, and I've been regretting it ever since. I left you behind, and I'm so fucking sorry for it."

I press a kiss against her wet lips, needing her to feel my remorse.

"I love you, Sienna. I have always loved you. I didn't stay in New York because I didn't want to be with you," I tell her while keep pouring down her cheeks. "And I didn't stay in New York for Callie. I stayed for me. I needed to deal with my demons without tainting everyone around me with them." I wipe away a tear from her cheek. "I stayed with Callie because with her I could be whoever I wanted to be. I could be her hero. I told myself I stayed because I wanted to chase her demons away, but it was always about my own demons."

She sniffs, swallowing her tears away, then gives me a tentative look.

"Do you still talk to her?"

I want to tell her no, to settle her clear unease and frustration. But I know I have to be honest with her.

"Sometimes. She's my friend." I press my forehead against hers. "And *nothing* more."

"I don't think I will ever like her."

I chuckle, because I can't really blame her. I'll probably never like any of her exes either.

"That's okay, baby." I pause, searching her honey brown eyes, wanting to take away the spark of insecurity that's still there. "I love you. I'm *in* love with you, Sienna Brennan. And only you."

"I love you, Reign Wolfe." With those words from her lips, and her body in my arms, the years' long ache in my chest finally begins to dissipate and for the first time since I was a little kid, I feel a peace settling inside of me.

36

REIGN

I watch as she brings the glass to her lips with visible skepticism that has me grinning in amusement. Her hair is up in a messy bun, giving me a clear sight of her slender neck, the one I want to press my lips against every chance I get. Over the last few days, I feel like the little chips of darkness have fallen off my shoulders, one by one, with every step I make. I feel lighter in every sense of the word, and when I look at the beauty in front of me, I know it's because of her. We've talked a lot, getting to know each other again by sharing every single part of our past. All the years we've been apart, all the ugly and the good stuff, but also reminiscing over our time together. My heart has fallen head over heels again for the girl that stole it first when I was sixteen. But then again, I guess I never really fell out of love with her in the first place.

Her brows move to her hairline, followed by a pleasant surprise sparking her honey brown eyes.

"I'm not a bourbon girl, but this is good!" She takes another sip. "It's caramelly, soft, sweet.

"I told you. Knox Ashford makes the best bourbon there is."

"If you can sell this exclusively in Boston, you'd get a clientele from all over the city." She holds the glass in front of her face, her elbow resting on her other arm with her hip against the workstation while I pull the other bottles from the box.

"I know."

"So, how much did he send you?"

"Fifty bottles." I wish the bastard would just let me place regular orders, but he refuses to sell outside of Louisiana. The only reason I got these fifty bottles is because he needed my hacking skills in return.

"Can you get more?" She licks her lips, and I stop doing what I was doing, feeling my dick stirring to life.

"Maybe." I turn around to push a strand of her hair behind her ear before pulling her into my body by her elbow, leaning against the back of the bar. "He wants to sell it exclusively in South Ridge, and bring some more tourists to Louisiana," I explain while my hands start to explore her waist.

"He's a smart man." She tilts her head. "How did you get him to agree to this?"

I move my face closer to hers, sucking in a big whiff of her sweet perfume. "You know I can be very persuasive."

She runs her hands up and down my arms, and I enjoy the warmth of her palms on my body before she smiles.

"I do, but something tells me you didn't persuade him by sticking your tongue in his pussy." She gives me a taunting look, her lashes fluttering. My eyes widen, and my breath catches in shock.

"When did you get such a dirty mouth?" Gone is that sweet girl with the cute smile. "I don't remember you using this foul language before."

She shrugs with a naughty glint. "It comes with the years."

"Hmm, is that so?" I muse before my lips move to the skin below her ear. "I like it," I say, while trailing open-mouthed kisses on her neck. "In fact. Turns me the fuck on."

In response, she turns her neck to the side, giving me better access while her hands snake underneath the hem of my shirt. I feel her breathing growing shallow as it fans my ear, and a moan escapes her lips that tightens my jeans around my groin.

"Reign," she whispers.

"Yeah."

"Killian is coming soon."

"He won't be in for another thirty minutes."

"Anyone can walk in."

"I locked the door," I reply with a smug tone while I continue to shower her with kisses.

She chuckles. "What for?"

"For moments like this."

"Moments like what? *Exactly*?" The amusement is audible, laced with a pinch of defiance, even though she knows it's futile. I can't get enough of this girl. I want to love her, kiss her, touch her every chance I get now that she finally lets me, resulting in us having sex whenever she'll let me. Which is anytime and anywhere. Because as much as she wants to scold me, telling me shit like *the elevator is no place to have sex*, she has been there and onboard every time I decided to show her differently. Not once has she told me no, or asked me to stop. She wants me just as much as I want her, and I'll be damned if I don't make up for the lost years for the rest of my life. Starting now.

"The moments when I want to fuck my girlfriend on top of the bar," I huff against her skin. My hands unclasp her bra so I can palm her breasts underneath her shirt.

"Reign." Her tone is laced with reprimand and desperation, giving me a choice of which one I want to listen to... It's not hard to choose when a loud moan echoes in my ear.

"Sienna."

"You can't keep fucking me in public." I take a step back, pulling my shirt over my head before throwing it on the floor, then do the same with hers until she's standing in front of me with only her jeans on. Her eyes are hooded, hazy with desire, and her puckered nipples are dying to be sucked.

My fingers reach out to unbutton her jeans while I press a kiss on her lips.

"You said that the last three times, but look at us now."

Her eyes close and her mouth moves again, though I don't know why because the surrender is clear in her entire stance.

"Reign, we are in a bar."

I peel her jeans off her hips, then lift her up to put her ass on the cold metal of the workstation to move them down over her knees and ankles.

"I know. It's *my* bar."

"People can see us through the window." She glances at the window with defeat in her eyes. But the good kind of defeat. The kind that says *I don't stand a chance against your touch, and I don't want to.*

"Who cares." I snicker while I start rubbing her pussy through her panties, making her whimper against my palm.

She gasps, throwing her forehead onto my shoulder while I push her hair back to give me full access to her neck.

"You're such a cocky son of a bitch."

"I know." I strip her from her panties, then run my fingers through her folds. "Can you shut up now so I can have sex with you?" I can't wipe the grin off my face when she starts to unbuckle my belt, eagerly pushing down my jeans and boxers. I feel her hands wrap around my hard shaft, moving it slowly up and down, making my hips jerk.

"You're awful."

"Shut up, baby." I crush my mouth down onto hers, delving into her with a craving that's shown by the frantic movement of my tongue against hers. Grunts are alternated with moans, and she arches her back when I slide my fingers inside her core. I start to fuck her pussy with my fingers, getting more turned on by every thrust wetting them with her juices.

"You can't say you don't like sex in public when you're this wet for me every single time, baby."

"Shut up, Reign," she scolds, pulling me closer by the back of my neck to lock our mouths again.

With one hand, I slowly run the tip of my dick through her folds, teasing her clit on every pass.

"Oh, fuck," she cries.

"Feel good, baby?"

"Yeah," she gasps, although it's more a plea than an answer. I stop in front of her center, cupping her face with my lips against hers as I push my dick inside of her, wanting to feel my body merging with hers. A shiver runs down my spine when I feel her wetness coat my shaft, making it easy to glide through her sweet pussy. I start thrusting, and her nails dig into my back before she drags them down like she's clawing me.

"Are you claiming me, baby?"

"Maybe." She sounds playful, and I sink my teeth into her neck, a carnal urge to do the same taking over. Her nails scratch the skin around my spine, having me cry out in pleasure, and the caveman in me is hoping she does it rough enough to leave scars on my back. I want her to claim me. I want her to claim my body like she already did with my heart.

Frantically, I pick up the pace as I wet my thumb with my tongue to press it on her sensitive nub. She lets out a frenzied screech when I start to slowly draw circles around it, flicking and taunting her clit over and over again. It doesn't take long until I notice the change in her moans, each one more desperate than the one before, telling me she's close. She holds on to my neck for dear life, and with every push, I feel my own release building alongside hers.

"I'm coming, Reign," she breathes against my neck with her eyes closed. She's completely at my mercy, and it only heightens the craving I have for her. "Don't stop. Please don't stop. Keep going."

It only takes me a few more thrusts, then I feel her explode in my hands, her walls milking my dick in a torturous way. She cries out and her quads tense, her legs shaking and still wrapped around my waist. I let out a feral grunt when my dick unloads inside of her while I keep chasing to drag it out as long as possible. When the last shudders ebb from my body, I drop my sweaty head into the crook of her neck while she runs her nails up and down my spine in a soothing way.

"You're so sexy." I grate my teeth against her skin, making her giggle before I bring my head up to drop a kiss on her lips. I reach out behind me for some paper towels, then roll some off, ready to slip out of her.

"No, wait." She keeps my hip in place, letting out a whimper. "Don't go just yet."

"What do you mean?"

"You feel so good inside of me." The lazy look in her eyes gets me hard again, but I know my brother will arrive any minute now.

"You're killing me, baby. But hold that thought. As soon as we're done here, I'm going to drag you home and do it all over again."

"Hmm," she muses, brushing her lips over mine. "That sounds nice."

She nibbles my lip in a teasing way, then takes the paper towel out of my hands and I slowly pull out of her. Licking my lips, I watch my cum drip from her glistening pussy, letting out a troubled breath.

"What?" she questions.

I shake my head. "There's nothing sexier than my cum dripping from your pussy."

She cleans herself up, wiping my juice from her folds, then throws it against my chest.

"You perv." She chuckles.

I catch it with a seductive grin before I throw it out and wash my hands while Sienna is getting dressed. When we're both fully clothed again, I hear someone knock, and I let my feet carry me to the front door to see who it is.

"What the hell?" I blurt when I notice the strawberry blonde hair that's familiar to me. She's beaming at me with blushed cheeks, her hand up in a wave before my eyes land on the man standing behind her. I've known him for years now, and the fact that he never loses his scowl has me laughing while I open the door for them.

Curious, Sienna moves closer, and when the blonde steps through the door, I give her a hug. "What the hell are you two doing here?"

"We were in the neighborhood."

37

Sienna

"**S**top bullshitting me."

"You can give me a drink first, Wolfe," she scolds playfully before her gaze locks with mine. A jealous feeling washes over me, not knowing this girl when, clearly, Reign is close to her. He offers his hand to the man following behind her.

"Is this...?" She gives Reign a side-eye and suddenly I'm feeling too much. My mind is running overtime, wondering who this girl is and, more importantly, *what* she is to Reign, and my stomach twists in a knot.

"Yes!" Reign huffs with a big smile. "This is Sienna, my girlfriend. Sienna, this is Callie. My–"

No-suh.

"Ex-girlfriend," I cut him off, rage settling in my chest. I clench my jaw and quickly yank my coat from the bar as I shake my head. I'm not dealing with this shit. Good for him that he's still on good terms with the girl who was a part of our break-up, but I sure as hell am not going to be part of it. I might have forgiven him, but this is pushing it for me. He should know that, and if he doesn't, he's wicked stupid.

"Sienna?" Reign gives me a puzzled look while I fly past the three of them, too angry to even utter another word. "Sienna! Baby, wait!"

I storm out of the Pack while I try to put on my coat with jerking movements, never missing a step forward. The last few days were amazing. Reign and I found a way to move past the heartbreak and start over. I tried to keep it casual at first, but the feelings he's giving me are hard to ignore and impossible to stop. I have never felt better before. But silly little me should've known there would be some wicked shit coming our way.

The cold air can't tame my flushed cheeks, the anger seeping out of me as I stomp over the cobblestone street.

"Sienna! Wait!" I hear her voice, and it only makes me grind my teeth, but there is a part of me that wants to turn around.

"Sienna! Please!" I want her to disappear. To go back to wherever the fuck she came from, but I also want to look her in the eye. To tell her to fuck off, woman to woman. But the conflict in me keeps my feet going with my hands balled into fists.

"Sienna!" she yells louder when the distance between us becomes bigger. "For fuck's sake, I'm pregnant!" My feet stop, and I stand there blinking at the street in front of me, until I turn around.

"What?" There is a confused frown on my face when I meet her gaze before my eyes drop to the small baby bump she seems to be carrying.

"Right." Callie saunters toward me, and I let my eyes roam over her body. She's wearing skintight jeans, with a bordeaux leather jacket and camel boots. Her hair is blonde, but there is a red glow over it that matches the freckles on her face. She's gorgeous. And she's nothing like me. We're like day and night. When she gets closer, she gives me a tight smile with a sarcastic look in her teal eyes. "It's not Reign's. In case you're wondering." Unappreciative of her timing to joke, I fold my arms in front of my body, popping my hip. She's a bit shorter than I am, but she holds herself with a confidence that I feel like matching. "It's the brooding man's who's scowling behind me." She pauses, pointing her thumb over her shoulder while she never looks away. "He is scowling behind me, right?"

I cock my head to look back at the entrance of the Pack, my eyes catching said brooding man she's talking about. He's huge, wearing a green short-sleeve shirt that brings out the tattoos on his arm. There is indeed a huge scowl on his handsome face, his eyes darkened against his dirty blond hair.

I nod in confirmation, and she glances over her shoulders.

"Baby, meet Sienna," she calls out, then twists her head back to me. "Sienna, my husband, Kane Carrillo." I watch him nudge his chin in greeting, his features never softening. The man is intimidating as fuck, and he's fucking twenty yards away from me.

"I'll be there in a minute," she tells him as she rolls her eyes, her voice low when she brings her eyes back to me. "He's a bit overprotective. We're working on it. I'm sure you are familiar with alpha assholes since you run around with the Wolfes."

"Pretty much." Unintentionally, I feel the corner of my mouth rise, but I do my best to keep a straight face.

"Look, I know you must hate me," she begins with one hand on her stomach, as if she's soothing her baby. "But Reign loves you. He told me a few months ago how you two were together before he came to New York."

My eyes widen, my slightly simmered anger flaring up again within a split second.

"What? You still see him?" I spin on my heels to leave, but she grabs my arm.

"Stop! It's not what you think." She lets go when I give her a dirty look, but I hold still to listen to her. "I needed his help. *We* needed his help to find my psychopath of a brother." She pushes out a breath, and a frown creases my face at her words. The features on her pretty face turn into a pinched expression, and as much as I want to hate her and tell her to eat shit... part of me is curious to hear what comes next.

"When I was eighteen, my brother sold me for the night. Whored me out like I meant nothing. Reign saved me that night. It bonded us. We became best friends, and for a while we were a little bit more than that." She pauses, resting her hand on my arm as if she wants to make sure I register what comes next and after what he told me, things are starting to click in my head. "I love him and I will always love him, but I am not *in* love with him." I can see the sincerity in her eyes, and my muscles relax a little. "Not like the way I'm in love with that gloomy crime lord still standing there. Is he still standing there?"

I nod, a smile haunting my face.

"For fuck's sake, Kane," Callie scolds, snapping her head back to her husband. "I'll be right in." They glare at each other for a moment, both their energies changing into something bigger. This tiny girl stands in front of me, unimpressed, peering at her husband like he's not at least a foot bigger than her. I can't help feeling in awe of her bold posture.

"I'll be fine," she finally growls.

"And I'll be fine standing here," he grunts back while I slip out a chuckle.

She snorts in annoyance before she rears her head back to me.

"He's an asshole," she discloses.

"Aren't they all?"

"Very true. Look, he never stopped loving you. He told me so himself. He's not going to drive off into the night with me." A genuine smile slides onto her cheeks and my anger disappears as quickly as it came. My gut tells me she's being honest and the scowling husband kinda proves the point. Not to mention the energy that two radiate when they look at each other.

"I promise," she continues. "Besides, my husband is a star at knife throwing."

I let out a laugh, appreciating her humor.

She shakes her head with a smile, though a seriousness is laced in her eyes.

"Not kidding, he threw a knife at Reign's head once for giving me a hug."

My eyebrows move up before I give her an incredulous look.

"You're shitting me?"

"Not even a little bit."

"That's... a bit much." I picture it in my head. "And weirdly sexy."

She wiggles her eyebrows at me. "I know, right? You don't have to like me. In fact, I understand if you want me to get the fuck out of here and never return. But I need Reign's help. And since your man is really good at what he does, there will be more than likely be more occasions when I need his help." She has a point. Reign doesn't just work for his brothers. He also sells his knowledge and skills at request. If people need to know something they can't figure out themselves, they call Reign.

"Riiight." I drag out the word before she continues.

"So, let's just have a drink. We can make it a mini double date. Just don't tell Kane or he'll be growling all day." She finishes with a whisper that makes me snicker. "If you want me to leave after that, I will, and you will never have to see my face ever again. What do you say?"

I hold her gaze. For the last few years, she has been the villain in my story. The one I hated something fierce for messing up my life, even though I know it was Reign who was the instigator in the first place. As much as we've been working things out, I still hated her with a passion, and while she's standing here in front of me, I still want to hold on to that feeling. But I can't. She seems fierce, like a badass. But I don't get the bitchy vibe from her that I expected.

"Okay."

Relief washes over her face, a happy spark moving through her gaze. "Thank you. I like your fire, though."

"Thanks." I smile, then look past her to Kane. "Does he always look this scary?"

"Pretty much. He's really a big teddy bear, though."

"A knife-throwing teddy bear?" I mock.

"Yeah, something like that." She laughs as we make our way back to the Pack.

"How far along are you?" I glance at the black shirt that's hugging her small bump.

"Sixteen weeks. Kane wants to lock me up and keep me safe until the baby is born."

"From the look on his face, I believe that within a heartbeat." We watch how he moves back into the bar, clearly satisfied now that his wife is following behind him.

"Yeah, he tried that once, though. Didn't work." She gives me a knowing look.

"I'm intrigued."

"Oh, it's definitely a good story, but let's keep that for when I'm actually allowed to buy you a proper drink." Amused, I nod as we walk back into the Pack, my eyes instantly locking with Reign's. He's giving me a troubled look, rounding the bar to close the distance between us.

"Everything okay?" he asks with his hands on my arms. He lowers his body to look me in the eyes, with his greens shooting me a questioning look. My heart swells when I see the concern dripping from them, loving how he's giving me his full attention.

"Ya-huh." He doesn't look away until he's satisfied, then pulls me against his chest in a warm hug before I feel his lips kiss the top of my head. With my cheek pressed against his heart, Callie finds my eyes, shooting me a wink that tugs up the corner of my mouth.

When she strolls to the bar, she places herself between Kane's legs, who's making himself comfortable by pouring himself a glass of the bottle of Royal Blue that stands on the bar.

"Oh my God," Callie screeches, and Reign and I break apart. "You got Royal Blue?" She snaps her head to Reign, who tugs me behind me as he walks back behind the bar.

"I thought Ashford didn't ship that stuff out of Louisiana."

"You know him?" Reign asks.

"We've met." She shrugs, examining the label on the bottle.

"You're a real *Donna* now, aren't you?"

"What?" she sputters. "No way."

"You're so full of shit."

"Takes one to know one. What did you blackmail him with?"

My eye catches the playful grin Reign gives her. "I gave him an offer he couldn't refuse."

She purses her lips, then points her attention to Kane sipping the liquid gold with a stoic look, though I don't miss how he brushes the skin on his wife's hip with his thumb. It's tender and unexpected, but it shows how much he adores her, and it melts my heart.

"This is bullshit," Callie huffs. "I finally can drink a Royal Blue in Boston and I'm fucking pregnant."

"You're *what*?" Reign blinks, an incredulous look going back and forth between Callie and Kane.

"Oh, yeah. Sorry, I was too preoccupied to get your girlfriend not to hate me."

"I don't hate you," I tell her, amused.

"Good, mission accomplished." She smiles, then her gaze locks with a gaping Reign. "Surprise!" She rubs her stomach with a beaming smile, and it doesn't take long before a wide grin splits Reign's face.

"Whoa, I did not see this one coming! Congratulations!" He offers Kane his hand, who takes it with a ghost of a smile seeping through his blank expression.

"Here." Reign grabs a new bottle of Royal Blue from the shelf. "Take it home. You can pour her a glass when she pushes that baby out."

He turns his attention to me, wrapping his arm around my neck to tug me against his side.

"I can't believe you're pregnant," Reign says, amusement audible in his voice.

"Neither can I," Callie counters.

"You know you're in trouble when it's a girl, right?" Reign turns his attention to Kane, who finally lets some emotion travel his face.

"Tell me about it. How are your brothers?"

"Good. Franklin and Connor are hitched."

"No way," Callie blurts.

"Ya-huh," I pitch in with a chuckle. My fingers hold on to Reign's shirt, loving him close to me like this. He starts to play with my hair, and I relax more with every stroke. The longer I stand there, the more comfortable I get, and the more I realize I was probably wrong about Callie.

"We didn't get invited to the wedding?" she asks, disappointed, then scowls at Kane. "Did you do something to put us on his shitlist?"

"What are you looking at me for, baby?" he growls.

"Because you're an asshole. Wouldn't surprise me if you pissed him off."

Reign and I laugh, then Reign explains. "They are not married yet, but something tells me Franky is about to pop the question any day now."

"Apologize," Kane commands with his lips close to Callie's.

"In your dreams," she counters, giving Reign and me a playful grin.

"Apologize," he repeats, tugging her closer against his body this time. Their chemistry is undeniable, palpable, and I keep my gaze trained on them in anticipation.

Finally, Callie rolls her eyes and snaps her head to her husband. Their lips almost touch until she closes the distance in a bruising kiss. Kane's hands quickly start to roam all over her sides until he pulls loose and lets out a grunt.

"That's all you get, baby," she says with victory in her eyes.

"Wow, Carrillo. You are so whipped," Reign taunts, and we all break out in laughter, except for Kane, who brings up his glass, pointing at Reign with a challenging look.

"First, shut up, Wolfe. Secondly, you're one to talk." Kane gives me a wink, his smile finally gracing us, albeit reluctantly, and I smile back in surprise. Something tells me the girl next to him is the only reason he lets out his playful stance, making me wonder how long they've been together.

"Touché, Carrillo," Reign replies, then tilts my chin with his fingers so he can plant an affectionate kiss on my lips. "But as much as I like having you two around and doing some catching up, you mind telling me what you're doing here?" He moves his gaze back and forth between them, and I notice how Callie's face falls, a serious look replacing her bright smile.

"We need your help," she says with a frown.

"I figured."

"It's about Cristina." She gives him a knowing look, and I feel him hold in his breath for a split second.

"Oh, shit."

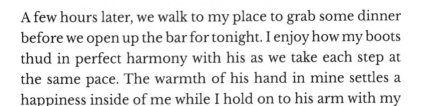

A few hours later, we walk to my place to grab some dinner before we open up the bar for tonight. I enjoy how my boots thud in perfect harmony with his as we take each step at the same pace. The warmth of his hand in mine settles a happiness inside of me while I hold on to his arm with my other hand, desperate to feel him close. The brisk air cools my whiskey-flushed cheeks, and I'm thankful I stuck it to two and not more.

"I like her." I glance up at him with a beaming smile before turning my focus back to the street. It's dark and the streetlights are creating shadow figures on the cobblestone. The streets are still crowded with people who are looking for a place to eat or those who need to commute home.

"I knew you would." I can hear the smile in his voice when he gives my hand a slight squeeze in appreciation.

"She's not as bad as I pictured her," I admit. "I'm sorry." In fact, she's nothing like I thought she would be. I wanted to dislike her, and I even stayed out of most of the conversation for the first ten minutes, but eventually, I couldn't hold back. She was sweet, friendly, and extremely funny when it came to burning her husband. She was entertaining as fuck with her bold comments and wit, a perfect combination for a badass crime lord, or lady, with the grace of a woman. And even her husband seemed to have loosened up more as soon as he saw Reign's hands on my body the entire time.

"Don't be. You had every right to be mad at me."

"Why didn't you tell me what happened to her?" I ask, referring to what she told me earlier about her brother. It was a story that kinda had me shocked, not even being able to imagine what it would be like to have a brother who uses you as livestock. My family isn't big, containing just me, my mom, and my cousin, Isabella, but still, it made me realize how lucky I am to have them.

I feel him shrug. "Not my story to tell."

I bark out a laugh, rolling my eyes.

"You Wolfe boys. You're as principled as Killian. He said the same thing when I asked him about Declan."

Immediately realizing my mistake, I come to an abrupt halt, feeling like the ground is about to swallow me whole. My head tells me to abort mission, to think fast and come up with something. Anything. When this came up last week, he was too distracted by our problems to dig into me more. Now, though, now I know he heard me clearly, and he's not going to let it go this time.

I just stand there like a deer in headlights as my body disconnects from Reign and he turns to face me. My lips part, unable to voice anything when I look into his deep green irises that now hold a confused glare that has me frozen on the spot.

"Asked him *what* about Declan?" He doesn't even ask me if we're talking about the same Declan. *The* Declan. The one his brother murdered over a decade ago. Because he knows. He knows exactly which Declan I'm talking about.

I shake my head with a tucked mouth as shivers run through every muscle in my body.

"Nothing." Part of me is still doing my best to find an excuse, an explanation, but I know Reign sees right through my lies.

Franklin is going to kill me.

"Asked him *what*, Sienna?" he grits out, this time taking an ominous step toward me. His energy changes to something huge, intimidating even. I know he would never hurt me, but I fear for those who he might hurt in this state, when I see how he balls his hands into fists.

"Nothing, let's just go home." I reach out to his arm in an attempt to drag him with me down the street, but he easily lifts it out of my grasp, making us switch places. I swallow, glancing around me. My heart rate speeds up when I look up into his sharp glare.

"Not a chance in hell, baby. What do you know that I don't know?" It's a snarl, and though I know it's not directed to me, it still makes me whine a little.

"I-I can't." I throw my hands up in anguish.

"Sienna," he growls, then closes the distance between us when my gaze moves to my feet.

"Just ask your brother."

He places two fingers under my chin, tugging it up so he can look me in the eye. Anger. Irritation. Desperation. Grief. I see his greens flash with every emotion, creating a big lump in the back of my throat. I know he deserves to know. In fact, I've been dying to tell him for years now, and when he felt brave enough to tell me about all the shit he went through, I wanted to break my promise so badly. To tell him why Franklin did what he did. That he isn't the villain in this story. But I also knew it shouldn't be me. That it should be one of his brothers who told him the truth.

"I'm asking *you*." It's an order, even though it comes from his lips in a soft and gentle tone.

"Reign, please," I beg.

"What don't I know about Declan?" I watch how his jaw clenches, and I close my eyes to prevent my tears from escaping. Rolling my lips, I go over how I want to handle this, wondering if there is a good way to deliver this information.

"Sienna?" This time it's a bark, making my lashes flutter, and I breathe in through my nose before I put on my brave face and shoot my eyes open.

"Why did you never ask Franklin, Reign?" He searches my eyes, his pupils dilating as they move back and forth over my face. I can see how he runs every memory of his past through his head, wondering what the hell he missed.

"What do you mean?"

"Why did you never ask Killian? Connor?" I pause. "Why do you ask *me*?"

He lets go of me, taking a step back as he runs a hand through his hair while shaking his head. My heart aches for him as I see how he's shattering slowly in front of my eyes, knowing whatever is coming next will change his life. I can see it in his stance, his entire demeanor. He knows, and when his eyes snap back to mine, I feel my heart literally stop for a brief moment.

"Tell me!"

I give him a sympathetic gaze, waggling my head.

"I don't think you want to know."

"Tell me!" he explodes, his eyes looking like they are about to pop out of his head, enough to scare me into opening my mouth.

"He raped Emma!" I wail. The frown on his face tells me it's not quite landing just yet, and I hold in a breath, waiting for him to connect the dots.

"Who did?" he croaks out.

I throw my hands up in despair.

"Who do you think, Reign?" I waver as he just holds my gaze with a pained expression. "Declan did!" I feel my tears push over the edge, now running down the cold skin of my cheeks. "*That* is the reason Franklin killed him.""

"What? He raped Emma?" He squeezes his eyes shut, pinching the bridge of his nose. "But she was... she was..."

"Twelve," I finish his sentence with a ton of bricks in my stomach. I've been through all the emotions he's feeling right now, never getting rid of the image of my best friend getting raped by that asshole. "Yes."

His glassy eyes lock with mine. He's looking at me, but his gaze is vacant as his vision grows wet.

"She never fully recovered, Reign," I explain. "It wasn't Franklin's fault. He went to Declan's house to make a deal with him. Something about drugs. When he looked through the window, he saw–" I snap my mouth shut, not wanting to spell it out. He covers his mouth with his hand, looking out onto the street while I continue. "He tried to protect her. Killian tried to fix her. No one could help her." He shakes his head. "She didn't kill herself because of what Franklin did. She killed herself because of what Declan did."

I wait for him to say something. Anything. But he just stays quiet, his breaths becoming shallower every second, and I see the exact moment it hits him right in the face. The precise moment he understands the context of my words, because I slowly see the blood drain from his face. Sweat forms on his forehead, and I can't stop the tears falling from my eyes as I watch the man I love fall apart in front of my eyes.

"I have to go." Before I can respond, he flies past me with big strides.

"Reign, wait!" I bellow at his back. I fear for what will happen when he's in this state, knowing he can be just as lethal as his brother when he's in this kind of pain.

"I have to go," he repeats without looking back at me. "Call Killian to pick you up!"

"Reign!"

With a vicious glare, he snaps his body toward mine, his finger pointing at my face, and I take a startled step back.

"Call Killian to pick you up, Sienna!" he growls.

He turns back around, moving away from me with big strides and broad shoulders.

"Reign!" When he doesn't respond, I bury my face in my hands, letting out the sobs that are sitting in the back of my throat. Every muscle in my body is tensed with the mistake

I just made. When I snap my head back up, my eyes catch a final glimpse of Reign as he heads around the corner, and I suck in a deep breath before I reach into my purse with shaking hands. I pull out my phone, calling the one person that can help me calm his brother down as I listen to the dial tone echoing in my ear.

"What's doing?"

"Kill, it's me." I do my best to hold it together, but regardless, my voice still breaks.

"What's wrong?" Killian asks with worry in his voice.

"I fucked up."

38

REIGN

You know those scenes in movies where the protagonist's world seems to stop spinning, and it looks like their head stops functioning? I always thought that was something that only happens in films, to actors. But as I keep blinking, that's exactly how I feel. Numb. Non-existent. Like someone has taken over my body and I'm just a passenger. I try to order my thoughts, but I just keep stomping down the street to wherever my feet take me. I keep walking like that for I don't know for how long until I find myself in the middle of the street and headlights coming my way. Snapping me out of my daze, my muscles freeze, and I just pause until the headlights hit me in the face, waiting for the car to slam my body against the floor.

The smell of burning rubber enters my nose when the car slams on the brakes with a screeching sound, making my skin peel, and I hold in my breath in shock. I expect my life to flash in front of my eyes, but I register nothing but the blinding lights moving closer until finally the car stops only a foot away from me. I lock eyes with the female driver, her gaze pale and terrified. For a brief moment, there is nothing but silence, until it's drowned out by the loud thuds of my heart against my chest.

"Are you okay?" the woman mouths to me.

As if I'm drowning, I feel my body crawl back to the surface, and I suck in a breath, experiencing how all my senses come back to life.

"Yeah." I nod, though still feeling a bit woozy while the adrenaline surges through my veins. "I'm okay." I offer her a tight smile and an awkward wave, then scramble back to the sidewalk. With a fast pace, I trot around the corner, then push my back against a brick wall, looking up at the sky.

What the fuck?

I close my eyes, filling my lungs with air as I exhale through my nose in an attempt to calm myself down.

Declan raped Emma? *That's* why she was depressed? Franklin killed him out of revenge for my friend? To protect her. Oh, I'm so fucked up. I'm such a tool.

I let out a feral grunt, pulling my hair. It feels like half of my life was a lie, and the worst part is the fact that I'm the only one to blame for it. Despair seems to hit me in the face like a cold cloth, slapping me awake after years of sleep.

I pull out my phone, knowing I have a lot of fixing to do while I still try to wrap my mind around the last few minutes. The dial tone sounds like a torturous gong in my head until I finally hear him answer the phone.

"Yeah?" His voice is composed, low, filled with authority, and it has never brought me more relief than it does now.

"Franky?" I try to keep a steady voice, but I fail miserably.

"What's doing, Reign?" There is a hint of worry in his tone now, telling me he can detect the distress in my voice even though I'm trying to hide it.

"Where are you?"

"I'm leaving the office and heading to the mansion with Kendall right now." I take a deep breath. "Why?" he continues. "What's going on? Are you okay?"

"Yeah. Yeah, I just need to talk to you." I slide my body down, until I'm squatting against the cold bricks.

"Something wrong?"

YES! Everything is wrong. I am wrong. I'm so fucking wrong. I'm so fucking wrong about everything. I'm an idiot. A shit brother. My mind is a mess, and I feel the strong desire to blurt it all out. To apologize. To ask him to forgive me. But as much as I want to break down right now, right here in the middle of the street, I owe my brother more than that. I owe it to him to look him in the eye and tell him what a fucking idiot I've been.

"In person," I tell him, pinching the bridge of my nose.

"What's wrong, Reign?"

"Nothing. Everything. I'm s−" I swallow my words, plastering a tight smile on my face to try and sound normal. "I just need to talk to you."

"Okay," Franklin concedes. "Meet me at the mansion in fifteen minutes, okay?"

I nod gratefully, as I straighten my legs again. "Alright, I'll see you there."

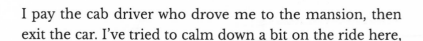

I pay the cab driver who drove me to the mansion, then exit the car. I've tried to calm down a bit on the ride here, ignoring Sienna and Killian's phone calls as I reversed the memories of my teenage years. I've been so angry at the world, at the ugly shit I've witnessed, the bad shit I've done, I couldn't look past my rage, blaming the one person who has always been there for me. Franklin moved mountains to help me in any way he could, and when I think about it, he's never stopped. No matter how badly I've treated him, no matter how much I piss him off. He is always there when I need him.

When I found out he killed Declan, I kicked him off the pedestal I'd put him on, throwing him in the bad guy corner with the likes of Jefferson. He disappointed me and broke my heart, but the more I think about it... the more I connect the dots... the more I come to the realization that *I'm* the one who disappointed *me*. I'm the one who broke my own heart, putting myself in the same category as Jefferson. As the guy who killed Nova.

I blamed Franklin for the pain, the guilt. But really, it was me all along.

With a frown to fight my emotion, I walk through the door of the mansion.

"Franky?" The echo of my voice reverberates through the foyer, and I stride forward toward Franklin's home office. Without knocking, I push the door open, my eyes locking with Connor, who's giving me a questioning look. He's sitting behind the big wooden desk, looking completely out of place with his ruffian appearance between the big bookshelves that surround the entire office. Like a bodybuilder in a library.

"Hey, asshole." Connor smirks before pushing his attention back to the papers in front of him.

"Where is Franklin?"

"He's still at the office."

"No." I grip the back of the stool in front of the desk, dragging out the word. "He said he was getting in the car thirty minutes ago."

Connor shakes his head, leaning back in the chair. "I haven't seen him yet."

A panicked feeling grips me tight, making it hard for me to breathe as a bad feeling settles in my gut like a parasite. Something is wrong. I can feel it.

Connor gets up at the same time we hear footsteps coming into the house, and Killian's voice reaches our ears. "Reign? Are you here?"

Connor rounds the desk with a frown knitting his brows together. "Are you alright?"

"Yeah," I huff, lying. "I just need to find Franklin."

"He's in here!" Connor calls out to my brother from the doorpost behind me.

"Reign? Oh my God, are you okay?" I turn around, my eyes landing on Sienna's tormented face, before I give Killian a pained expression.

"I'm fine. Or I will be."

"Reign. Sit down, man," he says.

"What's going on?" Connor moves his gaze back and forth to Killian and me at the same time that my phone buzzes in my pocket, telling me I have a message.

"He *knows*," I hear Killian say as I pull my phone out of my jeans, then slide my fingers over the screen to see who it is. It's a photo. Of Franklin. And Kendall. Tied up with blindfolds covering their eyes.

UNKNOWN NUMBER: Roses are red, lovers are dead. Thank you for giving me your brother to play, you can collect his body by the end of the day.

I stare at the coordinates behind it, feeling like they are about to dance off the screen. My breath grows shallow while my brain processes the picture in front of me, the same sense of panic showering me like it did earlier. It feels like my brain stops, my world stops spinning, but this time, my body doesn't freeze. This time, I feel the rage burning me from the inside out, liquefying my organs in the most torturous way.

Connor seems to notice the change on my face, because he tugs my phone out of my hand.

"Who's that?" He looks at the picture. "What the fuck?"

I hear Killian, Connor, and Sienna gasp at the picture, talking about the action we need to take, but they are slowly being drowned out by the memories haunting my mind.

"I'm too late," I whisper, staring at the floor. My thoughts are all over the place, and I fail at keeping them together, like I'm a little boy all over again. Only now, I have the strength of a grown man, and I let out a guttural growl as I start to push off all the stuff that's on the desk. My hands move over the shelves, throwing books through the room as I keep screaming like a wolf gone mad.

"What the fuck, Reign! STOP!" Killian's voice sounds like I'm inside a fishbowl and he's looking through the glass, but I ignore him, baring my teeth as I keep going. I had years to put on a brave face and ask my brother the question that has been nagging me since I was twelve.

Why?

What happened that night? Why did Declan have to die? Why did you kill him? But instead, my own stubbornness kept me away from my brother. The only one who always took care of me without any conditions, any requirements. I destroyed our bond, cutting off piece by piece the more I resented him for something he didn't even do.

"It's my fault. It's all my fault," I chant, dropping my body to the floor. Tears leak down my face as I hold my hands behind my neck. "It's my fault. I ruined us."

A pair of arms wrap around my body, and I hold on to them tight, thinking I might lose consciousness if I don't, while I keep sobbing. It feels like years and years of pain are now seeping out of the open wound I've been carrying around for so long, relieving a pressure I always felt weighing on my chest.

"It's okay, Reign. I got you," Connor whispers in my ear, and I look up at him.

"I was wrong, Con," I wail. "I was so wrong. I'm so sorry."

"I know. It's okay. It's okay. I got you."

"What are we going to do?"

He holds my face in his hands, and our eyes lock. His green eyes function like a mirror to mine, and I search for the anger, the pain, the disappointment in me. But all I can see is love. Loyalty. That unconditional bond I've always had with my brothers, in good and bad. Why don't they hate me like I deserve?

"We are going to get him back and you two can work your shit out, okay?"

I nod, taking a short breath. "How?"

Connor twists his head to Killian. "Any ideas?"

Killian looks pissed, his eyes showing the cunningness he's capable of, but I know it's not for me. It's for whoever captured Franklin and Kendall.

"Yeah," he nods. "I got a few ideas."

39

FRANKLIN

I swallow to get rid of the dryness in my throat, my eyes slowly opening due to the headache that's pounding against my scalp. The sweet smell of the chloroform sits in my nose, and I suck in a deep breath to get rid of it, feeling the tightness of ropes around my wrist. I register something like a warehouse, and my dizziness is quickly disappearing. Suddenly realizing we've been taken, my eyes spread wide, looking for Kendall. I find her sitting next to me, tied up like I am, but the scowl on her face tells me she's been awake for a while longer.

"Are you okay?" I grunt, my eyes roaming her body to look for any physical damage.

"I'm fine." She offers me a coy smile, then puts her glaring back in front of her.

I trail her gaze, then lock eyes with the face that once kidnapped my nephew.

"Bella," I hiss.

"Hey, *Franky*." There is a disdain in her voice that reminds me of something, yet I can't quite place it until she moves closer and I notice the curls that weren't there the last time I saw her. I narrow my eyes, flashes of Reign's foster home in Providence dancing in front of me. Rage forms a fireball inside of me while my heart is tapping against my ribcage, ringing in my ears.

"I remember you."

"I don't think you do, Franky boy." She saunters toward us with a cocky smirk.

"Oh, but I do." I give her a smile. "I knew you looked familiar when you had the guts to take my nephew, but I couldn't place you. But now I see the true bitch inside of you." I chuckle, then hold her gaze for a few seconds. "I thought you were dead, *Aubrey*."

A grin splits her face, a little impressed.

"I was." She shrugs. "In a way. But then, I was resurrected. Like a phoenix from the ashes."

"You look more like a duck." Kendall huffs. "A lot of quack. Not very impressive."

I do my best to keep my amusement inside that comes from my girl's snarkiness, but I can't help showing appreciation for her wit.

"Your wifey got a big mouth. Maybe I should do something about that." Aubrey's gaze turns vicious, and my amusement is quickly replaced by fear.

"Leave her alone," I bark, doing my best to pull my hands from the ropes around my wrists. It's too tight, and she grabs a piece of duct tape while my ribs slowly move up and down, placing it over Kendall's mouth. I try to calm her with a soothing look, but I can see the gutting fear in her eyes.

"Now we can talk," she says when she's finished. "How are you, Franky?"

"Peachy. How are you doing, Aubrey?" I play the game with her, not even thinking about giving this piece of shit any of my distress.

"Hmm, let's see. Got the big bad Wolfe tied up in my warehouse with his little wifey, so I'm doing pretty good."

"Not for long, you won't," I shrug.

"Oh, Franklin Wolfe," she says with a devilish chuckle, "always such a big mouth. You know, that smart mouth will get you in trouble one day. Tell me, do you even know why you're here?"

"Something tells me you have a sick obsession with my brother."

"Oh, that's not very sweet, is it?" She leans her hands on my knees, peering directly into my eyes. I always thought she had a crazed look every time I picked Reign up for the day, but now that she's only a few inches away from my face, I realize she's long past the crazed stage. Aubrey Brady is a full-blown psychopath.

"But no." She gets back up, walking away from me, then theatrically turns around. "My obsession is with *you*. After all, you're the one who ruined my life, didn't you?" *See, psychopath.*

"Enlighten me," I tell her with a bored look.

"You took Reign from me."

The absurdness of her words genuinely makes me laugh.

"Trust me, little girl, Reign wanted to leave just as much as I wanted to get him out of there."

"Ah, you see, but that's where you are wrong. The Reign *I* know would've saved me. Taken me with him. But you prevented him from doing that."

"You're delusional."

She looks up at the ceiling, her index finger on her chin.

"That's what my shrink said. He also said I was a bit crazy. But I guess getting fucked in the ass from age twelve does that to you, wouldn't you say?" she snarls.

I hold her gaze, unfazed by her comments, until I catch movement in the corner of my eye. My face falls when I notice a young girl in a crate in one of the corners of the warehouse.

"Who's that?" This time I can't keep my voice as composed as I want to.

She looks over her shoulder.

"Oh that? Novalee. My daughter. Or my sister. Whatever way you want to see it. Figured Novalee is a good name for her. You know, *Nova*-lee." She snickers with a rant.

"She sleeps in a crate?"

"Well, how else am I going to make sure she doesn't get in the way?"

My mind brings me back to the hell Reign was forced to live in, and my heart now slips into protective mode knowing that there is a kid involved.

"We can help you."

"You already did enough, *Wolfe*. If you didn't take Reign from me, this would've never happened. But without Reign there as a shield and my mom gone with the wind, my father thought I was his rightful property. Got my little girl to remind me of it every day." She says it as if it's the most normal thing in the world, making me understand there is nothing left to save.

"Your shrink is right. You *are* crazy."

"Maybe he is."

"Reign is going to kill you."

"No, he won't." She gives me an incredulous look. "He loves me."

Amused, I decide to indulge in her craziness.

"What makes you think that?"

"I know it. I feel it in my heart. He came back for me, you know?" A dreamy glow washes over her face. "He killed my dad in the process. He came to save me. When he knows I'm still alive, we can finally start our lives together with our baby girl."

"You mean *your* baby girl," I correct, and her vicious glare quickly returns.

"Reign will love it like it's his own. You know how big his heart is."

A huge smirk travels my face, a chuckle falling from my mouth that I'm unable to keep inside when I look at the stupid girl in front of me.

"You're underestimating one thing."

"What's that, Franky boy?"

My energy grows bigger, even though I'm tied to a chair. She notices the dark look moving down my face because I can see how she shifts on her feet.

"The loyalty of the pack," I growl, my tone growing more wicked with every sentence. "Reign might care about you. I will even entertain the thought of him loving you, considering your history and all. But he will *never* betray me. He will rip you apart when he finds out what you did to me. What you did to *her*." I jerk my head to Kendall.

Aubrey lifts her chin, doing her best to keep her indifference, but I see the uncertainty in her eyes.

"I guess we'll see about that," she mutters.

40

It took me a few minutes and two shots of Bourbon before Connor pulled me on my feet and I came to my senses. I vaguely remember how Lily took Sienna to the kitchen to stay with her and Colin, and by the time we walk in there, Killian is leading us back out, already having put everything in place to get our brother back. I could be surprised about how fast my brother put up a strategy to get Franklin and Kendall back in one piece, but really, I'm not. Killian is just as cunning and smart as Franklin, and with him being absent, Killian makes good use of those skills to lead us.

I slug forward, following my brothers outside where Callie and Kane get out of one of the SUVs on the circular driveway.

"What are they doing here?" I frown, never missing a beat, as we descend the few steps in front of the house.

"Keeping an eye on Colin and the girls," Killian replies. He gives them a tight nod in recognition, and I do the same. Callie sends me a comforting smile and a short wave before she disappears into the house, and we jump in the car. Connor climbs behind the wheel with Killian next to him while I place myself in the back. Four cars are behind us, with two finalizing the convoy that will be on its way as soon as Killian gives the signal to go. He opens the window of the car, holding up his hand, telling our men to wait while he puts his phone to his ear.

"Yeah. Be there in ten." He pauses. "Oh, and, hey! Don't screw this up. This is your shot to prove yourself."

He hangs up the phone, then signals for the cars to go.

"Who was that?"

"My secret weapon." The smirk is audible in his voice and Connor gives him a puzzled look, though we both don't bother to ask what he's talking about. Whatever he's got in store, the chance is that it will work best if we don't know. Make sure we can't give anything away.

I close my eyes, trying to get some rest for the next ten minutes, while at the same time, the door on the other side flies open.

"What the hell?" I snap my head toward the silky black hair flowing my way as I feel the car drive over the gravel at a slow pace. "Get out, Sienna!" I order.

"No!"

"What the fuck, Sienna?" Killian growls from the front.

"Baby, this is not a game. Con, stop the car!"

"No! Reign Wolfe, I just got you back. I'm not losing you again." Her eyes are glassy and breaking my heart all over again.

"For fuck's sake, baby," I cry, grabbing her hand. "You're not going to lose me. I'll be back before you know it. Connor, stop the car."

"No, Reign. I'm coming with you!"

"Stop the car, Connor!" I bark out, ignoring her pleading look. I need to keep my head straight and that ain't working if she's around.

"Reign!" Killian booms. He twists his body around to glare at the both of us, his finger pointed and reprimanding. "We don't have time for this shit." He directs his attention to Sienna. "Not cool, Sienna! You're one of us, and I love you like a sister, but right now you're not helping! You're only making this harder. You can come, but you're staying in the car or so help me God, I will put you in the trunk until we get my brother back." He pauses and I can feel her straighten her back next to me, bringing a ping of amusement on this gloomy day. "Got it?"

Like a little girl, she nods, clearly impressed by my brother's change in attitude toward her before he turns back around with a sharp movement. She glances at me, then crawls closer to hold my arm as she looks up at me.

"You think he's serious?" she whispers.

"Dead." I want to stay mad at her, but she's fucking cute as she throws me a shocked expression, not used to being on the other side of Killian's wrath. "And so am I. You're staying in the car, or we'll tie you up, gag you, and blindfold you before we throw you in the trunk."

"What?" she screeches. "You wouldn't."

"I would if it meant keeping you safe for the next few hours."

"And I sure as fuck will," Killian pitches in.

She holds my gaze with a dull expression, and I look into her gorgeous irises. I watch the golden specks dance around in the light of the moon before they are washed with a hint of guilt. "I'm sorry, Reign. I should've never–"

"I'm glad you did," I cut her off, cupping her cheek. "But right now, I need to focus on getting my brother back, okay?"

She nods.

"Sorry you had to witness that."

"I'm glad you did it." She shakes her head, then leans her temple against my arm. "It was about time you let out all that anger."

Maybe it's the alcohol that's giving me the ability to look past the cloud that has been blurring my vision for many years now, or maybe it's the fact that this new piece of information acted like a ray of sunshine in a pitch-black world. But either way, I know she's right.

I sigh, holding her hand in a tight grip. "I know."

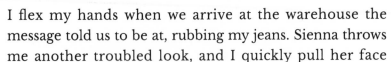

I flex my hands when we arrive at the warehouse the message told us to be at, rubbing my jeans. Sienna throws me another troubled look, and I quickly pull her face toward mine, planting a crushing kiss against her lips.

"Stay in the car, baby. I'll be right, back."

"You promise?" she whispers, holding onto my wrists.

"I promise." I give her a final peck, then exit the car with Connor and Killian.

"Are you ready for this?" Killian purses his lips, giving me a questioning look, while Connor comes to stand beside us.

"I guess." I take a step forward, ready to get this over with, but Killian's hand drops on my chest, holding me back.

"Look. There is a big chance a part of your past is in that warehouse. *Are you ready for this?*" His green eyes peer at me with a worry that guts me, making me feel like an asshole all over again. I treated my brothers like shit, lashing out because of my own pain, and they are still here to defend me. To take over if I decide I can't handle it. To do their best to keep the hard things away from me. But it's time for me to grow up. I'll always be the youngest Wolfe, the little brother. But I'm no longer going to let my brothers fight my battles for me. Whoever is inside those walls, they are dead.

"I'm ready," I say with determination while squaring my shoulders.

"Good. Let's go." Killian instructs our men to surround the warehouse while three of them guard the entrance as my brothers and I walk in. Like a rehearsed script, we walk in as a unit, each step taken at the same time with our fingers close to the guns in our waistbands. Our steps reverberate through the empty space, the air stuffy. It's dark and we slow down our pace to take in our surroundings until we are close to the middle of the empty hall.

Suddenly, a single light turns on, the bulb swinging from the ceiling. A cold shudder makes my skin tingle in an excruciating way as I stare at the sight in front of me while I hear my brothers breathing loudly beside me.

Franklin and Kendall are both tied up to a chair, Kendall's lips covered by a piece of duct tape. Both of them are squeezing their eyes shut, doing their best to adjust to the sudden flash of light.

"Evening, boys," Franklin smiles when his gaze lands on us. He looks completely unbothered, like all he needs is a glass of whiskey to have a good night, a pro at hiding his stress. But I know with Kendall in danger, his heart must be pounding like a madman's.

But that's not what shocks me. It's the blonde standing right underneath the light bulb. Her hair is different. She looks older. But I'd remember those eyes anywhere. They are still laced with that ominous glint, the vicious part that can't hide behind the sweet smile she's shooting me.

"You," Connor growls in recognition.

"Bella," Killian huffs.

"Aubrey," I stammer. "You're dead."

"Aubrey?!" Connor and Killian parrot in confusion.

"Really? Because I feel pretty alive," she beams with a smug grin. She's wearing white jeans with a white crop top showing deep cleavage, her new look finished with a fiery red leather jacket.

"Your hair."

She plucks a strand of her blonde hair. "You like?"

"I don't understand." I saw the records. I saw pictures of the dead body. I went through every database and came to the same conclusion; Aubrey Brady is dead.

"It's not that hard." She rolls her eyes, sauntering a little closer, and it's the first time I notice the gun resting in her palm. "I swapped some dental records and I'I faked my own death. Aubrey's life wasn't much fun anyway. Bella, on the other hand, she is fun."

"Bella," I repeat, remembering the name from a few months ago. "You kidnapped Colin."

"Yeah, sorry about that." My shock simmers down, quickly replaced by rage that's fueled by the thought of my nephew and how she kidnapped him to get to my brother.

"You drugged him."

"Don't be so dramatic. It was innocent. Just something to keep him unconscious."

"And the gifts?"

"Just wanted to let you know I was thinking about you." Her lashes flutter up and down, and I have a hard time figuring out if she's being serious or sarcastic. If she actually believes her crap or just enjoys putting on a show.

"Why are you doing this?" I keep a straight face, but really, I feel the blood boiling through my body. I know she's always been damaged and easily angered, but I don't understand why she would take Franklin.

She cocks her head with a crazed look, her eyes narrowing as a grimace travels across her lips.

"Why are you looking at me like that? Aren't you happy?"

"Happy?" If she thinks I'm happy with my brother and sister-in-law tied to a chair, she's more psychotic than I thought.

"Your brother ruined your life. I'm here to save you from him. We can finally start our life together."

I hear Killian snort and she snaps her gaze at him while I try to comprehend what she's saying, realizing she's not joking. She's dead serious.

"Together? Aubrey–"

"Aubrey is dead!" She cuts me off with a vile look. "It's *Bella*!" Her tone is agitated, and I know that's not a good combination with her mental state, so I throw up my hands, placating.

"*Bella*, I don't understand."

She clears her throat, then rubs her forehead as if she's growing more impatient by the minute.

"You said we would leave, build our own family. Look, I already started." She points her gun to a crate in the corner of the warehouse, barely noticeable if you don't know, but when you look at it, you can see the clear silhouette of a little girl with big eyes staring back at us.

"That's fucked up," Killian chimes in while Connor just keeps growling. His hands are balled to fists, his entire energy big as fuck as he keeps breathing through his nose with a deep scowl. He's ready to charge, to rip her head off her neck, and I know the only reason he isn't is because we need to get Franklin and Kendall first.

"Is she yours?" I swallow, trying my hardest to push away the lump that forms in the back of my throat as I look at the girl.

"Isn't she cute?"

"She is." I smile. I remember how sly she can be, being a direct offspring of her father, and right now, with my brother still on that side of the warehouse, the last thing I wanna do is piss her off. I gotta play the game to make sure she gives me what I want.

"We can make more, honey." There is a sincerity in her eyes that hurts, forming a big knot in my stomach as she keeps going. "You, me, her. Let's go like we were supposed to with Nova."

I shake my head.

"That was never the plan. I was going to help you. I was going to save you. But I never intended to start a new family." A pained expression forms on her already glaring face as she grinds her teeth together. "I already have a family."

"But you came back for me." She wiggles her head, looking at the floor, as if she can't believe what I'm saying. "I saw you. You killed my dad for me. *I* was your family." Her gaze lands on mine, the hurt clear in her amber eyes.

"I am." I slowly move closer to her. "You can be. But if you want to be part of my family, you can't hurt the people I love. You're hurting my brother. My friend." I point at Kendall. Her blue eyes are staring at me in horror.

"No! Your brother deserves it! He took you away from me!" Aubrey shouts. She quickly snaps her arm up, pointing the gun at my brother. We all get on edge, Killian and Connor taking a step closer, but I bring up my hand, telling them to stay back.

"Franklin tried to get you out!"

Her brows lift in surprise, but as quickly as they move up, they move back down, and she raises her chin.

"Lies," she sputters.

"He tried to get you out, but you were too old. He tried to get you out until you turned eighteen. And then you died."

She lets out a possessed screech, then points her gun to the ceiling and shoots twice. The loud sounds of the shots make me wince with dread gripping my heart.

"Shut up, Reign! You've always had him on a pedestal." She dangerously holds my gaze, her gun now pointed at Franklin again. "Too stupid to see he's the root of all problems."

Unable to hide my anger any longer, I take a big step forward until she shakes her head in warning.

"Aubrey, if you hurt my brother, I *will* kill you," I say through gritted teeth. I always knew she could be hysterical, the years of her childhood functioning as the foundation of a tight balance between a little troubled and insane. But never in a million years would I have expected her to come after my brothers. *My* family. That alone is enough for me to erase the little spark of hope I feel inside of me, wishing that, with the right help, Aubrey Brady could still have a better life. The look in her eyes tells me that's futile. There is no saving Aubrey Brady because she doesn't want to be saved. Her life damaged her beyond repair and now all I see is a threat. A threat to my world and my life, building out the urge to bare my teeth.

"Oh, I see how it is now." My body jerks to get closer. "Don't move!"

I hold still, with my hands up. "Calm down. Just let them go."

"Reign?! Are you okay?" My heart falls when I hear Sienna run into the warehouse, the footsteps of our men echoing through the air. For just a second, I close my eyes, not moving a muscle as I hear her come closer.

"Stay back, Sienna," I hear Connor grunt behind me.

"I heard gunshots. Oh my God, Kenny?" A gasp is audible and everything inside me wants to turn around, pick her up, and throw her in the trunk, like we said. But the psychotic look Aubrey is giving Sienna, with the corner of her mouth up and slowly dragging her tongue over her lower lip like Sienna is her next meal, tells me it's not safe to turn my back on Aubrey right now.

"Stay back," I bark in a lousy attempt to keep her as far away from Aubrey as possible.

"Well, well," Aubrey titters, "look what the cat dragged in. Sienna Brennan, how are you?"

"You," Sienna pushes out, shocked. "You attacked me."

I glance at Sienna, watching the horror drip from her face as she's looking at the girl from my past, and I feel my jaw clench when the memory of Sienna on the floor of that restroom flashes before my eyes.

"Geez, you people sure like to overreact. It was a little bump on the head." Aubrey rolls her eyes.

"You hurt her?" My chest slowly moves up and down.

"Honestly, Reign, if she can't even handle that, she ain't woman enough for you." Aubrey sounds bored, but I can see the amusement in her eyes.

"She's more woman than you'll ever be," I snarl.

She cocks a brow. "Is that so? You think she has the balls to do this?"

Her feet take big strides toward Kendall, and I hold in my breath until she places the barrel of the gun on her forehead. Kendall's blue eyes are looking like they are about to pop out of her head in fear as she jerks in her seat. Franklin's entire body tenses, the rage and nerves easily detected when you look at his flushed face.

"No!" I shout at the same time Sienna yells, "Stop!"

"You are dead, girl." Killian chuckles diabolically behind me.

"She's innocent," I plea. "Sienna, get in the car." I point my hand behind me, and I immediately hear her shuffle away from us, not putting up an argument.

"No, actually, Sienna. Stay." Aubrey smiles, like the sick bitch that she is.

"Leave," Killian presses with a grunt.

Aubrey shakes her head, her glare now aimed at Killian.

"Tut, tut. I said I wanted her to stay." She pauses. "How about a trade? Your brunette for my brunette?" She nudges her chin to Kendall.

"No," my brothers and I blurt out the word without effort, not because Kendall isn't worth a trade, but simply because we will never play into her hand. We will never give our enemy what they want, and this sociopathic blast from my past is no exception.

"I'll do it." I grind my teeth at the nobleness of Sienna's stupidity as fear showers my entire body.

"Don't you dare," I roar without looking back at her. When I entered this warehouse, I felt in control, confident that whoever was behind taking Franklin, we would defeat them. Yes, finding out Aubrey is still alive threw me off for a hot minute, but I still wasn't scared. But now that the girl I love is slowly dragging her feet past me, toward the woman who wants to harm her, makes me feel like that control is slipping from my fingers.

"Sienna." Killian tries to grab her arm, but she swings it in the air to escape from his grasp.

"Oh, such a noble little wifey," Aubrey taunts as Sienna takes another step forward.

"Sienna, don't you dare," I call behind her back, glancing at Killian in despair. He brings his gaze up and I follow it, noticing a figure on one of the beams. I suck in a breath, lowering my eyes again as I keep a straight face.

"Maybe I was wrong, maybe she is woman enough for you." Aubrey's eyes are fixated on Sienna, and my patience has reached its limit.

"Sienna, stop!" I lunge out, grabbing Sienna's arm before yanking her behind me.

Aubrey's arm tenses, the gun now aimed at my head.

"You really don't want to do that, Reign."

41

Sienna

Reign continues to shove me backwards until Killian pulls me behind him. We stand diagonally from Reign's back, giving me a clear vision of the stern features on his face. They were laced with fear a minute ago, but now they are different. More cunning, reminding me of the looks Killian normally gives people.

"I'm sorry, Aubrey," Reign says. His voice doesn't match his words, and he squares his shoulders. "I really, really am. I wish I could've helped you more. Helped you better. Helped Nova better. I failed you, and for that, I'm truly sorry. But you failed to have seen one thing from the start." There is a smugness in his tone that surprises me, making goosebumps pepper my skin as I watch his entire stance change. As if he's pushing out the full form of the Wolfe that's tucked inside of him. Killian lets out a chuckle that has me frowning, wondering if he knows something that I don't. "

"Now you sound all cryptic like your brother. Your *alpha*," she mocks. "It's pathetic how all you grown ass men let your life be dictated by one man. As soon as he leaves the building, you're nothing but a few stray dogs looking for your leader."

A devilish snicker falls from his lips, and I hold my breath.

"But that's where you are wrong. We are a pack. The *Wolfe* pack. You know what the characteristics of a pack are?"

"Please, do tell," she replies, swishing her gun in the air.

"Family." He pauses with every answer, raising the tension. "A team. Careful planning. Strategy and unlimited patience."

A big bark of laughter erupts from her mouth, sounding like a fucking witch.

"Not sure what that's going to do for you now?"

"You might think we are an unstructured group of dogs without Franklin, but we continue to function as a pack. With or *without* him."

A red dot falls on her chest, and she dips her chin when she notices it. Her eyes frantically start searching around her, and I do the same, keeping my head still to hide my confusion. Finally, she locks her gaze with mine once more, fear now written in it.

Reign smiles. "You didn't really think you could beat us, right? It's over. Aubrey. Drop the gun."

She holds still, as if she's going over her options.

"Drop the gun," Killian commands.

Aubrey's face grows more desperate, and she shakes her head. Her eyes are getting gloomy, and my heart starts to race, knowing she's about to lose it.

"You were mine, Reign. *Mine*. When you came to Providence, I knew you were going to be my savior, and you just bailed." She pushes the last words out with a growl, then stomps over to Franklin. "How are you going to pay for that? With his life or hers?"

There is no more threat in her action, just a clear promise, laced with determination as she pushes the barrel against his temple.

"No!" I yelp. With wide eyes, I register how she brings her finger to the trigger with a grimace. "

"Say goodbye to your brother, Prince Charming." The gunshot rings in my ears, and for what feels like forever, I just blink, a beep slicing through my mind in a sharp pain of stress while I look at Aubrey's paralyzed body falling to the floor. The smell of gunpowder attacks my nose, and I know right at that moment that it will forever remind me of the horrible sight in front of me. The girl is still conscious, but it's clear her life is slipping away. My eyes land on Franklin, a silent conversation forming between him and Reign, while my chest slowly moves up and down. Franklin swallows, breaking their connection, then nudges his chin to Aubrey on the floor, as if he tells him to finish it without uttering an actual word.

"Are you okay?" Reign swings his body to face me with a worried look.

"Yeah," I breathe, nodding, though it feels like a lie.

Satisfied with that answer, he looks up to the beams, and I follow his gaze.

"Is that—?" He looks at Killian. "The girl from the bar?"

A little shocked, I glance at the girl wearing all black and sitting with a rifle in her hand like it's her best friend. She has a smug smile haunting her scowling face, making her appear daunting in the shadows of the warehouse.

"Told you I had a secret weapon." Killian smirks with a wink, then slogs his way past us with an arrogance only Killian can.

Killian cuts Franklin and Kendall loose while Reign squats down next to Aubrey, cocking his head in a taunting way, bringing shivers that make my back shudder. Connor moves closer, placing a comforting hand on the small of my back as I keep my gaze trained on Reign and Aubrey, holding in a breath. I don't have to see the vicious smirk that I know is on his face, because I can hear it in his tone when he opens his mouth.

"At some point in our lives, we have to stop blaming everyone else for our misery. I wish there was something better for you. But I knew that very first day how much your dad's evil had already rubbed off on you, Aubrey. I desperately wanted to save you. But I never truly could." Tears are brimming my eyes, grieving for the ghosts of Reign's past. Now that he's told me everything, I realize how hard this must be for him. Especially for him, who always wants to see the good in people. He wanted to save Aubrey and Nova, protect them like his brothers have always protected him, but he never stood a chance.

"Help me." It comes out with a gurgle, her eyes widened in terror and the tips of her blonde hair now stained with blood. One last plea, even though she must know it's useless. I know she does. If Reign won't kill her, one of the others definitely will.

"You tried to hurt my pack. *No one* walks from that alive."

"Reign, no," she huffs, her words barely audible.

"Goodbye, Aubrey." He moves to get up, but with her last strength, she grabs his arm and he rears his head back to her.

"Take care of my girl, please." I want to hate her, but knowing her past and hearing the last words she's chosen only makes me feel sorry for her. It makes me realize we don't always control where we end up in life. Sometimes you just ride the wave of life and hope you end up at the beach, instead of drowning in the darkness.

Reign gives her a short nod, then gets up with a determination that makes him age within a split second. As if he's shedding the skin of his past, growing into the man he is today. With a pinched mouth, his piercing eyes find Killian.

"Kill her."

A wide grin splits Killian's face before he licks his lower lip, gloating over the opportunity his brother just gave him while Reign glances at Franklin holding Kendall in a tight grip. His eyes are closed and his lips are pressed against her dark hair. A small smile curls the corners of his mouth with relief, and he then moves his gaze to me. Closing the distance, he notices my discomfort as I watch Killian slash his knife across Aubrey's throat. My eyes won't divert, until Reign blocks my vision with his body, his hands on my arms.

"Don't watch, baby. Connor, get the girl." I glance at the little girl looking at me like a scared kitten, as if I'm hugging the devil. "Come here, baby." He tucks me into his chest and, grateful, I do as he says, wrapping my arms around his waist, and then, in the comfort of his arms, I finally give my tears free rein as he hums in my hair. "It's over, baby."

42

Sienna

H is soft hand brushing the skin on my back in even strokes wakes me up the next morning. My arm is draped over his stomach, my cheek pressed against his chest, and our legs tangled together. I look up at him and am instantly met by his famous boyish grin. His eyes still look heavy and hooded, as if he has not slept at all, but there is a tiny flare of lightness that wasn't there before.

"Good morning." He presses a lingering kiss against my forehead.

"Good morning." I stretch out, then snuggle closer against him. "Did you get some sleep?"

"Some."

"How are you feeling?" I pause, giving him a tentative look. "You know, about Aubrey."

He sighs. It's deep and hefty.

"It's hard," he admits, looking up at the ceiling. "But in a way, I also feel very liberated."

I comfortingly run my palm over his chest as I keep listening.

"For years I lived with the feeling that I should've saved her. That I should've done more. That, in a way, I killed her just as much as any other asshole in her life. The guilt has been dragging me down ever since that day, and more than I wanted, I kept wondering what I could've done differently. And every time, I came to the conclusion that there was nothing because she couldn't be saved, and then the next day, the same train of thought would start all over again. I never understood why, because physically, I could've pulled her out of there. But now that I've looked into her eyes for the last time..." He sucks in a sharp breath, as if he's bracing himself. "I know why. There wasn't anyone who could mend her broken soul. Not even me." I still hear the pain in his voice, and it's breaking my heart.

"You were only sixteen, seventeen. You couldn't do much more. She was eighteen when she faked her own death. She made her decision."

"I know." He nods. "But all those years I yearned a girl I thought I should've saved. I mourned my failure. Now I just need to grief the girl, you know?"

"I understand. And you should take the time you need for that." I offer him a comforting smile, and he replies by pressing his lips against mine.

"Thank you for understanding, baby."

When we break loose, he tucks me even closer against him, his warm body melting into mine. We lie like that for a few minutes, feeling content in each other's arms as we look up at the ceiling.

"Who was that girl, by the way? The one who shot Aubrey?"

A chuckle leaves Reign's lips, and I tilt my head to look at him.

"I haven't caught her name yet, but I know she's been following Killian around for a while. Something about wanting his help to avenge her family."

"No-suh!"

"Ya-huh. That night we were at the club?" I nod in recognition as he brings his gaze to mine. "She was there. And a few nights later, she was at a bar Kill and I were having drinks in. I guess she helped us in return for a favor or something."

"How old is she?"

"I don't know. But she looks like she's fresh out of high school."

I stay quiet for a moment. "Killian doesn't seem like the guy that goes out helping teenage girls looking for vengeance.

"I know." He snorts. "That's why I think there is more going on. I haven't had the chance to ask him yet. But that's not important right now." He quickly flips me on my back, pushing his body on top of mine, and I let out a playful shriek until his face goes serious.

"Are *you* okay?" he questions, cupping my cheek with a tender look.

I bite my lip, a smile tugging my mouth as I nod. I love how thoughtful he is, even though this was his war, never mine.

"Yeah. Yeah, I'm okay. I hope to never have to find myself in that situation again. But I'm okay." The tips of my fingers move up and down his arm. "Are you sure *you* are okay?"

"Not yet," he replies honestly. "But I will be. I just need some time. Can you give me that?"

My palms snake around his neck, and I guide his lips toward mine.

"I got all the time in the world, Reign."

43

When I stare at the morning sky, sitting on the bench in the garden of the mansion, for the first time in forever, I feel like the sky is exactly as it seems. Blue. Bright. Not laced with clouds. Not waiting to be pushed away by thunder. I still remember vividly how I felt a sense of relief when I killed Jefferson, but with Aubrey gone, it's like I've finally been able to let go of my past. With her death came the freedom to forgive myself, and to give the twelve-year-old inside of me a pat on the back. It was never my job to be their prince. To save them from the darkness. Unknowingly, I gave myself a burden that no twelve-year-old should carry.

I understand that now.

My attention moves to the side when someone sits down beside me, and I lock eyes with my big brother. After yesterday, we didn't get a chance to talk, both hell-bent on taking our girls home and sleeping the night away. But now that our eyes lock, really lock without any restrictions, a sense of faith showers over me. Knowing the future will be better after this.

"How are you holding up?" Franklin gets comfortable, his gaze pointed in front of him.

"I'm okay. Just trying to wrap my head around it all."

"We found a good foster family for the girl."

"That soon?" I snap my head to him. "You sure?"

"Positive. I made a few calls this morning. The woman who helped me get you and Killian back knows a young couple that wanted to adopt. They were eager to foster her. They will get a trial period, but if it turns out okay, they will consider adopting her as well. And I'll be checking in with them every week."

"Thank you."

"No problem."

"How is Kendall?"

He pushes out a breath through his nose, a smile tugging the corner of his mouth.

"She's good. She's a tough one."

"Don't I know it." I chortle.

"How is Sienna?" he asks.

"A little startled. But she'll be fine."

The silence returns, sitting between us like an awkward fifth little brother. With my finger, I draw letters on the wood of the bench, building the courage to bring up the big elephant in the room. After about a minute of silence, I push out a breath before sucking in another lungful of air.

"I know," I tell him, pausing for a second to find the right words. "About Declan." Pause. "Why you killed him?"

I slowly twist my head, watching Franklin nod.

"Sienna told me." There is no judgment in his voice, and it spurs me on to keep going.

"Why didn't you tell me, Franky?"

"Same reason you didn't ask me." He turns his head to face me, the features of his face blank, though I can see the kindness coming through. "You know, you and I have the same character. The same tortured soul with more empathy than necessary in our line of work. I didn't tell you because I knew your torment needed someone to blame."

"But it wasn't true," I counter.

"I know. But I'd rather you hate me than do things to others you'd regret even more out of rage. I knew I caused you that pain. If I didn't kill Declan, this would've never happened. I took responsibility. Gave you someone to kick at without getting you into trouble. You are not as cunning as Killian. You are not as brutal as Connor." He pauses. "I knew the reason you'd lash out at me was because you knew deep down you can never lose me. It would be the one thing that would break you forever if you lost anyone else. It was safe to be mad at me." My eyes grow wet with his confession, pain flying from my chest. I always thought that one day I kicked him off that pedestal, but hearing him reflect on it like this makes me understand I never really did. My brother has always been my big example, and he still is today. It's something that never changed, even though I tried my hardest to make that true.

"I'm so sorry, Franklin." My voice breaks as I latch my arms around his neck, taking him into the hug I've been longing for since the day I found out the truth about Declan. I've been craving to feel that brotherly bond and the comfort only Franklin can give me. "I'm *so* sorry."

"It's okay," he says in my ear. "You're my brother. I'd do it all over again if I had to."

My emotions take over, and I let them, sobbing against my brother's shoulder.

"I'm so, *so* sorry."

"I'm sorry too."

He just holds me, for as long as I need, literally having my back as I collapse in his arms. The leftover pain and grief finally seem to leave my body, making it so I can breathe again when I regain my strength. I break loose, wiping my tears away with the back of my hand, then stare into my brother's green eyes.

"Can you forgive me?"

He waggles his head. "There is nothing to forgive."

He looks away to gather his thoughts, then continues. "I don't expect you to be like our Connor and Killian. Or even me. We all have our qualities. But from now on, no more secrets." A scowl forms on his sharp jaw, and I can't blame him.

"No more secrets. I love you, man." I give him another hug, and he eagerly takes it as he squeezes my chest against his with a chuckle.

"I love you too, *tool.*" Our brotherly affection is interrupted when we hear the shuffle of footsteps behind us, followed by someone clearing their throat, and I look up to Callie's beaming smile.

"We're leaving."

"Right." I get up, pulling my friend into a hug while I shoot her husband a genuine smile above her head. I expect him to growl at me or bark something, but he stays quiet, though with narrowed eyes.

"No-suh," I huff, then pull back to look at Callie. "He just let me hug you without throwing a knife at me. I think we're making progress. Maybe next time I can greet you with a kiss on the cheek?"

"Don't push it," Kane now grunts, making me bark out a laugh.

"So, predictable, Carrillo." I let go of Callie, then offer my hand to Kane, followed by Franklin doing the same. "Thank you for protecting Colin and the girls, man. I really appreciate it."

He gives me a coy smile. "You're welcome. Sorry, I couldn't stop your girl from getting in that car."

"Don't worry about it. She's like this fireball." I nudge my shoulder against Callie. "You can't stop them when they get something into their heads.

"Don't I know it," he replies as Callie rolls her eyes at the both of us.

"Call me if you need anything else."

"Thanks, Reign." Callie twists her focus back and forth between me and my brother. "If any of you Wolfes are popping the question that comes with a ring, I want an invite." She points her finger at us, her lips pursed in a slight scowl. "I don't care if he's on your shitlist." She glances at Kane. "I can come without him. I'm not missing a Wolfe wedding."

Franklin and I break out into laughter as we all make our way to the front of the house.

"You got it, Callie girl," Franklin replies. I trail a bit behind them, a smile stretching my mouth, fueled by the lack of pressure on my chest. And when I see Sienna waiting for me on the gravel of the driveway, it only grows brighter. After years of sitting in the darkness, ruled by my past, I can finally live my life.

With her. The girl who has always been my light.

44

Sienna

"**R**eign, we need to set up. We're opening in half an hour."

I moan against his ear as his lips leave a trail of kisses down my neck. His hands are everywhere, touching every piece of bare skin he can find.

"We can do a lot in half an hour." He cups my cheek, holding my face in place for him to keep going without restrictions.

"Yeah, like count the money, set up the glasses, restock the shelves," I scold.

He grunts against my skin, biting, then brings his head up.

"You're no fun." He pouts.

"Tell you what," I say, softly pushing him away, "after closing, you can fuck me on the bar."

His eyebrows raise with excitement. "Really?"

"Really."

"Lay you out on the entire bar, spread you wide, and press my tongue against your pussy?"

I swallow, the image already making me drip with desire, then swat his arm.

"You're an asshole."

"I just want to make clear we're on the same page, expectation wise and all?" He smirks. "If you're giving me a free pass, I'm not just doing a quickie against the workstation. Nope, I want to have a memory of your ass on every piece of the bar."

My cheeks grow flush when he crowds my space once more, knowing exactly what he's doing. "Are we in agreement?" He presses a kiss on my lips. "Or do you want me to show you what I'm talking about right now?"

"Yes!" I huff, pushing him off with a chuckle. "We are in agreement. Now stop touching me." I jump off the workstation to create some distance between us, and he takes the opportunity to smack my ass, eliciting a shriek from my lips.

"Hold up." He yanks me back by my shirt, and I fall into his chest. "I got something for you."

"For me?"

He pulls a piece of paper from the back of his jeans, holding it in front of my face. I snatch it out of his hand with a suspicious look, then turn around to read it without him staring at me. My eyes bounce over the words as Reign snakes his arms around my waist, his chin resting on my shoulder.

"Ownership?" I screech, confused.

His grip tightens, preventing me from turning around.

"Look, I know you'd rather have your own bar, and Franklin did promise you a wicked bag of cash. If that's really what you want, we can still do that. But you're part of our family. You're part of the pack and everything in this bar is done by your hand. Killian agreed to take a step back, and I figured you and I can run this bar together."

"Together?" I parrot, still staring at the piece of paper.

"Well, yeah. Whatever way you're going to put it, at some point we're going to be married and half of this bar is going to be yours anyway. We might as well just start it together, too. Besides, it means I can fuck you on *our* bar whenever I want."

I blink, trying to comprehend what he's saying.

"We're going to be married?"

He clears his throat, straightening his back as he spins me in his arms.

"Listen, you can fight me on the bar thing, I don't mind. But the marriage thing is non-negotiable. You are going to be my wife. And I'm going to be your husband."

An amused grin tugs on the corners of my mouth and he grabs my chin, bringing his lips closer when he notices the playful glint in my eyes.

"Is that so?" I purr, resting my hands on his arms.

"You wanna fight me for it?" His lips brush against mine until they fall against my mouth in a longing, affectionate kiss.

"No." The answer is simple, because that's exactly how it is. My love for Reign Wolfe isn't fightable. It's unbreakable. "But does that mean this is also a proposal?" I hold up the paper.

"No, *this*[]—he grabs it from my hand—"is a promise. A promise that I will share everything I own with you. My house. My heart. My cars."

"Cars? As in plural?"

"Not the point. But yes, everything. *Including* my bar." He buries his hands in my hair, holding my head in place. "So, what do you say? Let's do this together."

I look into his piercing green eyes, feeling like a sixteen-year-old girl again. When he could make me sway with a single look, and he still can.

"We'll do it together."

45

EPILOGUE

Sienna

THANKSGIVING

I finish decorating the front door with fake fall leaves, then take the steps down to the floor. Colin flies past me with a salvo of giggles coming from his cute face while Reign chases him through the hall.

"No, no, no!" I lift Colin in the air, making him squirm in my arms when his uncle comes closer. I hold my hand up, giving Reign a reprimanding look, and he holds still, stunned.

"I spent the entire morning decorating the house. I'm not risking that because you want to play tag."

Reign cocks an eyebrow while Colin moves his green irises between the two of us in anticipation. It's eerie how much this tiny person looks like these four brothers, clearly blessed with the good genes that run in the Wolfe family.

"Excuse me, *miss*," he sasses. "We are not playing *tag*. We are playing *pirates*. And like any feared pirate"—his eyes narrow, his voice growing lower, and he hunches forward as he takes a step closer—"I don't listen to girlies like you!"

A feral grunt erupts from his lips, and I screech, followed by a squeal from Colin, and with the little man in my arms, I take off to the kitchen as fast as I can, with Reign following our tracks. Our shrieks are alternated with laughter as we storm through the swinging kitchen door, our amused panic greeted by five sets of eyes staring at us like we've lost our minds.

"Help! Help!" I yelp, my words almost drowned out by Colin's infectious laughter. "Pirate! Pirate!" I hide behind Franklin, and Reign stalks into the kitchen with big strides and a mischievous grin on his face. The look in his eyes screams trouble, and he lets out an unimpressed chuckle when he sees Colin and me hiding behind the big shoulders of his brother.

"Help us, Uncle Frank! Help us!" I whisper from his back.

With a big smile, he turns around. "Come here, I'll help you. Come, little Wolfe." He takes Colin out of my arms, and I shoot Reign a victorious look with my arms crossed in front of my chest. Franklin hands Colin over to Connor. Confused, I move my head back and forth between the two of them, but before I understand what's happening, Franklin pushes me right into Reign's arms, who leaps onto my neck with his lips. I shriek, and it's followed by laughs from everyone sitting in the kitchen, and Colin who's still shouting I should run.

"Too late for that, buddy," Reign explains, holding me in a tight grip as I glare at Franklin.

"Traitor." I stick out my tongue, and he just laughs.

"You didn't really think he was on your team?" Reign murmurs in my ear.

"I liked it better when the two of you were still hating each other," I joke.

Reign spins me in his arms, pressing a kiss to my neck, and I let my weight fall against his chest. I glance at the kitchen island where Lily is putting the final touches to the supper she prepared.

"Wow, Lily! This is amazing!"

Killian sneakily tosses a meatball in his mouth, but Lily catches him like the real mom that she is.

"Take your paws off, *Wolfe*." She slaps his hand, and he moves them out of the way, scorned, though a smile haunts his lips.

When the doorbell rings, I glance around the room. "Who's that?"

"For me." Killian's gaze is blank, though I notice a sparkle in his green eyes when he walks out of the kitchen.

"He invited someone?" I question no one in particular.

"Must be official, then," Reign pitches in.

Kendall, Lily, and I exchange a look, our eyebrows all the way up to our hairlines.

"Wait? What?" Kendall blurts, followed by Lily's, "No-suh!"

The brothers all keep their mouths shut, and we stare at them in anticipation until the kitchen door swings open. Killian walks back in with that same stoic expression on his face, but this time he's followed by a tiny brunette.

"Everyone," Killian booms, "this is Lexie."

She tilts her head in annoyance, a glare clear on her freckled face pointed at Killian. "It's Alexandra." Killian shrugs like an asshole, which doesn't surprise me before Lexie glances around the room.

"Hello," she says, a little bit shy. She's wearing a black bomber jacket, black jeans, and black boots, looking like the definition of a teenage rebel. The purity from her make-up free face makes me believe she's not a day older than twenty, and I blink in surprise. She holds onto the arm that hangs around her body, the awkwardness dripping off her entire stance.

When the room stays quiet for a second too long, I shoot her a beaming smile and offer my hand.

"Hi, I'm Sienna." My gaze turns grateful when I recognize her now that I can properly look into her eyes. "You're the girl that saved us. Thank you."

A coy smile forms on her lips, and she grabs my hand with hesitation, before the rest of the group follows right behind me and the ice seems to break a little. I keep my gaze fixated on her as she starts to joke around with Colin while Killian stays close behind her.

"Did you know about this?" I murmur to Reign.

"I know some of it."

Before I can ask him for an explanation, Franklin claims the attention in the room with his booming voice.

"Now that everyone is here, I have a few things to say." He raises his whiskey glass, then his eyes travel around the room.

"This year has been a lot. But in the end, we grew our pack, and I couldn't think of a better way. You all have my unconditional loyalty, because from now on, you are family, but there is one person who deserves most of what I have to give."

"Ah, man!" Reign whines, a grin audible in my ear. "You didn't have to put me in the spotlight like that!"

Franklin rolls his eyes, the rest of us falling in laughter. "Shut up, *tool*."

He puts his glass down, then goes down on one knee while he grabs Kendall's hand, who's still sitting on one of the stools. Her entire body freezes, and she gasps before throwing her other hand in front of her mouth while Franklin pulls out a small jewelry box.

"Kenny, I spent at least an hour today finding the words to tell you how much I love you, but I finally threw them all in the trash, realizing I'm not Reign."

We all chuckle.

"I don't have many words. All I know is that I love you, I refuse to spend a day without you, and I want to wake up next to you for the rest of my life." He pauses. "Will you marry me? Become a *Wolfe*?"

Kendall is lost for words, her tears finding their way out of the corners of her eyes.

"See, man. This is what you get when you propose in the fucking kitchen! Who does that?" Reign bellows like the fucking clown that he is.

Franklin snaps his head to Reign. "As soon as I got this ring on her finger, you better fucking run."

"I don't know, man." Killian pitches in. "He kinda has a point."

Franklin points his finger back and forth between his youngest brothers with a glare. "Dead. Both of you." When he puts his focus back on Kendall, she's sobbing into her own hand, and he slowly tugs her hand to snap her out of it.

"I kinda need you to say yes, pretty girl." He smiles, encouraging.

She nods, followed by a yes, and we all start clapping.

"One day, that will be us," Reign mumbles, his lips flush with my ear.

I twist my head to look at him, then crash my mouth onto his. "Can't wait."

Franklin slides the ring over Kendall's finger, then presses an affectionate kiss on her lips before he whispers something in her hair. When they break loose, the smile moves from his face, a blank expression back in place that would scare those who don't know him. He locks eyes with Reign before doing the same with Killian.

"Oh, shit," Reign and Killian both huff before they bolt out of the kitchen, with Franklin trailing behind them.

THE END

If you enjoyed Reign & Sienna, please consider leaving a review on Amazon. If not, please don't. LOL.

BILLIE LUSTIG

My brothers and I rule the underworld of Boston.
Some would say I'm the mysterious one. The one people
are scared of.
The one that unnerves people the most.
Lexie doesn't seem to care about my reputation.
If she does, she's great at hiding it.
She's young, bold, and nothing like the girls that normally
draw my attention.
She wants revenge, and she thinks I'm the man to help her
with it.
She won't take no for an answer.
I admire that. Respect it.
Even if it makes me want to wrap my hands around her
pretty little neck.
Lexie deserves her revenge and I'll help her this one time
—for a price—and then send her on her way.
Easy enough, right?

ACKNOWLEDGMENTS

If you stick it out until the end... my first thank you is for you, my reader. I wrote this with a constant knot in my stomach and I imagine it was the same reading it. The light Reign shines with a past like that is truly an inspiration and I love him even more for it. But man, his story is hard. So, thank you.

Thank you, Katie Salt, as always. You know how I struggled with this one and why, but you made me push through. Without you I'd probably tossed it all in the bin, running off to write a rom-com or something.

Thank you, Ellie Kent. And yes, I'm using your pen name, because everyone; she's becoming one. Thank you for your very necessary and appreciated cheerleading skills. You are always the first that makes me believe it's actually a good book, no matter what story I give you. You all eat it like candy and I'm grateful for you.

Thank you, Sheryn. I know you're busy as hell like we all are, but you still took the time to read my book. I appreciate you as an author, a human, but mostly my friend.

Thank you, Rion. Your friendship means the world to me, and I love how we're always on the same page. You read this while growing a human in your body and focusing on your own release. You're a supermom and a great friend!

Thank you, Brianna & Lauren. The two of you binge beta my books like I'm feeding you liquid gold and each one of you improves my books. I appreciate the amount of time you put into them.

And lastly, thank you, MacKenzie. Not only do I love your work as an editor, but your opinion means a lot. You pointed out what I was already doubting and helped me make it even better. Not to mention the timeframe we're working in. It's always a pleasure to work with you!

ABOUT THE AUTHOR

Billie Lustig is a dutch girl who has always had a thing with words: either she couldn't shut up or she was writing an adventure stuck in her head. She's pretty straight forward, can be a pain in the ass & is allergic to bullshit, but most of all, she's a sucker for love.

She is happily married to her own alpha male that taught her the truest thing about love:

when it's real, you can't walk away.

Check out www.billielustig.com for more info & sign up to my newsletter to be kept up to date or follow me on: Facebook, Instagram, Goodreads, Bookbub, Amazon and/or TikTok.

ALSO BY BILLIE LUSTIG

The Fire Duet:
Callous
Combust
Tormented
Torched
The Boston Wolfes:
Franklin
Connor
Reign
Killian
The Sisters of Sin:
Lush Rebel
Lush Angel
Lush Devil

ALSO BY B. LUSTIG

I created B. Lustig to publish books that give you a heavy dose of angst, big mouthed heroes and women that like to challenge them. These are the stories without the guns, criminals and dark worlds they come from. However, they bring you the same amount of sass and spice as any other Billie book.

Numbers:
8
9
5
7

Made in the USA
Middletown, DE
24 July 2022